Mission Renegade

Producer & International Distributor
eBookPro Publishing
www.ebook-pro.com

Mission Renegade
Charlie Wolfe

Contact: Charlie.Wolfe.Author@gmail.com
ISBN

MISSION
RENEGADE

CHARLIE WOLFE

PROLOGUE

The large, innocent-looking suitcase was pushed slowly on its four wheels by an elegantly dressed young woman whose bulging belly announced to the whole world that she was carrying a baby, or perhaps even twins.

Gentlemen who offered to help her were repelled by a fierce look and those bold enough to try and actually take hold of the suitcase handle were shooed away by a loud hissing sound emitted through thin lips enclosing her small mouth.

She struggled with the wheels that appeared to have a will of their own and looked as if they were arguing with one another about the direction in which to move. Finally, she reached the escalator leading to the second level of the large shopping center and realized the suitcase was too wide for the escalator stairs. She turned around, abruptly knocking over a toddler holding his mother's hand and, without an apology, headed toward the wide elevator. The toddler's mother sent a drop-dead look to the receding back of the woman who was entering the elevator.

If radiation detectors had been mounted in the elevator, they would be chirping like crazy with flashing lights, indicating a deadly level of radiation, but none were installed, so no one was the wiser about the imminent danger.

The woman entered the ladies restroom with her suitcase and barely squeezed into the stall reserved for the handicapped. She quickly removed the pillow that made her midsection bulge, changed her clothes to nondescript jeans and a tightly fitting top that accentuated her slim figure, removed the blond wig she had been wearing and passed a comb through her jet-black short hair.

She placed the pillow and old clothes in a plastic bag that she left in the corner of the stall next to her suitcase. She then set the combination locks on both sides of the suitcase to the code that would give her thirty minutes to get far enough from the shopping center.

She waited until she was certain the restroom was empty, opened the booth's door and exited. With a small screwdriver that she pulled out of her purse, she set the sign on the door to "occupied." She entered the next stall to relieve herself from the sudden urge to urinate.

She exited the washroom and made her way to the parking lot, went straight to her car that was still parked in the spot reserved for handicapped drivers, and without any visible signs of being in a hurry merged with the traffic on highway 55 and headed north on the I-5, trying to get as far away as possible from the Costa Mesa Mall.

PART 1. GETTING IN

CHAPTER 1

Six Years earlier, Las Cruces, New Mexico

Nagib Jaber was carrying out another series of experiments with the electrochemical cell he had developed under the supervision of his doctoral thesis advisor, Professor Jack Chen.

Nagib was well aware of the fact that his professional future as an analytical chemist rested on the success of these new measurements. If he could reproduce the results obtained in his earlier tests then he would be able to complete his thesis and after passing the final exam, get his doctorate and start looking for a well-paying job in industry or government.

The subject of his thesis was the design of a small, compact, pocket-size device that could be used for determining trace amounts of uranium in water or in soil. With such a device, surveys of uranium deposits could be performed in the field without the need to collect samples and transport them to a remote laboratory for analysis. This would enable the surveyors to track uranium bearing mineral deposits simply by following the increase in concentration until the main source was located and to carry out environmental contamination surveys quickly and cheaply.

Nagib was the only Palestinian student in Professor Chen's large research group that consisted mainly of Chinese students who erroneously thought that Jack Chen was also Chinese and applied in masses to join his prestigious laboratory.

Chen was originally from Israel, where Chen is pronounced with a hard CH and in Hebrew means "grace." His first name was Jacob, but he preferred the American version of Jack. The students who followed the numerous publications of this prolific scientist were unaware of this fact. Nagib, who was a graduate of Bir-Zeit University in the territory of the Palestinian Authority, also applied to Professor Chen for graduate studies assuming he was Chinese.

Professor Chen himself was quite indifferent about the nationality of his graduate students as long as they agreed to work long hours at a salary that just about allowed them to survive in Las Cruces where the cost of living was quite low. Chen used to joke that he preferred Chinese students because they did not complain and were just grateful for the opportunity to study and live in the United States. He also liked Palestinian students because, as he jokingly said to his American colleagues, they had no home to go to for their vacations thanks to the Israel Defense Forces.

In the case of Nagib this was accurate—his brother, Yassir, had been involved in the kidnapping and murder of an Israeli youth near Jerusalem and had been apprehended, tried and convicted by an Israeli military court. He was sentenced to a long prison term—capital punishment was not practiced in Israel—and the house of his family was torn down by bulldozers as a retaliatory act and as a warning to other would-be terrorists.

Surprisingly, Nagib and Professor Chen got on very well and occasionally shared a meal consisting of Middle Eastern special dishes prepared by Nagib or by Chen's Israeli wife. Nagib knew that as a graduate of Chen's laboratory, and with proper recommendations and references he stood a good chance of getting not only a good job but also a "Green Card" that would allow him to work in the U.S. and receive citizenship after a few years.

It was his dream to become a U.S. citizen and work in one of National Laboratories where nuclear weapons were designed and produced. He did share this part of his plan with his advisor but did not divulge the second part of his dream—to return to Palestine and seek revenge of the Israelis for destroying his ancestral home.

Five Years earlier, Albuquerque, New Mexico

Nagib decided he deserved a short vacation after successfully defending his thesis at New Mexico State University (NMSU) in Las Cruces the previous day. Indeed, while all his friends were partying and having fun, he had spent the Christmas and New Year school break studying day and night for his final exam. He passed it with flying colors despite his fear that the external examiner, an Israeli scientist called Dr. Benny Avivi, who was added to the examination panel, would give him a hard time. To his surprise Dr. Avivi was totally aboveboard and did not try to undermine his theory or question the validity of his experimental results.

Nagib wanted to spend part of his time in Albuquerque interviewing for a job as an analytical chemist and part having fun and skiing in Taos. While in Palestine he had never had a chance to ski, although every two or three years some snow did accumulate in his mountain village near Hebron and like the other kids from the village he liked to take a thick plastic sheet and slide down the snow covered hill on his backside.

He learned to ski in the mountain area of Cloudcroft in New Mexico and became quite proficient with the help of his girlfriend, Amanda, who was also a student at NMSU and came from a family of winter sports athletes. He was sorry to leave the sheltered life of a graduate student in Las Cruces and especially saddened that Amanda had ditched him in favor of a local boy who was her childhood neighbor, much to the joy of her conservative parents who did not encourage her relationship with a foreigner, especially a Muslim like Nagib.

Nagib had never lived in a city with more than two hundred thousand residents and viewed Albuquerque as a major metropolis with its own international airport, large university, and its position as the business and cultural center of New Mexico. He knew that job opportunities there were very good for someone with his credentials and the proximity of Sandia and Los Alamos National Laboratories were an added attraction for his long-term plan.

After a few interviews, he was offered a position as an assistant director and chief scientist in a medical laboratory that carried out bio-chemical tests. He was clever enough to realize that the fancy title was a kind of compensation for the meager pay and monotonous routine work and declined the offer saying he was more interested in real research and development.

Through the contacts of his advisor, Professor Chen, he was also interviewed by Geo Consultants Ltd. (GCL), a sub-contractor of Kirtland Air Force Base that carried out geological and environmental surveys in and around the base. Kirtland was quite unique as its runways were shared with the civilian ABQ Albuquerque Airport, making it a combined civil-military airport.

Employees of GCL were not required to be U.S. citizens and it was sufficient that they were legal aliens and holders of a Green Card on the way to full citizenship. The pay as a consultant to a sub-contractor was way below what an analytical chemist with a Ph.D. degree would normally receive but Nagib was pleased with the pay that was significantly higher than that of a graduate student and with the position that allowed him access to a military air force base. He reckoned that being close to the world's largest storage facility for nuclear weapons—he read this on Wikipedia—would also potentially help his long-term objective, so he gladly signed the employment contract.

Most of his work consisted of following a predetermined route that took him to several points near the large storage facilities in the base and then to its perimeter and finally to other points that were up to fifty miles from the base, mainly in the downwind and downstream direction. At each point Nagib and his driver/technician, Renaldo, who was also a Green Card holder originally from Chihuahua in Mexico, would collect samples of soil and vegetation and water from drilled wells—if possible—and carry them to the laboratory.

Nagib and Renaldo were also in charge of performing the chemical analyses to determine if there was any environmental contamination that originated from the base. The reports were passed on to their GCL supervisor who then arranged them in tables and graphs, added his own signature and delivered them to the environmental officer of the Kirtland base.

Neither the supervisor nor the environmental officer really understood the meaning of the numbers in Nagib's report, so after going through this routine for a couple of years, without seeing any significant variations in the numbers, Nagib suggested to Renaldo they reduce the amount of the tedious analytical procedures and just copy some older values.

Renaldo, who already thought he was underpaid for his efforts, gladly agreed to lessen the workload and agreed. This went on for another year without anyone noticing the fraudulent reports but then Nagib was offered a promotion and pay increase that would permit him to stay in the air-conditioned laboratory without having to travel on gravel roads to the remote sampling points. Nagib was allowed to hire Renaldo to help him in his new R&D job.

Nagib travelled back to NMSU to discuss his new appointment with Professor Chen. His advisor was glad to see that his former student was doing well professionally, so when

Nagib asked for his permission to carry out field tests with the pocket-size device they had developed jointly Chen immediately agreed. He also added that an application for a patent had already been submitted to the U.S. Patent Office, but as was the custom in his group, future proceeds, if any were forthcoming, would be shared between Professor Chen and NMSU.

Nagib returned to GCL with the news and proposed a special mission for discovery of leaks that involved release of uranium using the new device and suggested he should be put in charge of the project. Nagib's supervisor told him he would discuss this idea with his own boss and get back to him.

By now, Nagib knew that his supervisor would take credit for the proposal, just as he had done with the reports previously, but that did not worry Nagib as long as the idea was approved. He was keen to have the added responsibility as the new mission would give him a good excuse to enter the actual storage facilities under the guise of collecting samples for tracking leakage of uranium from stored weapons.

Nagib was certain his proposal would be approved as he had read—once again on Wikipedia—that Kirtland had suffered a shattering setback in 2010 when it had lost, temporarily one may add, its certification to manage and maintain the nuclear warheads stored on the site.

It took several months to be recertified but the lesson had been learned and now any idea, proposal, or suggestion that could enhance safety or security was almost automatically approved. Nagib was also aware of the jet fuel leakage incident that was discovered only in 1999, probably after decades of leaking. In this case some hazardous chemicals had reached the aquifer and endangered the city's drinking water reservoir and wells.

His supervisor at GCL had become accustomed to Nagib's presence and had forgotten that he was not yet a U.S. citizen, so he failed to note that fact when filling the forms that would enable Nagib to gain access to one of the most secure places in the U.S. nuclear facilities.

However, a routine check by the officer in charge of base security revealed this fact and the supervisor was removed from his position for gross negligence and lucky to escape charges of endangering the national security.

Nagib, who had not even seen the forms filed by the supervisor, was put under special surveillance through no fault of his own. Nagib now was faced with a dilemma—if he quit his job with GCL, under a cloud of suspicion, he may find it difficult to apply for a job with one of the National Laboratories after receiving a U.S. citizenship, but if he stayed on the job he would not be able to gain access to the part of the base that really interested him because everyone would be alerted that he was subject to entry restrictions.

Nagib was still responsible for carrying out the analysis of the samples that were collected in the Kirtland base and the vicinity. He was in charge of a small team of lab technicians and analytical chemists who did the work but was no longer in the field to collect the samples. He was instructed to closely screen the samples that were taken inside the storage facilities as they would indicate if any of the stored nuclear weapons caused contamination. This suited him well as he believed he would be able to learn about the construction of the weapons from the analysis of these samples but soon realized this was not the case. In fact, no traces of radioactive materials were found on the swipe samples that were collected in the storage facilities.

Nagib liked living in Albuquerque, where he had rented a studio apartment near the university and had made many friends among the student crowd. He was not an observant Muslim and enjoyed a few beers or cheap Scotch at parties, liked Mexican food that often contained pork and most certainly had fun with some of the female students who were intrigued by the handsome foreign man who had earned a doctorate and was gainfully employed.

Combining all these joyful deeds with weekend skiing vacations at the nearby Taos ski resorts, something that happened at least once a month in winter, kept him going. There was nothing he liked more than taking a good-looking, all-American, preferably blonde, girl to spend his days on the ski slopes and nights in a comfortable king-size bed after a good meal and a bottle of local wine.

The girls also liked this, but he seldom took out the same girl more than once or twice as he was not interested in a long-term relationship. So, he reached the decision to remain employed by GCL at least until he became a U.S. citizen.

Nagib had gotten used to the good life in Albuquerque and felt that he was given an opportunity to fulfill the American dream. He had almost forgotten his grand plan to avenge the destruction of his ancestral home. He was even considering settling down with a nice woman, preferably of a Palestinian Muslim origin but like himself not really devout and starting a family and a new life in the land of the free.

One day, out of the blue, he received a phone call from his father who told him that his brother, Yassir, who had been incarcerated in an Israeli prison for several years, was freed in a deal in which over one thousand convicted Palestinian detainees were released from Israeli jails in exchange for one Israeli soldier that had been held by Hamas in Gaza. Yassir was not allowed to return to his family home that was rebuilt in the village near Hebron in the West Bank and was sent to Gaza, where he had to remain in a kind of exile.

Nagib's father said that his brother had joined the military arm of Hamas and was the commander of a group that launched rockets into the Israeli territory. This was curtailed when an Israeli drone fired a U.S.-made rocket at Yassir's group just as they were getting ready to launch one of their rockets, killing its five members. His father said that his brave brother Yassir was now a martyr, a Shahid, and that it was Nagib's duty to avenge his death.

Nagib, who had loved his brother and admired his courageous fight against the Israeli occupation, was shocked by the news of his death. After this phone call, Nagib abandoned all the plans of settling down in the U.S. and continued to plot his revenge with even more determination and motivation.

Nagib and his father were both unaware of the fact the phone call was recorded by the Israeli army intelligence unit responsible for monitoring all calls from the Palestinian Authority, and that the transcription of the conversation was passed on to the Israeli Security Agency (ISA) and brought to the attention of the section in charge of following suspected terrorists and their families.

Forty something years earlier—October 8, 1973, six miles East of the Suez Canal

Sergeant Benny Avivi raised his head and peeped over the top of the protective armor of his vintage World War II half-track. He saw a Centurion tank moving rapidly along the dirt road leading from the direction of the Suez Canal to the point on the map that was marked as Tassa, which served as the temporary headquarters of the Israeli forces. Benny could just make out the tactical marking on the side of tank and knew that it was the tank of Colonel Dan, the commander of his regiment.

Colonel Dan had led his unit in to battle against the Egyptian forces that had crossed the Suez Canal in a surprise attack two days earlier. Benny exchanged a look with Captain Moshe, his company's executive officer. They had heard the call sign of the regimental executive officer who was now directing the remaining tanks of the regiment to hold the line firmly and stop the advance of the Egyptian tanks and infantry. Both immediately understood that the regiment commander was either dead or seriously wounded. The rest of the troops in half-track 3B were apathetic or in shock and did not understand what was happening.

A few minutes later Benny's company commander led the six half-tracks up the hill called Hamotal in the code maps. Benny saw half a dozen Centurion tanks that were arranged in positions facing west and south opposing the Egyptian forces that were now retreating to their original positions after failing to take Hamotal. Benny's crew had recovered by now from their state of shock and got busy carrying the dead and wounded soldiers from the damaged tanks to the half-track, evacuating them to the field hospital that was set up at Tassa.

Benny noticed thin electrical wires on the ground and was told that they were used by the Russian-made anti-tank wire-guided missiles that caused havoc to the Israeli tanks. The massive use of these relatively primitive yet effective anti-tank missiles had been something of a tactical surprise. It gave the Egyptians an initial advantage and caused heavy losses until IDF tank crews developed countermeasures that greatly reduced the success rate of the missiles.

March 15, 1974,
The Weizmann Institute of Science, Rehovot, Israel

After five months of emergency reserve duty, twenty-seven-year-old Benny Avivi returned to his laboratory at the renowned Weizmann Institute of Science where he was a doctoral student in the Chemistry Department. Many of his fellow students did not return to their studies after the Yom Kippur War, also known as the October War. Some Israeli students were dead, injured, pronounced as missing in action, or had simply lost interest in pursuing a scientific career after the sights they had seen in the war.

Some of the foreign students left Israel and returned to their home countries where life was not as exciting and wrought with uncertainties. Benny continued his research project and decided he could do more for his country as a scientist than as another sergeant in armored infantry.

Benny completed his doctoral dissertation in 1976, and then spent two years as a post-doctoral research fellow at one of the University of California campuses. After returning to Israel he accepted a position in the analytical chemistry department of the famous Israel Institute for Biological Research (IIBR) and eventually became the head of that department.

Benny also started a family with his wife, Anna, who held a Ph.D. in electro-optics and was employed at the Soreq Nuclear Research Center as a senior research scientist. As his retirement got close, Benny took a Sabbatical from the chemistry department of NMSU, and his wife got a temporary position as a guest scientist in the physics department. Benny was invited to serve as an external examiner during Nagib's final doctoral examination and thesis defense.

Benny's eldest son, David, had served as a squad leader in an elite Special Forces unit of the Israel Defense Force (IDF) and after that studied physics at the Technion before joining the Mossad as an analyst and later as a field agent. He had accrued a lot of vacation time and managed to get special permission to join his parents in Las Cruces for a few months and take a couple advanced courses in nuclear physics at NMSU.

David took a couple trips to visit the National Museum of Nuclear Science and History in Albuquerque and to learn about the Manhattan Project and the Cold War era. He also visited the smaller and less famous Bradbury Science Museum in Los Alamos.

Two years earlier, July 9, Albuquerque, New Mexico

Nagib received an invitation to pledge his allegiance to the United States of America and become a full-fledged citizen. The ceremony was something of a disappointment as he felt greatly superior to most of the other people who were sworn in with his group.

These were mainly people with menial jobs and little formal education whose main reason for being awarded citizenship was that their spouses, parents, siblings, or children were already U.S. citizens—in what is known as family unification. Nagib did like the proximity of the ceremony to the 4th of July celebrations and saw this as a sign from heaven to carry on with his plan.

Soon after becoming a U.S. citizen, he applied for a job at the two National Laboratories that were in the area—Sandia that was practically in Albuquerque and Los Alamos, which could be reached by car in a couple hours. Getting a job at Los Alamos would force him to leave the good life he had created for himself in Albuquerque, but he expected the work there would enable him to get closer to his objective of obtaining access to nuclear weapon designs and to fissile materials. To his pleasant surprise, he was invited to interview at both sites.

The job offer at Los Alamos was more attractive—the pay was higher, the scientific challenges were greater, the team leader, Dr. Brian LeClerk, was more outgoing and appeared to be sincerely interested in recruiting him, and most of all, he would be involved in research with real nuclear materials. So, as sad as he was to leave Albuquerque and relocate to the much smaller town of Los Alamos, Nagib accepted the job offer, and agreed to start work as soon as his security clearance was issued, probably, as he was told, at the beginning of September.

Nagib was surprised by the naivety of the U.S. authorities and by their approach as if being a U.S. citizen was a sacred religious affair. If you are one of us—a U.S. citizen—then you are entitled to a good job, you are welcome to work in our most closely guarded institutions, and welcome to share our secrets, but if you are not formally a full-fledged citizen then you are a potential spy and an enemy of the people and not to be trusted at all.

It seemed as if the authorities adopted a binary approach— trustworthy citizen or unreliable alien, while life itself was more of an analog situation and consisted of many shades of gray—not only fifty as some came to believe after reading the novel or seeing the movie.

Nagib returned to GCL and gave notice that he would be leaving at the end of August. His colleagues and friends gave him a little farewell party and wished him luck with his new job. Renaldo in particular was sad to see him leave—after all they had worked together for a few years and had even become friends. Nagib promised him that he would try to bring him along to Los Alamos, if he would be in a position to hire people and if Renaldo acquired his own U.S. citizenship.

Two years earlier, September 1,
Los Alamos, New Mexico

Dr. Nagib Jaber received a badge with his name as he entered through the security office of Los Alamos National Laboratory (LANL). He looked forward to start working in the analytical chemistry laboratory but was told that as a new employee he first had to receive several orientation courses.

First, he attended a general orientation lecture about the history of LANL, the lab as it was called by the veterans, and the pivotal role it played during World War II. He was surprised to see the contribution of so many Jewish scientists to the Manhattan Project from J. Robert Oppenheimer, Leo Szilard, and Edward Teller through the then junior physicists like Felix Bloch and Richard Feynman to mention a few. He was also shocked to learn how many of them were refugees that managed to escape from Europe as the Nazi party rose to power in Germany.

Next, he was given an extended course on radiation safety and the techniques for handling radioactive materials. The instructor emphasized the safety procedures that had to be followed at all times and noted that safety drills and exercises were conducted periodically. The Head of Security gave a series of boring lectures on the procedures for handling classified material and, in particular, warned the new employees about communications security when using a telephone, e-mail, the internet, and, especially, cell phones that he regarded as the invention of the Devil and the worst nightmare of security officers. He also explained that some areas were restricted and entering them required a special permit and he stressed that discussing work related issues was strictly forbidden outside the designated zone.

There were also more practical and useful bits of information delivered by the deputy director of Human Resources—the cafeterias and dining facilities, the post office hours, transportation to the lab, entertainment options, etc. This took a couple weeks and was concluded with a series of exams. Failure to pass any of those exams resulted either in repeating the course a month later without pay, or even dismissal from the lab and termination of the job before it began. Nagib had no trouble passing all these exams at the top of the class, so by mid-September he was granted permission to start working in the analytical laboratory and was told to report to Dr. Brian LeClerk.

CHAPTER 2

The Present, September 4, Los Alamos, New Mexico

After two years, Nagib was considered for promotion. He had proven himself as a meticulous analytical chemist who could be trusted to perform his duties with precision and accuracy second to none. He mastered the most advanced techniques practiced in the analytical laboratory and learned how to work with the most toxic radioactive materials with skill and confidence, while scrupulously observing all safety procedures.

His duties involved determination of trace amounts of uranium, plutonium, and other actinide elements in bioassays and environmental samples, as well as evaluation of the isotope composition of these elements in samples of materials used in the construction of nuclear weapons. He had not yet received permission to enter the most secure area of the lab in which actual weapon research was conducted, but he expected that after his promotion he would be granted free and unrestricted access to the entire lab.

One of the main lessons he learned from his work at the lab and at the Kirtland Air Force Base was that gaining access to nuclear weapons was not as simple as he had imagined, especially after seeing how easy it was to get a job at LANL. What was even more important to his plan was that he realized even if he could see the weapons in storage, it would be practically impossible to remove one. This was due to their weight and size on the one hand and to the security measures that involved armed guards, closed circuit cameras, and special alarm system on the warhead. He realized there was only one viable option and that was to capture such a weapon or warhead in transport to the lab for maintenance or from the lab to a military base.

This did not happen frequently as the lab was not involved in routine construction or dismantling of standard nuclear weapons. However, he did not even know where to start to obtain information on the transfer of a warhead, let alone arranging the logistics of stopping an armed convoy that escorted these items during transportation and getting away with a warhead. So, Nagib being a practical man decided to break down the problem in to two parts: first, get access to the information on the transportation of a warhead and then work out the logistics of overpowering the security detail and getting the warhead to a safe place.

Nagib had been in and out of the security office several times: first, when he was issued his badge, then for a few periodical reviews, and more recently, when he was dealing with enlisting his old friend Renaldo as a laboratory assistant. He noticed that one of the secretaries took a special interest in him and was more than willing to help him through the bureaucratic procedures of the security office. She was quite plain looking and Nagib had other things on his mind when talking to her but did not fail to notice her nametag that said Ms. Alia Elias.

He knew that Elias was a common last name in many countries and in his youth even knew a Christian family by that name that owned a souvenir store near the Church of the Nativity in Bethlehem. However, her first name, Alia, was quite typically Arabic and he knew of Princess Alia bint Al Hussein of Jordan, for example. So Nagib found an excuse to visit the security office and managed to exchange a few glances and some words with Alia. He then returned to the analytical laboratory and picked up the phone and called her with the pretext that he needed some help with the forms he was asked to fill for his forthcoming promotion and suggested they meet over a cup of coffee in the main cafeteria.

Alia was more than happy to accept, being thrilled that the handsome scientist asked for her assistance, and although she suspected he had reasons other than bureaucratic help for the meeting, she was willing to meet him. She glanced at his personal file and was aware that he was originally from Palestine and was glad and flattered that he took an interest in her.

Nagib was already seated at a small table near the window of the cafeteria when Alia arrived. He offered to get a cup of coffee and a pastry for her, but she said she had to watch her weight and preferred herbal tea, which he brought to the table. She addressed him as Dr. Jaber, but he told her to call him Nagib, which he preferred and asked her if he could call her Alia. She smiled shyly and asked him what he needed. Nagib pulled out the forms and said he was not sure about some items and she leaned over to have a better look at the form and he got a whiff of her delicate perfume. He knew then that she was really interested in more than just helping him and smiled discreetly to himself. After finishing with the forms he asked her if they could perhaps go out for dinner one evening and she said she was free on Saturday, so they exchanged cell phone numbers and she gave him her address and arranged for him to call for her at seven Saturday evening.

Nagib took Alia to the Pyramid Café on Central Avenue that served Mediterranean and Greek food and after having calamari and shrimp for appetizers they ordered couscous with lamb and chicken tagine for their main course and shared the tasty dishes. Nagib asked Alia if she drank alcohol and she laughed and told him that she was a Christian and liked red wine, so he took a look at the wine list and ordered a bottle of Argentinean Malbec. The dinner was delicious, and both were now more relaxed and thanks to the wine less inhibited and left the restaurant walking so close to one another that their shoulders "accidentally" rubbed each other.

Alia told Nagib that she had been married for less than one year to a no-good redneck, who loved rodeos more than he loved her and left her for the sake of an affair with one of the cowgirls who followed the rodeo show around the county. Their divorce was smooth and quick—they had no property or assets to fight over, and thankfully no children. After the divorce she took up her maiden name—Elias. Nagib knew he should go slowly and gently cultivate his relationship with Alia who had been hurt once before, so after dinner he drove her back home, shook her hand and thanked her for a delightful evening. She was a bit disappointed that he didn't try to kiss her but thought he had little or no experience with women and attributed it to his shyness.

A few days later he called her and invited her for another date. He suggested they meet on Saturday morning and drive to Bandelier National Monument, visit the Pueblo dwellings and have a picnic. She volunteered to prepare a cold lunch consisting of salads and sandwiches and he offered to bring a bottle of good wine and some cold sodas. The short drive to Bandelier was very pleasant. The sun was shining but not too brightly and they enjoyed the hilly views.

There were not many visitors at the site, so they took their time climbing up the wooden ladders to the small rooms carved in the soft rock. Nagib helped Alia, who made a big show of being afraid of heights, so when they descended back to the bottom of the ladder, they naturally continued to hold hands. They took one of the many trails carrying their picnic basket and a rug until reaching a secluded spot with a scenic view of Frijoles Canyon.

They spread the rug on the grassy terrain and enjoyed the food Alia had prepared while washing it down with the wine Nagib brought. They were both slightly intoxicated and lay on their backs, still holding hands, and looking at the clouds moving across the sky. Nagib turned on his side and gently caressed Alia's shoulders and then leaned over and kissed her neck working his way up to her cheek. She turned her head so their lips met in a long, deep kiss. Their kissing became more passionate but once again Nagib pulled back slowly, making sure not to offend her, and said that they'd better head back to town. Alia again attributed his behavior to lack of experience with women and reluctantly let him go. They drove back in silence as both pondered the next step in their relationship.

October 14, Los Alamos, New Mexico

Strangely, Nagib was getting fond of Alia and almost decided to forego his plan to manipulate her and use her for getting information on scheduled warhead shipments. Then another idea occurred to him—what if he made her an accomplice and full partner to his plans.

So on their next date—this time over dinner she had cooked in her apartment he waited until they were seated on her living room couch after dinner before bringing up the subject. He tried to probe and understand what she thought about the Israeli occupation, life in the U.S., and the unconditional support the U.S. gave Israel. He asked her about her life in the U.S. and she told him that she was born in Durango, which was a small village in south-western Colorado where her parents ran a mom and pop convenience store.

Her parents had immigrated to the U.S. from Beit-Jala, a small village populated mainly by Christian Arabs that was not far from the village near Hebron, where Nagib had grown up. At home, her parents spoke Arabic among themselves, but Alia, like many first-generation immigrants, insisted on answering them in English, so, she told Nagib, she could understand Arabic quite well but speaking it was sketchy. She attended a community college where she had met her rodeo cowboy and followed him to Los Alamos, where she managed to get a job at the lab. She told him that her pay was enough for her to rent her small apartment, own a car, and save a little money for the future. On the whole she was grateful to have her independence and felt that the U.S. had provided her with a better life than she would have had as an Arab woman in Palestine. However, she did have a serious grudge against Israel and the way they treated Arabs: a couple of years earlier she went on a trip to visit her grandparents who still lived in Beit-Jala. Although she was a U.S. citizen by birth, she was humiliated by the Israeli border control officers at Ben-Gurion Tel Aviv airport. She was taken to a side room, where she was questioned at length about the purpose of her visit, her relatives, and her ties with the Arab community in the U.S., and all details of her life. She was then asked to open her luggage that was scrutinized by a couple of giggling customs officials, and then subjected to a strip search by a female officer who wore latex gloves and probed her body, purposefully inducing pain in her most intimate organs.

Her cell phone was taken into another room and she imagined that her list of contacts and record of her conversations was copied. By the time she was allowed to leave the airport, she almost wanted to turn around and catch the next flight back home but knew her grandparents would be deeply disappointed. When she arrived at their humble home in Beit-Jala, the warm welcome and loving attention she received made her momentarily forget the disgraceful and humiliating treatment at the airport. When she left, two weeks later, to return to the U.S., she suffered a similar ordeal by the security officers checking departing passengers. She had tried to put the whole episode behind her, but when Nagib asked her about her feelings for Israel, it all came back to her so vividly that she couldn't hold back her tears.

Nagib hugged her and let her tears fall on his shoulder. He gently lifted her chin and looked into her eyes and when she managed a shy smile he kissed her eyes and then her lips in a comforting and soothing manner. Their kiss turned in to a hungry, passionate kiss, and Alia pulled him to his feet and led the way to her bedroom holding his hand.

Nagib knew he needed to act as if he had little sexual experience and played coy, letting Alia take the initiative. After all, she had been married and supposedly knew something about making love. He followed her lead and obeyed her tutoring and really enjoyed being seduced. Once in bed, he did not care about her plain looks and actually enjoyed her full figure that was a welcome change after the skinny all-American girls he used to date in Albuquerque.

In fact, since he had moved to Los Alamos a couple of years earlier, he had not formed a serious relationship and had gone a long time without a woman. So it was expected that their first sexual encounter would not last long—she ascribed this to his lack of experience while he attributed it to the long period of abstention. Both were young and energetic, so the second time around came shortly and this time both were more considerate and gentler, and with her firm guidance both were fully satiated, collapsing in each other's arms and snuggling comfortably.

Afterwards, when they were sitting quietly and drinking a cup of tea Nagib told her about his parents' house that was bulldozed to the ground by the IDF and about the death of his brother, the Shahid. Alia asked him if he returned to comfort his parents after their loss and he replied that he didn't want to be noticed by the Israeli authorities as he had grand plans for avenging the injustice brought upon his family.

She enquired what he had in mind but Nagib evaded the question saying that his plans had not yet been thought through and that he would be glad to share them with her. Alia offered her unconditional help to get back at the Israelis and held his hand tightly.

November 10, Los Alamos, New Mexico

Alia and Nagib decided to move in and live together, and as his apartment was slightly bigger than hers she terminated her lease and moved all her belongings to his apartment. They were required to notify the lab security office of their new status, but as both were employees of the lab this was not a problem and each kept their job.

Alia's colleagues at the security office were thrilled with the news and congratulated her on her choice of a handsome partner, especially after her unsuccessful marriage to the cowboy. Nagib's colleagues were also glad to hear that he was settling down. His supervisor, Dr. LeClerk, who Nagib informally addressed as Brian, invited Nagib and Alia to a poolside barbecue party at his house, and it was attended by the whole group of the analytical chemistry laboratory.

Alia called her parents in Durango and told them she had found the love of her life and they immediately invited her to bring him over for a visit. So, the following weekend Nagib and Alia left the lab after work on Friday afternoon and made the four-hour drive to Durango, arriving late in the evening. Despite the light snow the roads were open, so there were no delays. Alia's parents were thrilled when Nagib wished them a good evening in perfectly accented Palestinian Arabic, but somewhat disappointed when it turned out that he was a Muslim. However, seeing the radiant glow of their daughter's face and hearing that he was a non-practicing Muslim alleviated their concerns about the relationship.

When it turned out that Nagib's parents lived less than fifteen miles from their village of Beit-Jala, they started looking for common acquaintances and within minutes found quite a few—the game of Palestinian Geography brought them closer together. Alia's mother was busy in the kitchen preparing the favorite dishes that her husband and only daughter loved and blushed when Nagib gave her the ultimate compliment saying that it was just like his own mother's cooking. Alia's father was also glad to see that Nagib drank his share of red wine during the meal and then joined him on the cold veranda for a whiff of a nargilah. The weekend was very pleasant and Alia's parents smiled and did not protest when Nagib and Alia slept together in her childhood bedroom. On Sunday afternoon the young couple drove back to their apartment in Los Alamos and felt closer than ever and started to discuss wedding plans.

November 24, Tel Aviv, Israel

Dr. Eugene Powers was combining business and pleasure by attending a conference organized by Global Initiative to Combat Nuclear Terrorism (GICNT) in Jerusalem and spending a few days vacationing in Tel Aviv. The conference, like most other conferences of its kind, was ninety percent politics and ten percent science and technology.

The senior delegate of each country, and there were over thirty countries represented here, read a dry statement about the dangers of nuclear terrorism and the importance of stopping it. It was practically impossible to find differences between the statements, even with a magnifying glass, although with a scanning electron microscope one could find some fine nuances.

Eugene was bored out of his mind, but when his turn came he read the trite declaration drafted by the State Department and feigned as much passion as if Archimedes had just discovered the buoyant forces in his bathtub. He was glad when the conference was over and he was free to roam the beaches of Tel Aviv, that even in late November were crowded with fun seekers and health aficionados. He noted the large, practically windowless building close to the sea front and saw the armed security guards and knew that it was the Embassy of the United States. He was looking forward to having a home cooked dinner later that evening with his friend David Avivi, the Mossad agent.

David and Eugene became close friends when they had worked together in Vienna on the case that became known in the popular press as *Mission Alchemist* affair. So, when he rang the bell of David's modest apartment in Ramat Aviv and the door opened, he was received with big smiles and warm embraces by David and by his girlfriend, Orna. She had been the security officer of the Israeli delegation to the International Atomic Energy Agency (IAEA) when Eugene and his Russian colleague suspected some foul play with gamma radiation therapeutic sources and sought the help of Mossad. Orna had made the contact between Eugene and David and worked closely with them and the International Task Force.

After a delicious home cooked dinner the three of them relaxed in the living room and over a few glasses of chilled homemade Limoncello chatted about their present work in as much detail as they could, considering their occupation. Orna told Eugene that after the affair in Vienna she had been given a citation of merit and was invited to join Mossad and work with David, which she gladly accepted. David didn't say much about his work but let Eugene understand that he was still involved in chasing the "bad guys" that posed potential threats to Israel's security.

Eugene informed them that he was now posted in the Washington office of the NNSA, the National Nuclear Security Administration that operated under the Department of Energy. He said that his job involved a lot of travel to the National Laboratories that were supervised by the NNSA.

David told Eugene about the time he had spent in New Mexico, when his father was there on sabbatical, and Eugene mentioned that he had returned from a visit to Los Alamos just before heading to Israel. David knew better than to ask him what he did there, so they discussed the tourist sites of New Mexico. As they were parting, Eugene mentioned in passing that while visiting the lab he attended a presentation on advanced analytical procedures that was given by, what he jokingly called, "a former close neighbor of yours."

This intrigued David, who asked Eugene what he meant by that and Eugene said that he was referring to a naturalized ex-Palestinian scientist, who was a graduate of NMSU. Eugene said he did not remember the name of the scientist but would look it up and send it to David upon his return to Washington.

Eugene returned to his hotel on the beachfront and the next day went over to the nearby U.S. embassy and filed a report about his informal contact with Mossad agents. David filed a similar report about his own informal contact with an NNSA employee. Both reports were put on file and no action was taken.

November 30, Tel Aviv, Israel

David received the short e-mail message from Eugene with the name of the ex-Palestinian scientist from Los Alamos—Dr. Nagib Jaber. The name rang a bell, so he called his father, who instantly recollected that he had been on the examination panel in front of which Nagib defended his doctoral thesis.

Dr. Benny Avivi recalled that he had been impressed by Nagib's defense and by his maturity that by far superseded that usually shown by American doctoral candidates who were generally very knowledgeable about their specific

subject but without a wider viewpoint. Benny also remembered that when asked about his future plans Nagib had said
that he wished to become a U.S. citizen and work in one of the
National Laboratories, preferably in New Mexico.

David thought this piece of information was important
enough to pass on to the Israeli Security Agency, the ISA,
and perhaps get them to do a background check on Dr. Nagib
Jaber, so he called his friend, the "Fish," who was now in a
senior position at the ISA and told him the whole story. The
"Fish," who earned his nickname for staying cool under fire
like his cold-blooded namesake, said he would look into it
and get back to David if there was anything interesting to
report.

December 16, Santa Fe, New Mexico

The wedding ceremony was very modest and held in
the City Hall of Santa Fe in the presence of less than twenty guests. None of Nagib's relatives attended and from Alia's
family, only her parents were present. They invited some of
their colleagues from the lab who were mostly very conservative church-going types, so they were genuinely glad to see
the young couple getting a formal "stamp of approval" and
would no longer "live in sin."

At Nagib's specific request, Professor Jack Chen was the
guest of honor and informally even filled the role of the
groom's father. The professor was getting ready to collect his
retirement pension from NMSU and was looking forward to
move to the Pacific coast and continue life as a consultant

without any teaching responsibilities. Chen called for a toast honoring the young couple and wished good health, a happy life together, and prosperity. He proudly mentioned the fact that although Nagib was originally a Palestinian and he himself had been an Israeli, but both were now loyal U.S. citizens and living proof that there could be a chance for peace between their two nations. Although some cynics thought that moving millions of Israelis and Palestinians to the United States was not a practical solution, the small crowd applauded and Nagib's face lit up with a big smile, but inwardly he felt uncomfortable for the planned betrayal of his mentor.

December 19, Honolulu, Hawaii

After the wedding ceremony, Alia and Nagib travelled to Honolulu for a short honeymoon. Nagib felt that he could fully trust Alia with his real objective, knowing full well that as his wife she could not testify against him, even if she wanted to do so. He was not surprised at her subdued reaction—she said that she now knew him well enough to realize that he was after something really big, not just promotion to a managerial position in the lab.

She emphasized that she would not do anything against the United States that gave her parents financial and physical security and a chance to a better life but would willingly participate in a plan that would hurt Israel that had been so bad for the Palestinian people and humiliated her personally. She said that she thought he would be indebted to Professor Chen who did so much for him during his studies at NMSU and helped get a good job after his graduation.

Nagib said that he worked very hard for his Ph.D. and that Chen benefited from his efforts no less than he did, and in any case Chen no longer lived in Israel or even considered himself as an Israeli patriot, so he had no qualms about inflicting destruction on Israel. Alia realized that he was really agitated and told him that he could confide in her.

Nagib then told her about his turning point with regard to how he felt about the United States. He said that as a Muslim, not a religious fanatic just someone who was born as a simple Sunni Muslim, the American invasion of Iraq in 2003 allegedly to disarm Iraq of atomic, biological, and chemical weapons was an insult to Islam. But what really offended him deeply was the treatment Saddam Hussein received after he was captured, especially when a U.S. paramedic wearing latex gloves probed his mouth with a flashlight—and this degrading scene was recorded on camera and screened repeatedly on global television and all networks.

He said that even the worst serial murderers were not treated like this, as long as they were not Arabs. That was the moment he understood that he would never be considered as an equal in the U.S. and vowed to avenge this affront to his people and co-religionists. He told her that he had secretly named his plan Adrestia. When Alia asked him for the meaning of this word, he said that in Greek mythology Adrestia was the goddess of revolt, just retribution, equilibrium, and balance between good and evil. She was often portrayed as handmaiden of Nemesis, the famous goddess of revenge. He added that the presence of foreign non-Muslim forces, he used the term Modern Crusaders, on sacred Arab soil like Saudi Arabia with its holy places, and Jewish control of Jerusalem—Al Quds, he said—was unacceptable.

When Nagib laid out his plan to intercept a warhead during transport to or from the lab she told him that there was no chance he could get away with it without a large armed force to back him up with the heist and then to smuggle the warhead out of the U.S. and ship it to Israel. They discussed the matter and eventually came up with a few alternative plans.

One plan called for obtaining a compact nuclear weapon from a U.S. storage site in Europe. This would be viable if Nagib could get a proper security clearance and a pretext to visit the facilities in Europe as an expert in analytical chemistry and learn about the security arrangements and devise a way to steal or highjack a suitable item. This too, required the military and financial support of an organization not an act an individual could carry out. Another option was to purchase such a weapon from one of the republics of the former Soviet Union, but this had been attempted unsuccessfully by much better connected and well-funded terrorist groups and allegedly even by some sovereign states.

After a few sleepless nights and numerous daytime discussions, Nagib and Alia hit upon a new idea. This held a much lower physical risk to them and didn't require use of armed force. They would somehow get hold of classified designs for the most advanced nuclear weapons in the lab and use them to barter with a state that already had primitive nuclear devices or even inefficient weapons. They would hand over the advanced designs in return for a primitive device, even for an improvised nuclear device (IND). They could even make a demand that the IND would be delivered in an innocuous form in Israel, or at a site from which it could easily be shipped there. In order to do this they needed to gain access to the highly classified advanced designs and copy them.

They returned to Albuquerque airport on Christmas day—when everybody else was heading in the opposite direction to Honolulu. They drove back to Los Alamos and settled back in their apartment. One main decision they reached while discussing their plans was not to start a family until the smoke, literally, cleared out.

CHAPTER 3

January 30, Los Alamos National Laboratory

Nagib, who was no longer supervised by Dr. Brian Le-Clerk, resumed work in his new position as the head of the section in charge of developing better analytical procedures to determine the isotopic composition and state of the fissile materials, the enriched uranium and plutonium, used in the nuclear warheads.

This was part of the stockpile stewardship project for which the lab was responsible. It was well-known that nuclear weapons had a limited lifetime mainly due to the natural decay of the radioactive materials of construction as well as to chemical processes like corrosion or degradation. Therefore, samples had to be taken periodically from warheads that were dismantled for this purpose.

By "better analytical procedures," the management meant more accurate, more robust, higher throughput, faster and less expensive analytical methods. Nagib seized the opportunity to call for a meeting with the people from the operations division who were responsible for sending the samples and explained that no analytical result was worth the paper it was printed on—not literally, of course, as results were conveyed by computer software and electronic spreadsheets—if the sample was not a true representative of the bulk of the material. He insisted on having his own laboratory team collecting the samples.

The operations division people, especially their manager, Dr. Max Level, automatically objected saying that the responsibility for sampling was theirs, as had been the custom for decades. The argument went on and on for several minutes with each side insisting that they should be in charge of the sample collection and as they could not reach an agreement they decided to go to the senior management for a ruling and made an appointment with the Deputy Director of the lab for the next day.

Nagib returned home that evening and told Alia about the debate and explained that by getting responsibility for sampling, he would gain access to the actual warheads and the storage area which could help facilitate their plans. Alia said that the name of Dr. Max Level sounded very familiar but could not recall from where. She asked Nagib if he wanted tea or coffee and went into the kitchen to switch on the electric kettle and make two cups of tea.

Suddenly Nagib heard her laughing hysterically and when he rushed into the kitchen, he saw her bent over the kitchen counter and holding her belly. Nagib thought that she was ill or suffering cramps but saw that her right hand was pointing at the kettle and wondered if she had been electrocuted so quickly unplugged the kettle. With great difficulty, still laughing hysterically, Alia stood upright and pointed to the line signifying the maximum amount of water that should be used to boil water. He looked closely at the line that prescribed the words max level and also burst out laughing.

January 31, Los Alamos National Laboratory

Nagib and Max Level presented their arguments about taking the responsibility for sample collection and the Deputy Director listened impatiently to both of them and after ten minutes cut them short and said that he had more important things on his agenda. He ruled that for a trial period of five weeks, samples would be collected by Nagib's laboratory personnel and if this led to improved results, they would continue this practice but if no significant progress was found then the old procedures would be reestablished.

Nagib and Max were both displeased with this decision, which probably indicated that it was a wise one. When they left the Deputy Director's office, they set an appointment with their senior staff members to discuss the details for implementing the decision.

Nagib brought his chief analytical chemist who was in charge of carrying out the analyses and his senior technician who did most of the actual sampling. Dr. Max Level brought his own executive officer who was the mechanical engineer in charge of dismantling the warheads selected for periodic testing and evaluation and the chemical engineer who oversaw the sample collection.

Nagib emphasized that his team would not interfere with the dismantling procedure but would only be present as observers of this stage, and they would then guide Max's people to perform the sample collection to ensure that representative samples were collected from all the components of the dismantled warhead. Max did not like being supervised by people who knew nothing about the dismantling and sampling of the unique components, and he avidly rejected the notion of having his team's work criticized or even observed by academic laboratory types who knew nothing of the real world of nuclear weapons.

He expressly told Nagib that receiving samples and analyzing them in the laboratory was miles removed from physically handling and disassembling the delicate, highly radioactive components. Nagib said that he was well aware of that and his people would not touch anything or intervene with work, and as he stated before, would only ascertain that the samples collected were truly representative of each component. Max had to accept this as decreed by the Deputy Director, but then raised the point that Nagib had been concerned about and feared—allowing only people with high level security clearance to participate.

Nagib played it cool by saying that he would make sure that his staff got the appropriate clearance, worrying that he may fail to get approved which would undermine the whole exercise from his point of view.

February 21, Los Alamos National Laboratory

It took three weeks but two of Nagib's laboratory staff received the required security clearance and participated in the dismantling and sampling of operational nuclear warheads.

The samples they brought were no different than those that had been received by the analytical laboratory in the past.

Nagib was concerned that the whole matter would lead to nothing and it would be hard for him to explain to the Deputy Director what the fuss was all about. He decided that he personally had to get involved and that necessitated upgrading his own security level. He asked Alia, who worked in the lab's security office, if this could be expedited and she told him she would speak to her boss who was the Head of the Security Office, Colonel (Ret.) Dick Groovey. Her boss agreed to set up a meeting with Nagib and see what could be done.

Nagib entered the Security Office and was greeted with warm smiles from Alia's colleagues and then ushered into the conference room where the Colonel Groovey was seated. The Colonel picked up a thick file that was placed in front of him and looked at Nagib with a stern face. He asked Nagib to repeat his life's story and Nagib did so briefly, going over his early years in Palestine and describing his life in the U.S., emphasizing he felt privileged to be an American citizen and honored to be able to contribute to the security of his adopted country.

The Colonel's expression did not change throughout this whole tirade and he asked Nagib if he still had contact with his relatives in the Palestinian Authority. Nagib said that he exchanged a phone call with his parents on their wedding anniversary and they called him on his birthday. He stressed that they had not attended his wedding or even met his wife.

The Colonel stiffly admitted that Alia was a model worker and very dependable and reliable. He concluded the meeting by saying he would be able to issue the requested clearance if Nagib would successfully pass a polygraph test, to which Nagib promptly agreed.

February 23, Los Alamos National Laboratory

Nagib sat quietly while the security investigator who was a senior member of the American Polygraph Association hooked him to the polygraph. Nagib had prepared for the test by reading about the polygraph on Wikipedia (where else?). He knew that the machine recorded his blood pressure, pulse rate, respiration rate and skin conductivity—perspiration— while the subject being tested was required to answer some questions. He was also aware of the fact that the polygraph's reliability was questionable, and it was regarded by many scientists as nothing more than pseudoscience.

He was asked to answer some trivial questions, honestly at first and then to deliberately lie as part of Control Question Technique, he did so without flinching. Then the more serious part of the test began. He was asked about details of his personal history which he had no problem answering truthfully without hesitation. He was then asked the real key questions:

"Are you now, or did you ever work for a foreign government?"

"No."

"Were you approached by a foreign intelligence service?"

"No."

"Are you now or were you ever a member of a terrorist

organization?"

"No."

"Are you now or were you ever a member of the communist party or a sympathizer?"

"No."

"Are you now or were you ever connected to an extreme racist or Nazi movement?"

"No."

"Did you obtain your student visa or your U.S. citizenship under false pretenses?"

"No."

The questions were asked two more times. Nagib's reply to all these questions was negative and the investigator appeared to be pleased with the answers and thanked Nagib for his cooperation and released him from the machine. Nagib laughed to himself quietly—he was not an agent of a foreign government, was not contacted by intelligence services, was not a member of any organization—terrorist, communist, or racist—and did not lie on his visa application. He was never asked if he plotted to harm the U.S. or its allies, if he planned to betray the confidence of the lab or steal any secret information from it and use it.

March 3, Los Alamos National Laboratory

At last Nagib received the clearance to attend the dismantling of the nuclear warhead that was selected for a thorough analysis of its state of fitness, or degradation, as part of the stockpile stewardship project. All he saw were a lot of small components that were carefully dissembled from a strange looking device. He was impressed by the skill and confident way that Dr. Max Level's people handled these parts.

No one bothered to explain to him what each component was and what function it performed, and he did not want to raise suspicion by being overly inquisitive. After observing the procedure for a couple hours, he could not come up with astute remarks or useful suggestions, so he returned to the analytical laboratory and supervised the analysis of the samples that were collected.

He already knew the isotopic composition of enriched uranium and plutonium that were in the core, or pit, of each warhead type, as did anyone who could surf the net and read Wikipedia, so did not learn anything new from the analyses that were performed in his laboratory. He also read some things about the construction of atomic weapons—once again things that were common knowledge in the public domain. So far, he had not gained a single fact that could be used for bartering and he was deeply disappointed.

In the evening he returned home and told Alia about his frustration with the failure of their idea. He knew he would have to return to the Deputy Director and admit that Dr. Max Level knew his job, so he wondered if he could use this to befriend Dr. Level and get some useful information from him. Alia encouraged him to continue with the efforts to obtain classified information that could be used for bartering.

The next day, Nagib submitted his report to the Deputy Director of the lab, with a copy to Dr. Max Level. He was summoned to a meeting in which he praised Dr. Level's professional approach and said that there was no need for personnel from the analytical laboratory to be present during the dismantling process for sample collection.

Max was pleased with the report and even the Deputy Director smiled and said that it took an honest man to admit that he had been wrong. After they left the office, Max thanked Nagib for his frank report and said that they should meet for coffee or for a drink some time and asked him if he and his wife were free on Friday afternoon.

The two couples met in the Pyramid Café that had become Alia's favorite place after the first date with Nagib. When Max introduced his wife as Minnie, Alia and Nagib could barely suppress their laughter because both remembered the other line on the kettle that said min level.

Minnie, who had a degree in mechanical engineering, was also employed at the lab, so the four of them had a lively conversation about life in Los Alamos and work in the lab. The two couples hit it off despite the age gap between Alia and Nagib who were in their early thirties and the Levels who were in their early fifties. The Levels had a daughter who was attending college in Denver and came home only for Christmas and in the summer.

While the women were engaged in their own conversation, Max asked Nagib if their two departments could increase their professional cooperation and hold regular meetings and seminars on issues of mutual interest. Needless to say that Nagib was overjoyed with this suggestion but managed to appear as if he was considering the idea and asked if this wouldn't raise security issues. Max said that he would work through channels and try to obtain the Deputy Director's approval and permission from the security office. The two couples departed agreeing to meet again soon.

March 23, Los Alamos National Laboratory

The first meeting of Nagib's analytical laboratory people with Max's operations division personnel was held in a small conference room and kicked off on a positive note. After a short round of introductions, each section leader presented the responsibilities and capabilities of his group. It appeared as if some of the problems that arose in the operations division, like evident corrosion, and degradation of components could be addressed using analytical tools to study the extent of the problems and the rate of the processes.

Max said that viewing the blueprints and pointing out the areas in which the degradation was most prominent would be helpful and Nagib gladly approved. So, they agreed to meet on a bi-weekly basis and devise an action plan, pending proper approval from management and permission from the security division, of course. Max said that he would be responsible for carrying out the bureaucratic procedures to gain the necessary clearances.

April 20, Los Alamos National Laboratory

Max entered the small conference room with a big smile and immediately switched on his laptop and connected it to the overhead projector. Nagib could hardly believe his eyes—on the screen there was a detailed diagram of one of the most advanced warheads in the U.S. nuclear arsenal.

Max described each component, its exact dimensions, materials of construction, and once he started to describe the problems that were encountered enlargements of the relevant areas were displayed. Nagib had to clear his throat and drink some cold coffee before he allowed himself to speak. He said that they should address one problem at a time and asked Max where he thought they should start. Max zipped through the presentation until he found the best view of the problematic component and reviewed the problems that they had encountered with that component.

Before long, a brainstorming session was in full gear with the analytical chemists raising questions and making proposals after hearing the answers from the operations people who had hands on experience with the component. Nagib and Max exchanged a look that showed how pleased they were with the way the two teams were interacting.

When Nagib returned home that evening, he told Alia about the way the meeting had progressed and said they had struck gold or at least a gold bearing vein. Alia suggested that they go and celebrate at their favorite restaurant and Nagib readily agreed. So off they went, ordered the best and most expensive bottle of wine, and drank it raising toasts to each other. That night they got very little sleep as both were feeling a need for close physical contact and a strong desire for each other.

May 3, Tel Aviv, Israel

The "Fish" called David Avivi and apologized for the long delay, since it had been almost half a year since David asked him to check if the ISA had any information on Dr. Nagib Jaber. The "Fish" said that Nagib had left the Middle East several years earlier, which David already knew, and the ISA had nothing on him regarding any illegal activity. However, he added, his brother Yassir may he rot in hell, had been a prime target of the ISA.

Apparently, Yassir was convicted for kidnapping and murdering a young Israeli student near Hebron and given a life sentence by a military court. However, he was released from prison with many other terrorists in return for an Israeli soldier and banished from his home to Gaza. There were reports that he was killed by an Israeli drone while attempting to fire a rocket on an Israeli town near Gaza.

David asked if Nagib had any known contacts with Palestinian terrorist organizations and the "Fish" said that he was not suspected of any wrongdoings. David thought that this information should be passed on to the Americans and called his friend, Dr. Eugene Powers, in Washington, DC. Eugene received David's call and said he would look into the matter and get back to him.

May 4, Washington, DC

Eugene called the Deputy Director of Los Alamos National Laboratory and conveyed the information he had received from the Israelis. The Deputy Director said that he knew Dr. Nagib Jaber personally and that he was highly regarded as a responsible and trustworthy scientist and had recently been promoted to head his own section in the analytical laboratory.

He related the episode of the attempted cooperation with the operations division and told Eugene that Nagib had passed the polygraph test without a hitch. He commended Nagib's initiative to work hand-in-hand with Dr. Max Level and said that he believed this would further the lab's stewardship project.

Eugene asked him if the new information did not bother him at all and the Deputy Director invited him to come out to Los Alamos and interview Nagib himself if he still had concerns about him. Eugene asked if he could bring his Israeli colleague to the interview and the Deputy Director told him that only U.S. citizens were allowed on site, and when Eugene suggested locating the meeting off-site the Deputy Director cut him short and said that he needed to promptly leave for his next appointment.

Eugene got back to David and told him that he would personally go to Los Alamos to meet with Nagib but didn't tell him about the conversation with the Deputy Director.

May 30, Los Alamos National Laboratory

Nagib was deeply frustrated—here he had access to even the minor details of the most advanced warheads but could not download the information and certainly not remove it from the lab. He couldn't get an electronic copy of the blueprints, he couldn't photocopy the schematics, he couldn't smuggle a camera to take photographs, and most certainly couldn't get samples.

Even worse, he was "invited" to meet a big shot from the NNSA who was scheduled to come to the lab the following week. He discussed this with Alia after he got back home. She told him that she had overheard a conversation in the security office between the Deputy Director and her boss about the planned visit of the man from the NNSA regarding the reliability of key personnel with respect to national security issues.

Now Alia and Nagib connected the dots and got a picture they did not like one bit. They considered their options: should they flee immediately or find some excuse for avoiding the meeting or continue to bluff their way and decided to go with the latter option. That night they didn't get much sleep, but unlike the sleepless night they enjoyed a few months earlier, this time it was the fear of being found out, or even arrested that drove sleep away.

June 5, Los Alamos National Laboratory

Dr. Eugene Powers was received with formal politeness by the lab's Deputy Director and by the chief of security Col. Dick Groovey. He told them about his concerns that Dr. Nagib Jaber may have an urge to avenge his brother's death and the destruction of his parents' home by the Israelis, and what was even more disturbing that he may wish to take it out on the U.S. as it is the greatest supporter of Israel.

The Colonel repeated what the Deputy Director had told Eugene that there was no evidence that Nagib was not what he claimed to be—a loyal U.S. citizen—and that he had successfully passed the polygraph test just three months earlier. Eugene acknowledged this but said that in the Middle East revenge is best served cold and that Nagib may still harbor feelings of retribution and wished to personally assess Nagib's attitude by interviewing him.

The Deputy Director left the room and Nagib was called in to the Colonel's office. After the formal introductions Eugene told Nagib that his family's history worried the chief of security at the NNSA and that he wanted to clarify a few points.

"Dr. Jaber, are you still in contact with your family?"

"I speak to my parents on the phone once or twice a year. They are now quite old and suffering from different ailments, so I try to follow their health situation."

"How do you feel about the death of Yassir, your only brother?"

"I am sad that he died the way he did, but he believed he was fighting for a good cause, so he was probably glad to sacrifice his life."

"What do you think about his cause?"

"Obviously I don't condone it or believe in it. I don't think that killing an Israeli or firing rockets at residential areas are good things."

"Have you visited your parents at all since you came to study in the U.S.?"

"No, at first when I was a doctoral student I couldn't afford it. After graduation, when I was employed by GCL and had applied for a Green Card I couldn't take the time off and was afraid that I would lose my temporary status."

"Why didn't you visit them after your brother's death, when you were already a full-fledged citizen and had a good job here at the lab?"

"I didn't see a point in returning to Palestine—my brother was dead and there was nothing that could be done. I had also heard that Arabs were treated badly by Israeli authorities, even if they were U.S. citizens and did not want to suffer humiliation."

"I understand you are now married and that your wife, Alia, is also employed here."

Here the Colonel intervened and said, "Alia is one of the best workers in my office and she was born in the U.S. and raised here, not naturalized."

Nagib added, "She feels like an all-American girl and has done her utmost to forget her Arab heritage. She can barely speak Arabic although she understands quite a lot."

"Why didn't you invite your parents to come to your wedding? Is this how you respect your parents?"

"Dr. Powers, I already told you that they are old and frail and for them to apply for a visa and travel so far would be more of a punishment than joy."

"How do you feel about the U.S. government and its policy of almost unconditional support for Israel?"

"I am grateful to the U.S. for the opportunity it gave me to obtain a good education, work in a challenging job, and get a chance for a better life than I could ever dream of in Palestine. I feel that I should repay the U.S. government by working in this place and contributing, albeit a modest one, to this country's security."

To this Eugene said, "Nagib, I am impressed by your patriotism." But thought that Nagib had been a little too glib. He concluded by thanking Nagib and the Colonel for their time and said that he had a plane to catch back to Washington.

Nagib went back to his laboratory very pleased with himself, believing his replies in the interview were perfect, especially after hearing the last comment made by the man from the NNSA. When he returned home that evening and told Alia about the interview, she responded with a huge smile and said she had heard Colonel Groovey muttering something about bureaucrats from Washington going around casting doubt about the patriotism of honest, hardworking, loyal Americans and had figured out that he was referring to Nagib.

They had a good laugh about the level of security in one of the most secret facilities in the U.S. saying that here were two amateur spies operating freely inside the lab without getting caught, just because they were American citizens and, therefore, considered beyond suspicion.

Nagib said that in Palestine, the authorities would not bother to interview him politely in a nice, air-conditioned office, but would simply throw him in to a cold cellar and threaten to pull out a few fingernails until he proved his innocence or admitted his guilt.

It was Friday night and Alia told Nagib he deserved a special treat for his brilliant behavior during the interview. Nagib smiled and asked what she had in mind and she shyly said she would try to match his performance by doing what women did to please their husbands in the "old country," and told him to relax on the sofa and close his eyes.

She took a keffiyeh that they kept in a drawer in their bedroom and tied it around his eyes making sure that he could not see anything. Then poured him a tumbler full of the finest whiskey they had in the house, added a couple ice cubes and placed it in his hand. She brought her laptop, and on YouTube she found belly dance music with a darbuka drum solo and switched on the speakers. Nagib started smiling as his expectations were building up.

Next she went to the bedroom, put on her most delicate perfume, removed her clothes and wrapped all the scarves she could find around her naked body. By the time she returned to the living room Nagib had finished his drink, so she gently kissed him on the lips and removed the tumbler from his hand and refilled it. She glanced at his crotch and was pleased to see a bulge forming there. As if by mistake, her elbow rubbed against it and she was rewarded by a sharp intake of breath and a sigh.

She said that Nagib could now look but not touch and removed the keffiyeh from his eyes and used it to tie his right hand to the sofa. When he saw what she was wearing he knew that this would be a night to remember but did not know what else she had in stock for him.

Alia slowly started gyrating her hips to the sound of the rhythmic music allowing her breasts to move unrestricted under the scarves. She moved toward Nagib and ordered him to remove one scarf without using his free hand, dancing closer and closer to him until he could catch the edge of the scarf with his teeth. She then moved sensuously away so the scarf fell off. She continued her ritual until the last scarf was removed.

By that time, Nagib was moaning with expectation and told her to free him, but Alia placed her finger on his lips and told him to be patient. She bent down and removed his shoes and socks while her forehead pressed upon his erection. Nagib wriggled on the sofa and tried to pull her against him with his free hand but she smacked his hand away and told him to wait. She untied the keffiyeh from the sofa, placed it on his eyes again, and instructed him to stand up. She then slowly continued to remove all his clothes and told him to sit back on the sofa.

By now, Nagib's erection had reached unprecedented proportions almost causing him physical pain. She was pleased by his reaction and in a low husky voice instructed him to take her on the carpet without removing the blindfold. She pulled him on top of her and within seconds both exploded in the most intense orgasm.

After they caught their breath, she removed the blindfold, hugged him tightly saying she would never let him go. He smiled and told her that whatever happened they would be together forever. They got up from the carpet and walked hand in hand to the bedroom where they continued their lovemaking.

When they woke up it was almost noon and after having coffee, they had a serious discussion about the future. Alia repeated her idea that they settle down in Los Alamos like good Americans, start a family and lead a normal life, and forget about the plan.

Nagib said he was tempted to do that but the urge to inflict damage on the Israelis would not fade away. Alia insisted they had a great opportunity to live happily in the U.S. and should let others avenge the injustice inflicted on the Palestinian people, but Nagib remained adamant it was their duty. She promised him more pleasures like they had the previous night, but by now the fires of passion that had driven him senseless before had cooled.

He repeated his speech about honor of his people, respect to family values of revenge, and duty to their homeland and the Palestinian people. Alia said that she would follow his lead and felt that the immediate danger of being exposed had passed, but nevertheless they should act quickly.

CHAPTER 4

June 6, Washington, DC

Eugene called David from his office and related his impressions of the interview with Nagib. He said that Nagib had been very smooth with his answers as if they had been rehearsed. Eugene was mainly bothered by the fact that at no stage had he shown any emotion, even when describing his relations with his parents and deceased brother.

However, the Colonel practically swallowed every word spoken by Nagib as if it was delivered by the Pope—Col. Dick Groovey was a devout Catholic—himself at the Ecumenical Council. Eugene told David that he thought they would have a problem convincing the Deputy Director and the Colonel that Nagib's access to classified information should be restricted, or even that a new thorough security investigation should be initiated.

***

David's concern that Nagib was up to something increased after the conversation with Eugene. He asked Haim Shimony's secretary to arrange a meeting, saying that it was not urgent, but she knew that Shimony, who was now Chief of Mossad, respected David's intuition and scheduled the meeting for eight that evening.

When David arrived at the Chief's office a handful of people, some wearing IDF uniforms and some dressed in civilian clothes were just leaving. One of them was the "Fish," David's old friend from the ISA. David greeted him warmly and asked him if he could stay for a few minutes and participate in the meeting.

The "Fish" asked David what it was about and when David told him it concerned Nagib Jaber he readily accepted the invitation. Once they were seated in the Chief's office, David related the news he had received from Eugene and expressed his gut feeling that something fishy could be going on.

The Chief said he had great respect for the American approach to security issues but felt that they were a bit gullible in their belief that anyone who received U.S. citizenship and took the required oath would be loyal to his new country and take no notice of his past and forget where he came from. He mentioned a few well-known cases of espionage by nationalized citizens who passed classified military, security, and commercial information to parties in their original homeland.

Some did this willingly and voluntarily, and some did it for financial gain while others were coerced to do so. The Chief suggested that the "Fish" should carry out a thorough investigation and profile of Nagib's background, family, and personal history, and also look in to Alia's background. In addition, he proposed to send David to the U.S. to personally meet with Eugene and see if he could find more about Nagib.

This latter detail was very sensitive since Israel vowed not to operate clandestinely on U.S. soil after the embarrassment caused by the Jonathan Pollard affair who was the only American ever to receive a life sentence for passing classified information to an ally of the U.S.

June 14, early afternoon, Los Alamos National Laboratory

Nagib sat in the office of his new friend, Dr. Max Level, for an informal meeting about ways and means to improve the performance of their groups by carrying out joint work. They drank some reheated coffee from the filter machine that tasted bitter and burnt and joked that its acidity was the best way to exterminate microbes in the gastrointestinal tract. Nagib couldn't help recalling the freshly brewed, dark, bitter coffee he had consumed as a youth in Palestine and that Alia prepared for him and served with sweet pastries whenever she wanted to pamper him.

Nagib, as usual carried a small memory stick with 16 GB, in blatant disregard of the security regulations that did not allow the use of any such items. He felt quite secure he would not be found out as the memory stick was part of a pen he had received from one of the vendors of chemical equipment at a conference on analytical chemistry in which he presented his research as a graduate student.

He explained to Alia that one never knew when an opportunity to copy classified information would present itself, so he was always prepared to seize such a chance. Max was in a very good mood as he was looking forward to a long vacation in Paris with his wife Minnie, due to begin the next day. The phone on Max's desk rang and he picked up the receiver. After a short conversation Max apologized to Nagib saying that some emergency in the deconstruction workshop needed his immediate attention. Nagib rose to leave the office but Max told him he would be back in a few minutes and they could continue their discussion.

Nagib noted that Max neglected to log out of his computer and quickly moved into Max's chair, removed his pen from the lab coat's pocket, and inserted the memory stick into the vacant slot. He entered the directory in which the classified files with the latest designs and blueprints of nuclear weapons were stored and started to download them to his memory stick. He didn't have time to see exactly what those files contained so he just copied them blindly.

He knew that the breach of rules would be noted by the security system's software but hoped it would take several minutes to block the computer and even longer to discover the physical location of the offending computer. As soon as the download was completed, he removed the drive, assembled his pen with the hidden drive, and returned to his seat. A moment later, when Max returned to the office Nagib said he had to leave at once as one of his assistants called about a problem in the analytical laboratory. He wished Max a pleasant vacation and told him they should celebrate after he returned from Paris.

Nagib went to the security office and stopped by Alia's

desk. He was welcomed by all the girls in the office, who still envied Alia for her handsome and successful husband. When Colonel Groovey heard the commotion, he peeped out of his own office and greeted Nagib, whom he regarded as a major asset of the research and development division. Nagib smiled at all of them and asked Alia if they could have a word in private and they stepped out of the office for a moment.

Nagib told her that the opportunity they had waited for presented itself and explained what he had done in Max's office. She paled and said that he may find himself in deep trouble and would probably be caught. He said that the temptation was too large to ignore and surreptitiously placed the pen with the memory stick in her pocket. Both realized that their life in Los Alamos was over and they would have to flee as quickly and as far away as possible. He said they should leave the lab immediately, return to their home to pack a few things, then draw as much cash as they could from the ATM machine, and try to disappear for a while until they could make plans to leave the country.

She returned to her office said that she was not feeling well and had to leave early. Nagib was already waiting in the parking lot and they took off.

Meanwhile, a security guard, Albert Danillo, arrived at Max's office in response to the alarm triggered by the security system's software that an unauthorized media storage device had been connected to a computer on the classified network. He found nobody in the office and was told that Dr. Max Level had left for the day. The guard looked around and everything appeared to be in order so he reported to his superiors that everything looked to be in order and that he would further investigate the matter the following day.

No one bothered to tell him that Max was going on vacation and would only return a few weeks later because the people in Max's section were often harassed by the security guards and particularly disliked Albert who was always after them for one reason or another.

Max drove to his house where Minnie was already waiting with the packed suitcases and they drove to Albuquerque international airport to catch their flight to Paris via Chicago. He knew nothing about the events that had taken place in his office and with a clear conscience was determined to enjoy Paris.

PART 2. GETTING OUT

CHAPTER 5

June 14, late afternoon, Los Alamos

Nagib and Alia placed their laptop in its soft case, packed a few things in a couple carry-on suitcases, and as there was nothing of sentimental importance in the house, they left everything undisturbed as if they planned on returning to it shortly.

They decided to head to California assuming they could blend in with the local large Arab and Muslim community and then plan their next step. They thought the easiest way to get there would be by taking the I-40 that in that part of the world was also part of the historic Route 66, and drive through Arizona and Nevada until they reach the junction with I-15 in Barstow and then head to Los Angeles.

They did not know how long it would take the lab security office to discover what had really happened but estimated that at most they had a couple days before a nationwide man-hunt began.

By the time they left Los Alamos and got on the I-40, the sun was setting in the west and they headed directly in that direction driving at a pace that kept them flowing with the interstate traffic. Although they were in a hurry, they did not want to draw attention to themselves by driving too fast or too slow.

According to the electronic map, the distance to Los Angeles was eight hundred and eighty-four miles and the estimated driving time was just under fourteen hours. They figured that if they took turns driving and stopped for gas and services every three or four hours, they could get to Los Angeles just after the morning rush hour ended.

The drive was very smooth and they made good time so they were quite relaxed when they reached Kingman, Arizona. As they were passing through this little town it was close to midnight and there were very few cars on the highway. In one section of the road the posted speed limit was thirty mph and they were doing about thirty mph when a police car that was hidden behind a large billboard on the side of the road pulled out and followed them quietly for a couple minutes.

It then switched on its flashing lights signaling them to pull over to the side of the road. It was Alia's turn to drive while Nagib took a nap and for a second she panicked and considered trying to outrun the police. Nagib woke up, quickly assessed the situation, and told her to stop by the side of the highway. The patrol car pulled up behind her and she could see in the mirror that the grossly overweight policeman barely managed to get out of his car and saunter over to her car. He held a large flashlight in his left hand and his right hand rested on his pistol.

He politely asked her to hand him her driver's license and car registration. When he saw that her name was Alia Jaber, he took a long look at Nagib and asked them both to slowly step out of the car without making any sudden movements. They gingerly complied being careful not to do anything rash. He then asked them what they were doing in Kingman in the middle of the night and Nagib said they were on their way from New Mexico to Los Angeles, where his uncle was in hospital with life threatening injuries after being a victim of a hit-and-run accident and they were hoping to reach him before he expired.

The policeman had heard that one many times before so said that he understood their urgency but as they broke the speed limit they presented a hazard to all other people on the highway and it would be in their better interest to spend the night in the local police station until brought before a judge in the morning. Nagib and Alia were flabbergasted and at a loss.

Once the policeman was convinced they were not driving under the influence of alcohol or drugs he told them that there was an alternative. When they asked him what he meant, he said that they could pay a fine of two hundred and fifty dollars on the spot and he would take care of all the paperwork in the morning and mail them a receipt.

Nagib and Alia exchanged a knowing look and said that they would pay but he need not bother with the receipt. This was accepted and a quick cash transaction was made and within ten minutes they were once again on their way to Los Angeles. Nagib said that this reminded him of the roadblocks in Palestine where the police of the Palestinian Authority regularly supplemented their meager income by shaking down innocent drivers. The rest of the trip was uneventful, and they made sure to slow down every time the highway passed through one of the small villages along the way.

June 15, Pasadena, California

Just before noon Alia and Nagib checked in to a small motel in Pasadena. They paid cash and told the woman at the reception desk that they would stay for a night or two. She acted as if she couldn't care less, which indeed was the case, and mumbled that check-out was eleven in the morning and that the ice machine and snack dispenser were in the lobby.

Once in the room, Nagib removed the battery from his cell phone and told Alia to remove the battery from hers and said that they would go out later, trade in their car and get an older model that would leave them with some extra cash and also purchase new SIM cards for their cellphones. They went to sleep for a few hours.

When they woke up, Nagib took out the laptop and powered it on, removed his pen from his shirt pocket and took the top off exposing the memory stick. He inserted it into the USB slot of the laptop and opened the directory with the classified files. Until that moment he only had a vague idea about the blueprints and designs he had downloaded.

The laptop was an old model and rather slow, so they waited impatiently for the directory to open. When the list of files was displayed, they could barely keep themselves from shouting cries of joy. One file was called, *The super high yield (SHY) device*, another was named *Dial a yield lightweight (DAYLIGHT) multi-purpose device,* and there were several other files with strange names and acronyms. Nagib was fascinated by something that was called a *suitcase omnipotent bomb (SOB)* that was described as a remotely controlled, powerful, portable, tactical device that could be clandestinely placed behind enemy lines or carried into enemy territory practically unnoticed.

He told Alia that this particular design would be greatly suitable for their purposes if they could get their hands on such a device or convince a friendly partner to manufacture it. Nagib connected with Wikipedia and under the heading of Suitcase-nuke found some interesting data. The website mentioned the reports attributed to General Alexander Lebed who was a high-ranking officer in the former Soviet Union about missing suitcase bombs.

These reports were treated on the whole by analysts merely as gossip, but no one was sure that there was no substance in them. Nagib added that there were claims by the Ce1nter for Defense Information—sometimes referred to as the Center for Disinformation—that replicas were hand-carried on domestic flights for exercise purposes.

Alia asked what explosive strength such a device would have and Nagib replied that yields of several kilotons could be achieved. Nagib continued his search on Wikipedia and saw that the U.S. had developed a lightweight device named Special Atomic Tactical Munition—ironically the acronym SADM had nothing to do with Nagib's hero, Saddam Hussein. The bare warhead allegedly weighed fifty pounds and was shaped as a cylinder that was only eleven inches by sixteen inches cm and could be placed in a suitcase.

However, the advanced classified design that he had downloaded was about the same size and weight, but its yield was supposedly much larger than the old SADM. Nagib said that the information they had was invaluable to countries with budding nuclear ambitions and even to countries with small arsenals of nuclear weapons. Alia said that she thought that non-government organizations like Al Qaeda or the Islamic State, not to mention Chechens, Kurds, and others, would find the small device much more suitable for their purposes.

Nagib thought about this for a minute and said that it was probably true but fissile materials, plutonium or high enriched uranium, were needed and as far as he could tell those non-state entities did not possess this essential component.

Alia asked Nagib how he intended to guard the information he had downloaded. Nagib said that so far, the only copy was on the memory stick that was concealed in his pen and that he had not copied it even to his own laptop. He added that presently the folder with all the classified files could be opened by anyone who possessed the memory stick and that the first thing they needed to do was limit access to the folder and protect it with a password.

Alia said that this could easily be done by anyone with minimal computer skills but could be undone just as easily even by a teenage hacker. Nagib, who was an accomplished analytical chemist but not an expert in computer security, was at a loss. There was nobody he could approach with the classified folder and ask for assistance in securing the information, and then Alia hit upon an idea. She told Nagib to access the internet and download pornographic material.

Nagib was surprised at the suggestion made by his shy and reserved wife and asked her what she had in mind. She answered he could then find a young hacker and tell him he wanted to hide these files from his wife and pay him for his services, provided he taught him how to encrypt files. Once he had the know-how and the program, he could apply it to hide the classified folder. Nagib liked the idea and downloaded some erotic clips from the internet, and while online looked for the addresses of a nearby internet café where he could seek the help he needed.

The couple was so elated by the wealth of information they now owned that they decided to celebrate before going out. After a long hot shower that they shared in order to save water, of course, they made love inspired by the erotic video clips they had just watched and took a short nap. When they awoke, it was close to four in the afternoon. Alia waited in the motel while Nagib drove to the internet café they had located. He took his laptop to the pimpled youngster who was at the desk and described his problem.

The guy looked him up and down, snickered, and said it would cost him fifty dollars to do what he requested, and Nagib managed to drive the price down to thirty in cash, with no questions asked. The guy took the laptop, hooked it to the internet and downloaded a short program. He then loaded the pornographic material into the program, showing Nagib each step of the way what to do, and within five minutes the porn files disappeared from the directory.

Nagib asked the guy how to retrieve the files and the youngster smiled and said that this would cost him another thirty dollars. After some haggling, the guy agreed to show him how to do the retrieval for twenty dollars. For an additional cost Nagib purchased another two memory sticks from the youngster and returned to the motel. When he told Alia about the whole affair she laughed and said that bargaining was no longer limited to the Middle East or the Far East, but that it was well worth the fifty dollars it cost. They encrypted the classified folder and files on the memory stick hidden on Nagib's pen.

After that, they left the motel looking for a used-car lot. They entered the first used-car dealership they found. The salesman, dressed like a cowboy, greeted them with a false smile that displayed white even teeth, obviously the work of an orthodontist and as false as his smile.

Nagib told him they were short of cash and needed to trade their new, expensive Toyota for a reliable, cheap car. The dealer exuded a few more smiles and made them an offer that would have been considered insulting under other circumstances, but they were in no position to refuse. Nagib managed to increase the price by a few hundred dollars but the dealer knew they were in trouble and refused to budge any further. He said he'd sweeten the deal by selling them a cheap Nissan. Nagib asked if there was a guarantee on the car, and the dealer assured him that he offered a "five-fifty guarantee" on all the cars he sold for no extra cost.

Nagib asked if he meant five years and fifty thousand miles, and with a small smile the dealer replied that he meant five minutes and fifty yards after they drove off the lot. Nagib did not see anything funny in that but signed the ownership transfer papers and left in cloud of smoke from the Nissan's exhaust.

June 18, Los Alamos National Laboratory

The head of security at the lab, Colonel Groovey, looked as if he was about to have a massive coronary. His face was crimson red, his blood pressure skyrocketed, and the uncontrollable tremor of his hands indicated he may not live through the day.

The security guard, Albert Danillo, stood in front of him and could barely refrain from wetting himself. Albert had been to many ball games where the unruly fans uttered a never-ending stream of curses at the referee, his mother, and his whole line of ancestors whenever he ruled against their home team, but until today he had never heard anything like it off the sports field.

The Colonel's tirade went on and on and the expletives were literally and figuratively a masterpiece of the English language. Had someone bothered to record what was said in the Colonel's office, it definitely couldn't be described as a conversation, and used it as an example in a class on English literature, it would have certainly won the first prize in any contest.

The intimidated guard tried to explain that he was convinced no harm was done and it was only a system error that
triggered the alarm that someone had inserted a memory
stick into Dr. Level's computer. He said he intended to investigate the matter the next day when Dr. Level returned to
work as no one told him the good doctor was on his way to an
extended vacation abroad.

The Colonel called him a stupid, asinine, dumb idiot and
added another few invectives unfit to print, and told him he
would stand trial for treason, no less, because his negligence
had caused more harm to the national security than anyone
since Klaus Fuchs passed the secrets of the atomic bomb to
the Soviets during the Manhattan Project. Groovey picked up
the phone and summoned two security guards to escort their
former colleague to the local police station, where he would
be charged with a dozen different variations of breaking every
law in the book.

After Albert was taken away, the Colonel started to prepare
his own defense in view of his pending interrogation by the
DHS, FBI, CIA, NNSA security division, local police, and any
other law enforcement agency that had jurisdiction at the lab,
or cause for investigation of the removal of highly classified
information pertaining to national security from the lab.

The Colonel had already received a detailed report on the
classified material downloaded from the files on Dr. Level's
computer. He also knew Dr. Level was questioned in Paris
by the head of the local CIA station and described what had
happened in his office.

Dr. Level was already forcibly placed on a plane that was

on its way from Paris to Washington. What really concerned the Colonel was that the real culprit had been identified as Dr. Nagib Jaber—the very same person whom he had personally interrogated and judged to be "an honest, hardworking, loyal American."

There was no doubt that Nagib was responsible for the fiasco. This was based on Dr. Level's testimony and on the fact Nagib and Alia had disappeared from their home and work without giving an explanation. Adding insult to injury, the Colonel recalled that on the very day the event occurred he had welcomed Nagib when he visited Alia at the security office. He was stunned when he realized Nagib would have had the offending memory stick in his pocket.

He murmured quietly, "I should have shot the bastard on the spot." He seriously considered using his gun to shoot himself and avoid the embarrassment that was inevitable.

The extent of the damage was still being assessed by the NNSA, but it was already obvious that the most advanced and detailed designs of nuclear weapons had been copied.

Two task forces had been nominated by the President himself. One team was in charge of locating and arresting Dr. Nagib Jaber and his wife, Alia, and recovering the sensitive files before they were distributed. This task force included representatives of the FBI, DHS, and the NNSA, as well as some other government agencies. They had a directive signed by the President that allowed them to enlist support from any local police force they saw fit, but at the present time they had no idea of the whereabouts of the culprits, so they did not know whose help they would need.

The second task force included representatives from the NNSA, NSA, DHS, CIA, and other agencies that could help in finding the motives and objectives of Nagib. While the first task force had to focus on physical evidence to find the culprits, the second task force had to rely mainly on intelligence and psychology.

June 18, Los Alamos, the First Task Force

The first task force convened in Los Alamos. They used one of the rooms in the Bradbury Science Museum as they expected they would have to question people who didn't have the necessary security clearance and access to the lab.

The representatives had arrived from Washington that morning or the previous night and after having a light lunch got down to business. Despite the objection of the DHS, the FBI was put in charge of the task force. Its representative, Penny Grant, was a no-nonsense former field agent who had risen through the ranks by a combination of intelligence, intuition, and ruthlessness. Her first order of the day was to post an all-points-bulletin with the names, photos, and descriptions of Nagib and Alia. This was immediately distributed to FBI and police forces nationwide.

In addition, all border crossings were alerted, especially those that were close to Los Alamos, like the crossing point between El Paso, Texas, and Ciudad Juarez, Mexico. The task force members were aware of the fact that it would take only five or six hours to reach that crossing from Los Alamos, and that the culprits could be long gone, but wanted to cover that point because it was the closest crossing.

Colonel Groovey was summoned to the conference room and asked to provide as much background information as possible on Nagib and Alia. The Colonel knew that the only way he could redeem himself, at least partly, was by full cooperation with the task force. He was very frank about the fact that Alia was employed in his own office and that he had been grossly mistaken to trust her.

He reiterated what had occurred during the two interrogations of Nagib—first the polygraph examination that he had passed with flying colors and next the session with Eugene Powers, where Nagib had impressed him as a loyal patriot. The Colonel admitted that he had been negligent and did not notice any signs that there was a renegade in their midst. He said he had believed that Nagib and Alia would be grateful to the U.S. for giving them a real opportunity to lead a better life than their parents had in the old country, and was, therefore, surprised that they had turned out to be traitors.

The main impression he left on the members of the task force was that he was totally unfit for his position as head of security in a sensitive facility like the lab. Penny expressed the general feeling by designating the Colonel as "a stupid, narrow minded bureaucrat, who was suitable, at best, for marching up and down the square." As in the memorable Monty Python film.

The next person to be questioned by the task force was Renaldo, the technician who had worked with Nagib in the Kirtland Air Force Base in Albuquerque, and later followed him to the lab. Renaldo said that he was shocked by the allegations of Nagib's misconduct—rumors had spread throughout the lab that Nagib was wanted by the security authorities. He alleged that although he had been Nagib's best friend for many years they had drifted apart after Nagib's marriage. He added that he had felt that Nagib was reverting to his Arab heritage and had become less appreciative of his adopted country.

Renaldo stated he had no real evidence for the statement and it was more of a gut feeling. He mentioned he was under the impression Nagib was very curious, perhaps even overly nosy, about what was going on in areas where weapons were handled. He went so far to say this was also the case when they worked in Albuquerque but refrained from confessing they had connived to provide false analytical data to their GCL employer.

The task force members had all read Nagib's Resume but wanted to gain a less formal insight. Minnie Level was the best friend of the couple and was summoned.

Her husband was still detained in Washington for further questioning, but she was allowed to return to their home in Los Alamos. Minnie described how Nagib and Max had grown close at work and that their friendship gradually extended to include their spouses.

She said that the Level couple regarded the Jaber couple as their protégés and tried to help them assimilate in the small community of Los Alamos. She said they sometimes went out to dinner together, but that due to the age difference and mentality gap they were not that close. She added that to the best of her knowledge Alia had no close female friends and Nagib also kept pretty much to himself. Finally, she said that although she did not know exactly why they had to return from Paris prematurely and why Max was detained and questioned she did figure out that it was due to something bad Nagib had done to her husband and she felt as if he had betrayed their friendship.

Penny tried to console her by saying Nagib had betrayed much more than friendship but promised he would be brought to justice and made to pay for everything. This interview was not very helpful.

The report of the interview of the FBI agent who was sent to question Alia's parents in Durango was presented to the task force. It was obvious that her parents knew nothing of their daughter's plans and even less of their son-in-law's actions.

A search of the Jabers' house, as expected, did not provide any clues with regard to their whereabouts. A court order was issued that allowed the investigators to get a list of all the calls made from their home phone and their mobile phones, but no useful information was obtained from these lists. A similar permit to get their bank records and credit card transactions showed the maximum amount of cash withdrawal from their account was carried out on June 14 from the ATM machine located at the employees' union of the lab. The New Mexico department of motor vehicles provided the details of Nagib's car—it was a newer model black Toyota with four-wheel drive. Alia's car, an old green Ford, was found in the lab's parking lot.

Meanwhile, reported sightings of the culprits started flowing into the task force temporary office. They were supposedly seen in Colorado, Texas, Utah, and Las Cruces, New Mexico. This last location appeared to be credible as they knew that Nagib had attended school there and received his doctorate from NMSU. But this lead, like all the others, turned out to be a case of mistaken identity. The only report that seemed to be substantive was from a traffic police officer in Kingman, Arizona. The officer said that around midnight of the 14th he had spotted a car that exceeded the speed limit and stopped it for examination.

The driver was a woman who had a foreign name, probably something that sounded Arabic, but he was not sure if it was Alia Jaber. However, he said that his recollection of the couple exactly fit the photos posted on the APB. When asked what he had done after stopping the car he said that as their papers were in order, and they were not intoxicated, he let them go with an informal warning. He also recalled that they gave him a story about an uncle who was hospitalized in LA in critical condition after being involved in a hit-and-run accident, but added that he did not believe this story he had heard so many times from speeding drivers. He neglected to mention the cash "fine" he had received as he knew that this would be considered as a bribe and lead to his dismissal from the force, if not to a severe punishment.

Penny wondered out loud if Los Angeles was indeed their true destination or just the first excuse that came to mind when they were stopped by the police. She said that her intuition was that the destination escaped their subconscious and called for an enhanced effort to locate them in the large LA area.

She directed the junior FBI representative of the task force to call the LA branch of the FBI and have them search for the Jaber couple and for the black Toyota they had driven in. The junior agent called ahead and said he would be arriving that evening and expected full cooperation of all the police departments in the LA metropolitan area. He said they should focus on used cars dealerships as he assumed the couple would need to get rid of the Toyota and get a cheaper used car and some cash.

The border crossings did not keep records of U.S. citizens going into Mexico or returning to the U.S. and usually just glanced at the car's registration and asked the occupants if they were U.S. citizens. In some cases, when the driver or passengers looked suspicious, they also requested to see some proof of citizenship, but on the whole the traffic flowed freely.

The FBI saw no point in asking the Mexicans for information as their cooperation was less than enthusiastic. At the suggestion of the representative of the Department of Homeland Security, Patrick Batterson, prize money was promised to whoever would provide information on the two fugitives. The reward for information on Nagib was one hundred thousand dollars and on fifty thousand dollars on Alia. Posters with their photos and promised rewards were distributed to all border crossings, but as feared by the experienced FBI people, the number of false sightings grew exponentially compared to the reports after the APB was published.

This once again demonstrated that greed was the strongest incentive for getting the public's cooperation. These reports were now a nuisance because every law-enforcement agent knew what would happen if it turned out that a true lead was not pursued, or more specifically if the media found that out after damage was done. As far as Penny was concerned, the manpower dedicated to sift through all these reports and follow up on those that appeared to be serious could be put to better use in the field, but like any other committee the politics involved meant that she had to acquiesce with the DHS.

She began to regard Mr. Batterson in the same light as she considered the Colonel—a bureaucrat with no imagination whose potential for causing harm should be curtailed.

June 18, Washington, DC, the Second Task Force

The mission of the second task force was to study the motives of Nagib and Alia Jaber and to try and predict their target. The members included Dr. Eugene Powers from the NNSA who had been appointed as its chairman, Brian Blade from the CIA who was addressed by everybody by his nickname BB and representatives from the DHS, FBI, NSA, State Department, and the Pentagon.

Eugene, who had interviewed Nagib in person just a couple of weeks earlier, recounted his impression of Nagib. He said that Nagib was very intelligent and managed to deliver his answers quickly and with what appeared to be complete frankness. He relayed the impression Nagib had made on Colonel Groovey and mentioned his own reservations about the smoothness of Nagib's response to all queries as if he had rehearsed them. He also mentioned the fact that he had conveyed his uneasy feeling to his colleague, David Avivi, from the Israeli Mossad.

He assured the skeptical members of the group that David could be trusted and related their mutual involvement in the case known as *Mission Alchemist*. Eugene also said they would need the cooperation of the Israelis to carry out a thorough background investigation of Nagib that would be vital in understanding his motivation. BB was especially dubious because the CIA had come to expect the Israelis to cooperate fully only if it were in their own interests and he wondered out loud if any foreign countries were involved in this case.

The DHS representative added they should focus on dangers to U.S. citizens and property and not worry about what happens in the remote Middle East, where tribal wars between Jews and Arabs and between Muslims of different sects were constantly raging.

The NSA delegate said they had checked Nagib's international e-mail messages and phone calls—officially they were only allowed to monitor the international communications or those involving a foreign national—and found nothing at all since he had joined Los Alamos National Laboratory. He did mention that Alia had some relatives in Palestine but had not maintained any contacts with them after her visit several years earlier.

The Pentagon representative said he had reviewed Nagib's work as a contractor in the Albuquerque air force base, before joining the lab, and got the impression he had been a hardworking, highly motivated employee with good professional skills.

The State Department delegate simply nodded and said he

had "no comment."

Eugene said they would work on getting information from the Israelis through official channels and summon the Israeli military attaché to their next meeting but decided to share his concerns with David without informing the committee.

The task force members discussed their next steps for quite a long time until a consensus about the priorities was reached. They agreed that the designs of nuclear weapons in themselves were useless unless fissile materials could be obtained. They also postulated that all nuclear materials in the U.S. were well guarded and, therefore, the designs themselves did not pose an immediate threat to the security of the United States.

The CIA representative, BB, raised the point that these designs would be worth a fortune to terrorist organizations that could get hold of fissile materials or to state entities that did have the necessary materials but could only produce primitive atomic weapons. He continued to name the three states that suited this profile: Iran, Pakistan, and North Korea. He added that a fanatic Muslim would rule out North Korea, but that they had no evidence that Nagib was a devout Muslim and even had ample evidence to the contrary—he liked to consume alcohol and had never refrained from eating pork products.

The senior officer from the Pentagon said military intelligence believed that Pakistan had already produced an arsenal of nuclear weapons that included multiple Megaton hydrogen bombs. Iran was, therefore, the most likely state that would be willing to purchase the stolen designs. Iran had a diplomatic delegation at the United Nations in New York and several of its members used their diplomatic immunity to carry out subversive operations like industrial espionage, purchase of sensitive items, and export them illegally with the help of fake export licenses and front companies. They also actively encouraged people to convert to Shiite Islam and turned them in to "sleeping agents," that could be called upon to carry out seditious acts.

Eugene said the NNSA was also concerned Iran would try to obtain detailed designs of advanced nuclear weapons despite its commitment iterated in the nuclear deal that was signed in 2015 not to pursue a military nuclear program. The State Department representative nodded and again said that he had "no comment."

When Eugene asked if anyone had practical suggestions, the members of the task force unanimously agreed there were only two operational items: find out more about Nagib and Alia in order to understand where they were heading, and increase the surveillance on all Iranian diplomats that were involved in illegal activities on U.S. soil.

Eugene's determination to contact David and the Israelis grew stronger and he started thinking of covertly inviting David to the U.S. to unofficially advise him unbeknownst to the committee.

CHAPTER 6

June 18, Pasadena, California

Nagib and Alia discussed their options. Unknowingly, their conclusions were quite similar to the discussions that took place at the meeting of the second task force. Nagib said that the information they had on the memory stick was worthless unless they could find a suitable partner willing to help them take revenge on Israel or its strongest supporter—the United States of America.

Alia repeated her objection to do anything that would harm the U.S., as it was a haven for her parents. They agreed that the most likely buyers of the advanced designs were Iran, Pakistan, and North Korea, but did not rule out powerful organizations like the Islamic State that may be able to get hold of the fissile materials.

Nagib had read the scientific literature and knew that with the proper facilities, a nuclear device could be constructed even with materials extracted from irradiated nuclear fuel. After some deliberation on the pros and cons of each of these options, they decided to focus on Iran and the Islamic State, as these two entities were considered as dire enemies of the Jewish state of Israel.

Alia said that they should not rule out Pakistan because it had a strong incentive to improve its nuclear arsenal as a means of retaliation to its much bigger neighbor, India. She added that she had read somewhere there were strong anti-American feelings in that country, and there were rumors that even inside the government there was a powerful anti-American faction. Nagib said he knew nothing about this, but they should not rule out this possibility.

The simplest way to make contact would be to go to one of the many mosques or Islamic Community Centers, ICCs for short, in the Los Angeles area, but as Alia was a Christian and Nagib had drifted far away from his original religion and now saw himself as an atheist, this approach could be dangerous.

Furthermore, like every American, and certainly every Muslim in America, they knew that after 9/11, these places were normally under surveillance by the DHS and FBI. They also realized that the religious institutions were riddled with informers and planted agents, so they decided to stay away from anything that was identified as a conspicuous Islamic center.

There was a large community of former Iranians in Los Angeles but some, especially those that arrived in the late 1970s and early 1980s, were sympathizers of the Shah, some were fully Americanized and some were even Jewish, so finding the right contact would not be easy and could even be dangerous. Alia suggested that they travel to New York and try to contact official members of the Iranian UN delegation but Nagib said those would probably be under close surveillance.

Then they considered crossing into Mexico on the way to

Cuba or Venezuela, where it would be easier to find Iranian representatives and where the U.S. law enforcement agencies could not operate freely, if at all. They ruled out this option as they believed the border crossing would be too risky, as they were sure extra precautions would be taken to block this route.

That evening, while watching the news on TV in their motel room they were glad to see that there was no mention of their action and their photos were not shown. During a commercial break a short advertisement promoting tourism to Turkey was shown. Alia excitedly told Nagib that this would be the ideal place to make contact with Iranians and with Islamic State operatives. In addition, many Americans travelled to Turkey, so they would not stand out there. The problem then was getting out of the U.S. without being apprehended.

They knew it would be impossible to get an airline ticket and board a plane in an American airport because their description and passport information would be flagged. They did not have the contacts, or the cash needed to purchase forged passports, so they figured their most promising route would be to cross into Canada and try to make their way to Turkey, indirectly, from there.

June 19, Washington, DC

David Avivi passed through the passport control at Dulles International Airport, collected his luggage and handed his customs form to the officer and was waved through without any delay or even a second glance. He had been briefed by Dr.

Eugene Powers that his presence in Washington was informal and he should contact him on his private cell phone after settling into his hotel. The Israeli embassy was informed that David would be in Washington on semi-official business: on the Israeli side he was sent on a mission by Haim Shimony, the Head of Mossad, but as far the U.S. intelligence community was concerned he was there as a private individual.

If his presence would be exposed, an embarrassing scandal could develop, so very few people at the embassy were aware of his visit. David went to the car rental desk and was told that his reservation was upgraded from his nondescript compact car to a red four-wheel drive Jeep Wrangler. To the surprise of the agent at the car rental desk, David said he preferred an intermediate size car and was told that a Chevrolet Cruze would be ready for him in ten minutes. He took the Washington Dulles Access Road to I-495, headed north and then switched to the I-270, getting off the highway at the Montrose Avenue exit and made his way to the Hilton hotel in Rockville. He preferred this location, far away from the center of Washington, DC, yet readily accessible by the Twinbrook Metro station.

This would be an ideal place for meeting with Eugene without drawing unwanted attention. He called Eugene, who was just leaving his office, and they arranged to have dinner in a small Mexican restaurant that was a short walking distance from David's hotel.

On the phone, Eugene did not tell David exactly what documents were downloaded by Nagib, only hinting they were pertinent to nuclear weapons. David said the disappearance of the ex-Palestinian scientist with highly classified documents was considered to have possible implications on the security of Israel and Mossad took this situation very seriously.

Before leaving Israel David had been briefed by the "Fish" and was given a thick file the ISA had gathered. It included information on Dr. Nagib Jaber, his family, his childhood friends, and particularly on his brother's criminal and terrorist activities. The file noted that the two brothers had been very close although their interests in life differed radically—Nagib had been the studious, rational, cool-headed type while Yassir was hot-headed and dropped out of school early and then became deeply involved with the Palestinian cause.

The ISA had also constructed a thorough record on Alia's relatives and had a report of her visit to her grandparents. David had all the data on his laptop, and it was in encoded format, so that no unauthorized person could access it.

When David arrived at the restaurant Eugene was already seated at the bar and sipping an ice-cold Corona beer in a chilled frosty glass. David sat down beside him and ordered the same. The cool beer was especially welcome considering that outside it was one of the ninety/ninety days—ninety percent humidity and ninety degrees Fahrenheit—Washington was noted for.

While seated at the bar they chatted about the weather, family affairs, the flight, and the tourist attractions but once they were seated at their corner table and ordered their dinner, they got down to business. Eugene told David about the disappearance of Nagib and Alia and said they had probably copied secret files that contained highly classified information.

David tried to find out what kind of information, but Eugene refused to elaborate and said it was very sensitive and could affect not only the U.S. national security but also destabilize the world. David could put two and two together and assumed the files may include technical details of modern nuclear weapons but kept this thought to himself.

Eugene then told David about the task force and its two main objectives—discovering the motivation and possible targets—and related his idea to involve the Israeli intelligence agencies and the objections of the other committee members. He explained it was his own initiative to invite David as his own private consultant and discretion was called for.

David said that his participation was approved by the Head of Mossad in person, but he was directed to keep a low profile and refrain from doing anything that would deleteriously affect the delicate U.S.-Israeli relations. So, by the time they finished their dinner the ground rules for cooperation were set, and now came the time for serious discussions.

They left the restaurant and took a stroll through the quiet neighborhood speaking in low voices. They passed Congressional Plaza and reached a sports bar and pub. They found a quiet table, far away from the TV screens showing some rerun of college football games and ordered another beer. There was no one seated near them and they felt they could talk freely.

David summarized the information collected by the ISA. Nagib had left Palestine over a decade earlier when he was in his early twenties, and never returned there. He'd never been in trouble with the Israeli or Palestinian authorities but his brother, Yassir, was a notorious terrorist in the eyes of the Israelis or a revered martyr in the Palestinian view. The two brothers admired each other's lifestyle and achievements— Yassir regarded Nagib's scientific career with great pride and Nagib respected Yassir's total dedication to Palestine.

David said that Nagib did not follow in his brother's footsteps and was not involved with any terrorist organization, even after his parents' home was demolished by the Israelis. The ISA noted that this was exceptional because Arab youths that went through similar experiences usually were short-tempered and sought revenge. The psychologist employed by the ISA emphasized that this type of behavior, lack of reaction, would be frowned upon in Palestine and Nagib would be considered as not man enough had he not lived abroad.

The psychologist added that in Arab culture "revenge should be served cold," namely the longer a person waited to avenge an offence the better. He said it could not be ruled out that Nagib had waited for the proper circumstances to exact his reprisal and seized it when presented with the opportunity.

David said that when he asked the psychologist what form the retribution could take, the answer was the longer the open sore festered the more toxic it became. The ISA did not have much data on Alia's family and only said that her parents, like many other Christians who felt unsafe under the Palestinian Authority's rule and immigrated to a place where they hoped their children would have a better future. Many took up residence in South America, especially in Chile and Peru, and others moved to the United States or European countries like

Germany or Scandinavia, usually joining family members that had preceded them.

There was record of Alia's visit to Israel and Palestine a few years earlier, but her grandparents were no longer alive and her remaining uncles and cousins refused to cooperate. Eugene thanked David for the update and said it may be the key to understanding Nagib's behavior that was supposedly out of character. He noted that none of his friends or colleagues had ever heard him say anything against Israel or criticize the support it received from the U.S.

They recalled that Nagib's doctoral advisor, Professor Jack Chen, was a former Israeli who had helped Nagib with his career and was the guest of honor at his wedding with Alia. So, it was unclear what Nagib had in mind and what he really thought about Israel.

David asked Eugene if the task force had developed any insight about possible targets and was told there was a general feeling he would try to sell the classified data to an entity, sovereign country, or clandestine organization that would help him take revenge. They did not believe he did this solely for money and considered he would want to be involved personally in the final act.

Although Eugene did not say it in so many words, David was now convinced more than ever that the classified material involved nuclear weapons, and as only a memory stick was taken, he knew it could only be technical information like blueprints or schematic designs. He, therefore, suggested there were a very small number of entities that would be interested in the stolen files. Eugene agreed and said that the task force decided to focus on Iran and the Islamic State movement.

David concurred but said that North Korea or even Pakistan should also be considered, not because they had any direct conflict with Israel, but because they could use some advanced designs to improve their own arsenal of nuclear weapons and their stature in the world.

Eugene reacted by saying he had not mentioned advanced designs, but David responded he had figured it out and did not want to force Eugene to divulge classified information. They agreed to meet again the following evening and David returned to his hotel and had a good night's sleep despite the jet-lag.

Early the next morning David called Eugene on his private phone and told him he had to leave the U.S. as some crisis regarding a Mossad operation in Europe was developing. David didn't mention that a Mossad collaborator inside the German police had alerted his Israeli girlfriend, who was actually a Mossad agent, that there were rumors of an operation by a fanatic Muslim faction, with ties to the Islamic State, against the moderate Muslim Ahmadiyya community that was about to hold a joint rally with the Jewish community for Peace-in-the-Middle East.

June 19, Oregon

It was close to one thousand miles from Pasadena to Portland, Oregon, and Nagib and Alia once more took turns driving and napping. They had left Pasadena the previous evening, avoiding the rush hour traffic, and made good time travelling along Highway 5, stopping briefly at the outskirts of Sacramento for coffee and services.

The old Nissan they got from the used-car dealership in Pasadena did not cause any trouble despite their concerns about the five-fifty guarantee. They did not want to check in to a motel and waste too much time, so they continued north until they reached Medford, OR, where they parked in a quiet corner of a rest area and took a nap.

Alia lay on the back seat and Nagib tilted the driver's seat as far as it would go and within minutes he was snoring, as if he had no worry in the world. When dawn approached, they woke up, had a steaming cup of coffee, then continued north to Portland. As they passed through Eugene, OR, Nagib muttered a juicy expletive.

When Alia asked what came over him he said the town's name reminded him of the guy from the NNSA who had interrogated him and appeared not to believe him. When they passed close to Lebanon, Oregon, Alia started laughing and when Nagib asked her why she was so happy she said that they were almost home as they were just close to Lebanon.

Nagib joined her laughter and was pleased that she was taking the whole affair in stride. As they reached Portland, they debated whether to check in to a motel there or make an extra effort and cross into Canada before resting.

June 20, Vancouver

The additional six-hour drive from Portland to Vancouver was beyond their strength, so they checked in to a cheap motel, paid cash, and went to their room. After resting for a few hours, they woke up, took turns in the shower and went out for dinner at a fast-food joint near the motel. They turned in for the night and woke up refreshed, with renewed energy but with the same old worries.

They realized that the sooner they got out of the U.S. the better chance they had of avoiding being captured. Their biggest fear was that their photos and passport numbers were sent out to the U.S. and Canadian border crossings. They decided to try and blend in with the many Canadians returning to Vancouver from their good paying jobs in the U.S. and weave in with the busy afternoon traffic.

They were surprised and relieved when this simple ploy succeeded and after entering Vancouver found a nice motel, and celebrated their escape from the U.S.

They saw that their cash reserves were almost depleted and what they had left would barely suffice for airfare to Turkey. They couldn't use their credit cards because they suspected those were closely monitored, and although they were out of U.S. jurisdiction, they feared the U.S. authorities would drum up some fake charges and get the Royal Canadian Mounted Police to detain and extradite them.

Their only asset was the car they had bought in a trade-in deal in Pasadena, so Nagib drove to a used car lot in Vancouver and the dealer at first did not want anything to do with it but when Nagib said that he desperately needed cash, a transaction was made for about half the book value of the car.

Now they faced a new problem. Ever since 9/11, all airlines were suspicious of passengers who paid cash, or of travelers who bought one-way tickets, and of travelers that purchased their tickets shortly before travelling. In addition, passengers with Arab-sounding names were immediately suspected. Nagib and Alia suited all four criteria.

However, when they checked the price of airline tickets from Vancouver to Istanbul, they discovered that buying a one-way ticket was much more expensive than buying a round trip. A little further search of the web found a special deal on tickets to Frankfurt, Germany, and figured they could fly to Germany and then continue their travel with one of the European low-cost airlines to Istanbul.

These airlines did not care if you just purchased a one-way fare so they could save a considerable sum of money. They still had to overcome the other problem, so they decided to concoct a heartbreaking cover story. They would claim they had been on vacation in Vancouver when someone broke into their hotel room and stole their credit cards.

Fortunately, they had some cash and by selling their car—they had the documents to prove that—they raised some more. They received a message that Nagib's father was in a hospital in Istanbul and tradition dictated that Nagib as the eldest son, had to see him before he passed away. That would also explain why they couldn't wait for new credit cards and clarify why they had to pay cash as well as explain their Arab sounding names. They hoped this would be convincing and as a back-up Alia was ready to shed tears because of the bad fortune that transpired while narrating her story.

Obviously, they couldn't buy their tickets online because using their credit cards would instantly alert the authorities, so they entered one of the few remaining travel agencies and explained their predicament. The polite travel agent examined their U.S. passports, found nothing wrong, and was favorably impressed by their appearance as solid citizens, so she didn't even mention the problems they had anticipated. They handed her the cash, received the printed tickets, and walked out of the office holding hands.

There were direct flights from Vancouver to Frankfurt but the cheapest fare they found was operated by Icelandair and scheduled to take off early the following morning. They were not worried about the stopover in Reykjavik, because they were convinced that no one would be looking for them there.

June 21, Los Alamos

The first task force, responsible for locating Nagib and Alia had made some headway about locating the couple. They had been traced to California, the used-car lot in Pasadena, where they had traded in their fancy Toyota for a cheap sedan, which had been found by the Pasadena police, that alerted the junior FBI agent.

The car dealer instantly recognized Nagib from the photo the agent had shown him but said he did not get a good look at Alia. He described the car he sold he sold them as an old Nissan in excellent mechanical condition and gave them the license plate and registration number. He added they looked pressed for cash and he was very pleased with the good deal he had made with the trade-in. When asked if they gave an address in Pasadena, he said he thought they mentioned a cheap motel nearby, and when asked if they said where they were headed he answered they didn't speak much. He neglected to repeat the joke on "the five-fifty guarantee" which was not really surprising.

The FBI agent looked at his map and saw that there were only two motels near the dealership. The woman at the reception desk of the first motel sighed when the agent approached her and showed her the photos of Nagib and Alia. She mumbled something about police harassment and confirmed they had stayed a few nights at the motel. She mentioned they had paid cash and kept to themselves, adding that those were the kind of guests that were most welcome. She said she knew nothing about their past, present, and future plans, and really couldn't care less where they had come from and where they were going to.

The FBI agent didn't even bother to ask to see their room and reported the news to the senior FBI agent, Penny, who was in Los Alamos.

The meeting of the task force proceeded. The fact that the couple had been seen in Pasadena a mere two days earlier was encouraging as it indicated they were in no hurry to leave the country, because this could have been done easily before anyone had an inkling they had gotten away with the classified information.

To Penny and the more experienced members of the task

force, this indicated that they were dealing with amateurs who were bound to make more mistakes. Furthermore, they had a good description of the car the couple had purchased. However, in two days they could easily be a thousand miles from Pasadena, or perhaps just a couple of blocks away from the motel in which they had been staying. The police force in Pasadena and the neighboring towns were ordered to search for the car but no trace of it was found.

The DHS representative immediately made sure that all border-crossings from California to Mexico and all airports in California were put on alert to watch out for Nagib and Alia, or for all young couples who even vaguely fit their description just in case they managed to acquire fake passports. He added that these passports may be under different names, not necessarily as a married couple, so the authorities should be really alert.

In June, close to the height of the tourist season this led to many unpleasant moments because innocent citizens were aggravated by the intrusive questioning. Several adulterous couples who were just trying to get away from their spouses for a fling in Baja, California, or a vacation in Hawaii, were embarrassed by the attention they received. Many threatened to write to their congressman, and a few were detained because they refused to cooperate and caused a scene.

There were some unexpected side benefits for the DHS—drug smugglers were caught, wanted criminals gave themselves in, Muslim agitators were stopped, and even a few patients who had escaped from their mental asylum were reprimanded.

Penny called for a wider search and the photos of the couple and details of the car's registration were sent to the crossing points on the Canadian border and to airports in a radius of five hundred miles from Los Angeles.

PART 3. GETTING AROUND

.

CHAPTER 7

June 22, Frankfurt, Germany

Nagib and Alia landed at the bustling Frankfurt airport, through which some sixty million passengers pass every year. The flight from Vancouver to Reykjavik and the short layover there were tiring but uneventful.

Airport security in Canada was not nearly as rigorous as in the U.S., and although a few brows were raised when they presented their airline tickets paid for in cash and purchased the previous day, their heartbreaking story about Nagib's father dying in Istanbul and Alia's tears about being robbed and losing their credit cards was accepted and they passed through airport security and passport control without a hitch.

After landing in Frankfurt, as they were only in transit on their way to Turkey, they did not even have to go through German passport control. However, when they proceeded to the gate where their low-cost flight was scheduled to leave for Istanbul, they saw that the flight had been cancelled and far worse, the airline had gone out of business. There were a few other stranded passengers at the desk by the gate and a young lady, dressed as a stewardess, sorry, cabin attendant, who was a representative of the now defunct airline. The young lady was in tears and told the angry passengers that their tickets were not worth the paper they were printed on, if they bothered to print the electronic tickets, and she herself had not received her salary over the last three months.

She said that they could sue the company but doubted whether this would solve their immediate problem. She added that statistically Istanbul was the busiest route from Frankfurt and assured them they would be able to get to Istanbul and suggested that they try to get on another flight, but she had no specific information regarding the alternatives. Alia and Nagib were at a loss and tried to plead with the young lady to no avail. Nagib said that they could either try to get on another flight or go look for a cheap hotel or a bed and breakfast until they could get on another flight, or perhaps reconsider their original plan.

Alia said that she felt safe so far away from the Los Alamos and the U.S. and that she wouldn't mind spending some time in Frankfurt. Nagib was concerned that the long arm of the law, or the intelligence services, would catch up with them and in addition was worried about their dwindling finances, so was quite reluctant to take the chance.

But then Alia said that she had some distant relatives, second cousins she believed, that had a small business in

Frankfurt. She knew that they had accepted the teachings of Mirza Ghulam Ahmad who claimed to be the metaphorical second coming of Jesus. The Ahmadi religion embraced some of the principles from other religions and adopted the teachings of monotheistic and Eastern sages from Abraham, Moses, and Jesus to Confucius, Buddha, and Guru Nanak, to name a few.

She added that the Ahmadiyya Muslim community was known for its tolerant approach and quest to end religious wars and was, therefore, accepted by most European authorities as being a potential bridge between the local governments and the more fundamental and fanatic Islamic movements.

Nagib said that he preferred zealots that had their mind set on destroying Western civilization, or at least were actively fighting against Israel, but she responded by saying that these would probably be under surveillance by the Bundesnachrichtendienst (BND) that was the Federal Intelligence Service and the foreign intelligence agency of Germany. When Nagib asked her if she knew how to contact those relatives, she said she could call her father and ask him if he had their phone number or knew their address.

Finally, Nagib acquiesced and said that a few extra days would give them time to formulate their plan and perhaps also enable them to make contact with the Iranian or Islamic State people, who were bound to have representatives in Germany.

In order to leave the airport, they had to go to the passport control booths and wait in line with the non-EU residents. The line was quite long but moved quickly with typical

German efficiency. They noted that some people, especially those with Arab features, were questioned at some length and sometimes escorted to another office, so they were a bit tense when they reached the booth in which a tough looking blonde with a sour face was sitting. However, she took a look at their U.S. passports, held up each passport with the photo page, compared it to their faces, and when she was satisfied with the resemblance she smiled, stamped the passport, and wished them a good day and a good stay in Germany.

They went to a moneychanger at the terminal and exchanged some U.S. dollars for Euro notes, collected a tourist map, then boarded the train that connected the airport to the city.

As soon as they got off the train at the central train station they were surrounded by a mass of people of all colors, sizes, and ages who spoke at least a dozen different languages. Arabic was quite prominent among them and Nagib relaxed a little feeling secure in this crowd.

They entered one of the small electronic stores and bought a couple SIM cards with prepaid calls that they inserted into their American cell phones. It was getting late in the evening and they easily found a very cheap hotel right near the station. No questions were asked when they asked for a room and paid cash. When the young man at the reception desk spoke to them in Arabic they pretended not to understand and said they were American tourists who were trying to save money by staying in inexpensive hotels. The desk clerk didn't make much of it and just handed them the key to their room.

They had a short rest in the room and then showered in

the rusty bathroom and went out for a pizza and beer. After they had returned to the room, Alia called her parents' store in Colorado where it was only early afternoon. Her father answered and said he was relieved and surprised to hear her voice and told her about the visit by the FBI.

Alia said that it must be some big mistake as she was on a planned vacation in Europe with her husband. She said she wondered if they had relatives in Europe and wanted to contact them to strengthen the family ties. Her father said he only knew of some family members in Germany but had last heard from them quite a while ago and didn't have an address or phone number but remembered the name of their business was, "Sayed and Sons, Oriental Foods Imports" in Frankfurt. He added that Sayed was his cousin on his mother's side, and he had become an Ahmadiyyan so most of the family, who were Christians, didn't want anything to do with him, and regarded him as a traitor to the faith.

He also said that Sayed was a good man who believed in justice and fairness. Alia told him not to worry about her and that she would be in touch soon and he should not mention this phone call unless he was directly asked about it. She refrained from telling him that they were in Frankfurt and had plans to go to Turkey.

A short web search yielded the business phone number and address of "Sayed and Sons, Oriental Foods Imports." It was too late to call the shop but decided to go there the following morning, case the joint, and decide whether they should contact Sayed and his sons.

June 22, Los Alamos and Washington, DC

At last, the task force in charge of tracking Nagib and Alia had a breakthrough. The wider net cast by Penny had come up with information that the couple had crossed into Canada and were probably in British Columbia.

The cooperation of the RCMP was pitiful at first, when they thought the U.S. authorities were after the couple for some trumped up allegations. However, this attitude changed when the head of the FBI personally called his opposite number in Ottawa and hinted at the kind of sensitive classified information on nuclear weapons Nagib had downloaded from a computer in one of the most secret and supposedly well-guarded facilities in the United States.

It didn't take the RCMP more than a few hours to locate the used-car dealer who had bought the old Nissan from Nagib and only a short time to find their motel. A quick check of the passport control database at Vancouver airport showed that they boarded a flight to Frankfurt via a stopover in Reykjavik. The record showed the ticket had been purchased at a local travel agency. The police inspector who was put in charge of the investigation in Vancouver drove over to the travel agency and was told that the agent who had sold the tickets had already left for the day. He was persistent and called her at home.

She clearly remembered the nice, polite couple and after hearing their story of being robbed and about Nagib's father in Istanbul had felt sorry for them and gone out of her way to assist them. She said that generally someone paying cash and buying a ticket for the next day would raise her suspicion—she was actually directed to call her manager in such a situation—but the couple was so nice, she repeated that, and saw they were under real stress that she decided to act on her own volition and help them. She said that she had worked out the cheapest and fastest route would be with Icelandair to Frankfurt and from there a low-cost airline to Istanbul that was their final destination.

The investigator called his boss who passed the information on to the chief of the RCMP, who in turn called the head of the FBI, who delivered the news to Penny in Los Alamos.

She told her boss that the matter was now out of her hands as her task force could not operate overseas and proposed to close down her group and reassign the responsibility to the other task force that was better suited to handle international affairs.

By the time these events had unfolded it was close to midnight in Washington, DC, so Penny called Eugene on his private cell phone, apologized for disturbing his sleep and updated him. She said she had checked with the airline that the plane had landed on schedule in Frankfurt, and the two Jaber passengers had disembarked there. Eugene asked her if there was any record of them boarding the flight to Istanbul and was told she had not checked that as the FBI did not have the connections to do so.

He then enquired if the FBI had put Alia's parents under surveillance and she answered that they didn't have the manpower for that, and added they didn't even have a court order to tap their phone. Eugene was truly disappointed and hung up after thanking her for her efforts.

Despite the late hour Eugene called the NSA member of his task force, an engineer by the name of Brad Evans, explained the situation and asked him to check whether an international call had been placed to Alia's parents' phone. Brad said he'd get back to him shortly and then reported that no such calls were made to their home phone or cell phones, but a call from a mobile phone with a German SIM card was made to their store about twelve hours earlier. Eugene asked if the call was recorded and Brad said that he would have to check that early the next morning. Eugene thanked him and told him to update him as soon as he had the information.

June 23, Frankfurt

In the morning, Nagib and Alia rose early and used public transportation to get to the store of "Sayed and Sons, Oriental Foods Imports." The storefront was very modest—the text on the sign barely fit above the narrow door and store window. It was located in a small quiet street amid a neighborhood in which many Turks and other Muslims lived.

At first, there were few people on the street this early, half an hour before most stores opened for business, but gradually more and more people filled the narrow sidewalks. Nagib and Alia wandered around the block and tried to understand the ebb and flow of people and traffic. If they could ignore the signs in German and only look at the people in the street, listen to them speaking, and smell the odors they could easily imagine they were in Turkey or somewhere in the Middle

East, perhaps even in Palestine.

Fifteen minutes after the store opened Alia and Nagib entered it. There was one other customer who was being served and after she had filled her basket with products and delicacies and paid the cashier, Alia approached the man who appeared to be the elderly proprietor seated at a table behind the cash.

In halting Arabic, she asked him if he was Sayed. He looked up, saw a young woman dressed in clothes that were obviously American, and replied courteously that indeed that was his name. She introduced herself and the old man rose from his chair and greeted her with a perfunctory kiss on both cheeks and enquired about the health of her parents.

Alia told him that they were well, had made a good life for themselves in Durango, Colorado, but missed the old country. Sayed said that he too missed it but did not want to return there, even for a visit, until peace prevailed in the Middle East. Alia called Nagib over and introduced him.

So, here in Frankfurt stood the three of them—Sayed the Ahmadiyyan, Alia the Christian, and Nagib the Muslim—related by family connections, but with little in common.

Sayed complained that since his conversion most of his relatives did not speak to him, so he was glad to see Alia. He then mentioned that his son, Ammer, had taken one step further away from his Christian roots and converted to Islam, mainly under the influence of his Muslim wife, Zenab.

Sayed asked them what they were doing in Frankfurt and Nagib said they were on vacation in Europe and also planned to travel to Turkey. When Sayed enquired what they did for a living in the U.S., Alia replied that she worked in the office of the chemical firm in which Nagib was employed as a scientist.

This was, of course, true but she did not reveal the fact that they had worked in one of the most secret facilities in the U.S., and certainly did not disclose that they were wanted by U.S. authorities for espionage and high treason. Nagib said they were robbed on their way to Germany and their credit cards were stolen so were very short for cash as they could not access their bank accounts.

He asked Sayed if they could stay with him for a few days until they replaced their stolen credit cards with new ones. Sayed said that he lived with his wife in a studio apartment above the store and had no room there but his son, Ammer, had a large house in a nice suburb just a few miles from the city center. He got on the phone and called his son explaining the situation. Ammer said they were welcome to stay with him and that after work he would come over to the store and pick them up and take them to his home.

Nagib and Alia were overjoyed to hear that and said they would go back to their hotel and bring their stuff back to the store in the afternoon.

They spent most of the day in a park that was very popular with Muslim women with babies, toddlers, and young children. Some of the children were obviously Muslim but there were quite a few that were fair-haired and others that that were evidently of African origin.

They found a bench in the shade that was slightly removed from the playground the noisy older children used. Nagib sensed that Alia was in a thoughtful mood and scarcely responded to his words. He followed her fleeting looks at the children and recognized what was on her mind. He held her hand in his and gently caressed it, saying that the world wasn't a good place for children and their mission was more important than raising a family. Their successful completion of this mission would bring immense joy to many children and adults.

A tear formed in the corner of Alia's eye and she asked Nagib to hug her tightly and rested her head on his shoulder.

It was early evening when Alia and Nagib were taken by Ammer to his house, which was a large, single family home. His wife, Zenab, met them at the door with a big smile and welcomed them. She showed them to the guest bedroom, that until a couple of years earlier was their teenage daughter's room, who was now a student at the Free University of Berlin.

She offered them tea before dinner, and although Nagib would have preferred a chilled beer he refrained from mentioning it in case his hosts were devout Muslims. Alia had told him that Sayed was now a follower of the Ahmadiyya sect after converting from Christianity, but they had no idea what Ammer and Zenab believed in until Sayed told them earlier that they were Muslims.

After the four of them sat down, they had a traditional dinner that consisted of a tasty chicken dish with rice, called Maglouba, and had sweet pastries and dark, bitter coffee for dessert, and they chatted.

Alia and Nagib repeated the story they had told the old man about being on vacation in Europe and enquired what their hosts did for a living. Zenab said she had been a schoolteacher, but after her two kids left the house she volunteered in a Muslim welfare organization that provided advice and modest financial support for immigrants who came from Arab countries to Germany.

The work was organized by a community center that operated side by side with a mosque. Zenab added that her husband was very pleased with her job and, secretly, that he was one of the biggest donors of money to the organization. She told them she was born in Germany but that her parents came from a refugee camp in Gaza to which her grandparents had fled in 1948, when the Israelis drove them away from their home in Jaffa.

Ammer said that after he had met her he, too, became a Muslim. That was more or less at the time his father had also abandoned his Christian faith. He said that he had great respect for his father, Sayed, who had emigrated from Palestine when he was a young man, actually just a teenager, and established himself as a merchant in Frankfurt. He said that the sign "Sayed and sons" was no longer accurate, as he himself did not work in the store and his only brother had died in a traffic accident while driving on the autobahn under the influence of alcohol.

Ammer told them that he was an electronic engineer by training and an entrepreneur by profession and his own company was one of the major suppliers of communications equipment to the German police and military. He added that his company had over fifty employees, almost all of them of Arabic origin, but said they had a few native Germans in the sales and marketing division and, of course, in the front office and on the board of directors. He was the founder, owner, and CEO of the company.

Nagib asked if he had international connections and Ammer replied that his company did a lot of business with the Muslim world, especially with Iran, Turkey, Egypt, and also dealt with North Korea. Working with North Korea and Iran was especially lucrative as they could charge a premium on merchandise that these countries could not buy on the open market.

The women cleared the dishes and the men lit cigars and continued to talk. Nagib probed Ammer gently and asked what he thought about the situation in the Middle East and particularly in Palestine. Ammer responded in a detached manner without committing himself that the situation was not good and was getting worse.

Nagib said he felt that he was brainwashed by the American media that was generally biased toward Muslim-bashing and objective news was hard to find and wondered if Ammer could bring him up to date on what really was going on there. He added that his own family's history in Palestine was very sad and described how the Israelis bulldozed his parents' house and murdered his brother, Yassir the martyr, in cold blood.

Ammer asked him if he intended to get back at the Israelis or forget about the injustice inflicted on his family and settle down in America. Nagib said he was a proud man and would certainly not behave like a lamb led to the slaughter as generations of Palestinian had done and hinted he may have a way of avenging the mistreatment of his people.

Ammer asked what he had on his mind, but Nagib would go no further. Ammer then said he had connections with all kinds of elements that were similarly motivated to make a point for the just cause of the Palestinian people and Islam.

Ammer and Nagib knew they were on sensitive ground and behaved in the manner that two porcupines made love— very carefully. Nagib told Ammer he had obtained sensitive, highly valuable, classified information that could be used for bartering with suitable partners.

Ammer enquired what kind of partners and Nagib responded he would have to sleep on it before taking the next step. Meanwhile, the women returned from the kitchen and joined them, and the conversation shifted to other topics.

June 23, Washington, DC

Brad, the NSA operative, called Eugene and told him that the phone call from Frankfurt to Alia's parents was not recorded as the phone number was not considered as important and no "trigger words" were used. Eugene knew that by "trigger words," Brad referred to words that would obviously imply acts of terror like: "bomb," "explosive," "detonate," "target," or those that are indicative of illegitimate deeds like "kill" or "eliminate," or "numbered bank account."

This may have worked in the Twentieth Century before even the most stupid terrorists and dumb criminals knew about the extensive network of eavesdropping by "big brother," but would not be very useful nowadays. Although the system was now operational in many languages, there were very few fish that were caught in the net—the big ones completely avoided using electronic communications and the small ones got through the large holes in the netting.

Eugene said he was disappointed but not surprised as Nagib and Alia were sophisticated people who knew all about the NSA and its powerful algorithms. He said he would send an FBI agent to interview Alia's parents and try and find out where she was calling from and what they discussed.

In the afternoon, Eugene received a call from the FBI agent who interviewed Alia's parents. He reported he was under the impression they had been seriously intimidated by the second visit of FBI agents in less than a week and were fully cooperative. He said he had recorded the interview and had it on tape and promised to send a transcript of the entire interview.

Alia's father said he had taken the phone call and repeated the conversation as best as he could remember it. The agent said that in his opinion the most important part was the sudden interest she had shown in her European relatives, especially those who lived in Frankfurt, and added that the details were in the transcript.

Eugene asked him if any specific names or addresses were mentioned and the agent said the name of "Sayed and Sons, Oriental Foods Imports," appeared to be the only obvious point. Eugene copied the name, thanked the agent, and hung up.

Eugene knew that late afternoon in Washington was close to midnight in Frankfurt and wondered who he could call for local assistance. He thought the CIA would have a large office in Frankfurt in view of the importance of the city as one of the busiest airports in the world and the main hub of Lufthansa so despite the hour called the CIA representative.

Greg Dower was not very happy when his encrypted phone rang and at first wanted to ignore it, but as the caller persisted, he picked it up and mumbled, "What?"

Eugene introduced himself and apologized. "Sorry to wake you up in the middle of the night but we have a situation that requires immediate action." He went on to describe the importance of the classified information stolen by Nagib and Alia. Greg asked him to hold on for a minute while he washed his face and swallowed a couple aspirins. He then said, "I'll call my team first thing in the morning and check the information. Do you want to involve the BND or local police?"

Eugene thought for a moment and replied, "No, not yet. Please use your own people and update me as soon as you find out anything about Sayed and Sons, Oriental Foods Imports."

June 23, close to midnight, Frankfurt

As soon as Eugene hung up, Greg called the office of the Director of the CIA in Langley. After mentioning it was an urgent matter directly related to national security he was put through to the DCI. The instructions delivered were very clear: terminate the culprits with extreme prejudice and recover or destroy the memory stick.

Greg asked if this included the woman and was told in no uncertain terms that she deserved the same treatment as her husband, as both were dreadful renegades and outrageous traitors. The DCI added it was entirely up to the agency to prevent an incident that would not only be a great embarrassment to the U.S. but also posed a clear and present danger to national security and global interests of the U.S. He blamed the bungling NNSA and its lapse of basic security concepts regarding screening the people it employed and the control of classified information.

When Greg said the FBI was also involved, the DCI said he expected them to drop the ball every time a pass was thrown in their direction, so he was not surprised. Greg Dower knew that his future in the CIA rested on his ability to handle this case and promised himself to do his very best to succeed.

Next, Eugene called David Avivi on his cell phone. David saw the caller's "private number" and at first hesitated whether to answer as his own people had "caller identity"—assumed names, but still a name on the screen. He decided to take the call despite the late hour in Frankfurt. He was surprised but glad to hear Eugene's voice.

Eugene gave him an update on the recent developments and asked if Mossad had any assets in Germany that could be enlisted to help locate the couple without notifying the local police. He had no idea that David was in Frankfurt, so when David said that he personally would coordinate the search he was pleasantly surprised.

When Eugene told David he had also involved the CIA, David said that although he had great respect for the CIA he preferred to operate independently in order not to compromise Mossad assets. Eugene said he fully understood but proposed to give Greg Dower a heads-up about this in order to prevent "friendly fire" incidents between the CIA and Mossad operatives.

David consented but had his own reservations about the capabilities of the CIA that tended to do everything with a lot of fanfare that was anathema to a secretive organization like Mossad.

Despite the late hour in Germany and in Tel Aviv, David called the head of Mossad, Haim Shimony, on his private line, known only to a handful of people from the Prime Minister down. He told Haim he assumed that the information stored on Nagib's memory stick would be of great importance to Israel's security. He said that Eugene never explicitly mentioned the type of information, but he surmised it was concerned with nuclear weapons, and probably with the most advanced designs in the U.S. arsenal.

Haim instructed him to try and get hold of the data and that he shouldn't worry too much about the fate of Nagib and Alia. He added that if taken alive, they could become an embarrassment to the U.S., so as good friends the Mossad should make sure they did not talk after being captured, and cynically said that dead men didn't talk.

June 24, morning in Frankfurt

Sayed descended the staircase from the little studio apartment he shared with his wife just as he had done every day for the last five decades. Although his son, Ammer, who was a wealthy businessman had pleaded with him to close the store and come and stay with him in his large house Sayed had refused to do so, saying that a man lived as long as he had a reason to get up in the morning.

Sayed quoted an old proverb that said a man was like a top—referring to the cone-shaped toy with a point upon which it is spun—as long as it continued spinning it stood upright but as soon as it stopped spinning it would fall down. With some difficulty Sayed lifted the heavy metal shutter and opened the store. As usual, there were a few of the regular customers waiting to buy their daily perishable products.

Sayed did not notice that some other people were keeping a close watch on his store. An Israeli Mossad team sat in the back of an old van parked across the street from the store. They could see through the dark windows without being seen and kept an eye on the street and the storefront.

In front of them a black Savana van, belonging to the CIA, also with dark windows, waited by the sidewalk with its hazard lights flashing as if the driver had just stepped out for a moment. Both teams knew of each other's presence but did not communicate directly or even acknowledge each other.

Unbeknown to them were a couple of men in typical Arab garb that were also surveying the store while pretending to be engaged in an idle conversation and having a smoke. These were members of a radical Islamic faction that wanted to know what Sayed, the Ahmadiyya do-gooder, was up to.

Radical Muslims hated Ahmadi Muslims and regarded them as infidels, even worse than Kefirs, as evident by the Ahmadi mosque that was destroyed in Aceh, Indonesia, by radical Islamists. Further up the street were a couple of German youths. The boy was a skinhead dressed in leather clothes from top to bottom and his girlfriend wore a thin vest that just managed to cover her pert little breasts and displayed an impressive set of tattoos that covered her arms. They too were trying to figure out what was going on in the store, and also keeping an eye on the two radical Muslims. Occasionally a police car drove by but did not stop. It was very disappointing for all these groups that nothing, except the routine business, was going on at the store.

While all this action, or more precisely lack of action, was taking place near Sayed's store, his son, Ammer, and the house guests, Nagib and Alia, were having a serious discussion.

At breakfast, Nagib said that he had reached a decision to confide in Ammer and told him that it was quite a long story so Ammer called his office and said he wouldn't be in and instructed his secretary to cancel all his appointments for the day.

Nagib then gave a brief account of his own history in the United States, beginning with his days as a graduate student at NMSU and ending with his employment as a research scientist at Los Alamos National Laboratory. He added that almost from the very beginning of his studies in the U.S. he had been plotting his revenge against the Israelis for destroying his parents' home and arresting his brother. After his brother's release from prison his passion for retribution abated a little but when his brother was murdered by an American-made rocket fired from an Israeli drone he decided that his reprisal would be of unimaginable enormity and unprecedented magnitude.

He added that Alia was in cahoots with him about

vengeance against the Israelis due to the humiliation she had personally suffered when she visited her family but did not want to inflict damage on the U.S. that afforded a better life for her parents.

Ammer was impressed and asked, "What have you got?"

Nagib responded, "Blueprints of the most advanced nuclear weapons in the U.S. arsenal."

Ammer whistled out loud, his face blanched and said, "I am curious. How did you get these designs?"

Nagib told him the whole story about using the opportunity of a lifetime to download the plans.

Ammer, who was a shrewd businessman was skeptical and asked, "Are you sure that these are genuine designs?"

Nagib was slightly offended and said, "These are as genuine as you can get. I vouch for this."

Ammer remained skeptical and said, "In my business there are several stages of developing a product. First, you have an idea then you examine its theoretical feasibility and design a prototype. Sometimes the prototype design is never even built, in other cases it is abandoned after initial testing and is produced only after modifications and successful tests. Are you sure that what you have is indeed the final, tested, and approved designs?"

Nagib's face turned red as blood rushed to his face and declared, through practically gritted teeth, "The blueprints were stamped as *highly classified, sensitive, top secret*. Of course, they must be the real thing."

Ammer, who saw Nagib's reaction, realized that he hit a sensitive spot—after all, Nagib had risked everything he had worked for all his life as well as the prospect of leading a normal family life with Alia for these blueprints. He decided to drop the discussion on the verification of the true value of the designs. He asked, "Have you considered who would be interested and willing to pay for the blueprints?"

Nagib simply responded, "Any country or organization that has nuclear ambitions."

Ammer then asked, "Nagib, what do you think the designs are worth?"

Nagib replied, "I am not interested in money, only in revenge. I would be willing to trade these designs for a chance to get back at the Israelis. I have talked about this with Alia and we thought that the Iranians would be very interested in the blueprints as would be the Pakistanis. Perhaps other countries with aspirations of becoming nuclear powers like Saudi Arabia, Turkey, and Egypt would be interested. We believe that the Islamic State would also be very keen to lay their hands on such a design and would use it to blackmail their enemies in Iraq and Syria and force them to surrender control of their country to ISIS forces under threat of annihilation by nuclear weapons."

Ammer said that it was quite a long list, and Nagib said he had only mentioned the Muslim countries, but North Korea was also a good candidate for bartering. Ammer said that he needed to think about this astounding information and added that he wanted to make a few discreet phone calls. He then raised an issue about the safety and security of Nagib and Alia, and by connotation about his own safety.

Nagib said that he was sure the U.S. authorities are

searching for him and assumed it was only a matter of time before they tracked him to Germany. He said they hadn't had time to prepare their disappearance from the U.S. when the opportunity to get the classified documents presented itself, so he presupposed the authorities could be close.

Ammer was worried that his involvement in their escape would be discovered and suggested they borrow one of his cars, originally registered to his firm, and drive to his country home that was a small cottage on the outskirts of Boppard.

When they asked where Boppard was, he told them it was a small town on the bank of the Rhine River, a little south of Koblenz. Ammer told them he would join them in the evening, and perhaps bring some colleagues who may be interested in the proposition. He added that he did not want to have long discussions on his cell phone.

He gave them a cell phone that had a SIM card registered to his firm. Nagib and Alia quickly packed their belongings, got in the car, and set their Navigator program. They saw that it should take them about an hour and a half if they took the direct route on the highways passing near Mainz, but they preferred to take a scenic route through some small villages and enjoy a taste of rural Germany on the way.

June 24, evening, near Boppard

Alia and Nagib enjoyed the sites of the tranquil countryside and small picturesque villages they passed through on the drive to Boppard. They particularly liked the last part of their journey in which the road ran close to the Rhine River and in parallel to it. They caught glimpses of old castles that were built on mountain tops, some of which were in ruins but others seemed to be teeming with life.

They were impressed by the busy boat traffic along the river where large barges loaded with commercial goods and raw materials made their way up and down the river amidst smaller pleasure boats and some larger cruise ships packed with tourists on the crowded decks. Most of all they enjoyed their freedom. For the first time since they left Los Alamos just over a week earlier, they did not worry that someone was following them closely.

They stopped for coffee a couple times, bought some food at a local minimarket, found a quiet spot overlooking the Rhine near Bacharach and ate the sandwiches they made for themselves, washing them down with a bottle of white wine. Nagib said that this was their chance to enjoy alcohol without being frowned upon by fanatic Muslims.

They reached Ammer's cottage situated along one of the small roads that branched westwards from the main highway that followed the western bank of the Rhine. The cottage was quite secluded and afforded them a high degree of privacy. They got there in the late afternoon and decided to take a nap before Ammer's expected arrival in the evening.

They settled in the guest bedroom, as directed by Ammer, and showered together to "save hot water" as they joked and then made carefree passionate love. After a short nap they showered again, separately this time, then sat on the veranda with cups of coffee and watched the daylight fade away.

For a long while they just enjoyed the silence that was only occasionally disturbed by the sound of a car engine in the distance and by buzzing mosquitoes. The evening was so pleasant they didn't even turn on the lights and just sat there talking quietly and making plans for their future.

After sitting like this for close to an hour they heard a car engine and saw headlights approaching the cottage, so Nagib got up and switched on the lights. The car came to a stop and when the driver got out they saw that it was Ammer. They greeted each other and Alia thanked him for his hospitality, but Ammer seemed to be in a hurry with no time for small talk.

He told them he had arranged a meeting with two potential customers who could be interested in their blueprints. When asked where they were, he stated he had dropped them off at a nearby restaurant because he did not want them to see where his cottage was exactly located. He added they were probably hungry and the meeting in the restaurant would be like killing two birds with one stone.

Alia shuddered at that, not because of the cliché but because a mental picture of two dead bodies, their own, came to her mind. Ammer said they should follow him in their car but join him about fifty feet from the restaurant as he thought it was better if the customers did not get a look at the car they were using.

They arrived at the restaurant and followed Ammer to the patio that afforded a view of the Rhine River. There were two men seated at the table nursing cups of coffee. The men rose as Ammer, Alia, and Nagib approached and Alia saw that one of them was obviously an Arab or an Iranian, while the other had distinct oriental features that she recognized as Korean or Chinese.

Nagib noticed that despite the warm June evening the Korean was wearing a jacket, while the others were in casual clothes. Every fine hair on the back of Nagib's neck was raised as he was sure that this guest must be carrying a gun that was scarcely disguised by the jacket.

However, Ammer did not seem concerned at all and made the introductions in English. One of the guests was introduced as Mahmoud and presented as an agent of the Iranian Revolutionary Guards (IRG), and the other one was said to be an operative of the North Korean State Security intelligence agency and he went by the name of Kim. Ammer said he had already told his guests about Nagib and Alia and their merchandise, as he called the blueprints.

Ammer suggested they should first eat and then discuss business and said the restaurant was actually a Weinstube (wine cellar), but had a nice assortment of typical German dishes, including some that did not contain pork. This last remark was addressed to the Iranian and added that they served pretty good poultry dishes. Within a few minutes a waitress arrived to take their order and they made small talk until their meals were served.

The serious discussion started after the meal. Kim wanted to know exactly what type of information Nagib had while Mahmoud was more interested in the price. Nagib said to Kim that he could provide a sample to prove the quality of his data and answered Mahmoud by saying it was not only money he was after, so the monetary price was not an issue.

Ammer intervened and said there need not be a single buyer and a deal could be made with both parties, and perhaps others who shared the same cause. Both Kim and Mahmoud strongly objected and said they wanted exclusivity because if the information became common knowledge they would lose their advantage, but said they could reach an agreement between the two of them as there was no conflict of interest between their countries.

Nagib didn't like the drift of the conversation and became very quiet. Ammer once again intervened and said this was just an introductory meeting and they should meet again after each party consulted with their governments. He used his credit card to pay for the meal and asked Kim and Mahmoud to wait a few minutes while he drove Alia and Nagib to their car.

In the car, he explained to Nagib he had brought both in order to have them compete with one another while bidding for the classified information that Nagib had and thus get a better deal. Nagib was shocked by the speed the events were taking place and said so to Ammer, and he also said they should have discussed this before being put in an awkward situation. He added that he suspected the Korean had a gun he did not bother to conceal and that worried him deeply.

Ammer said that he need not worry because he only intended to get the negotiations started that evening. By that time, they reached the car.

Nagib and Alia drove back to the cottage and on the way there he told her about his concerns about Ammer and the rapid pace of the developments. Alia said that Ammer was family and, therefore, could be trusted, but Nagib said normally that would be true but their situation was certainly not normal and the temptation to cut them out of the deal and take all the money could blind even the most loyal family member.

He asked her if she had noticed that Kim was carrying a gun and Alia said she had not, and that projected a new light on the meeting. Nagib said he would feel safer if they left the cottage before dawn and contacted Ammer again without disclosing their exact location.

Alia agreed and they retired for the night, setting their alarm to wake them at four in the morning.

June 24, evening, Frankfurt

Watching Sayed and his storefront was an exercise in frustration for the Americans, the Israelis, the Islamists, and the German racists who were all stalking the small store. Fortunately, they all managed to avoid each other, and more importantly not attract the interest of the local police.

The Mossad team reported to David who was not pleased with the lack of progress and instructed the head of the team to plan for what he called "application of persuasive measures" in questioning Sayed just before midnight. He was not aware of the fact that the CIA team had similar plans, as the coordination between the two groups was less than first-rate.

However, these plans were preempted by the Islamists fanatics that did not want to question Sayed, did not want to wait until midnight, and were only interested in intimidating him because of his moderate beliefs in the will of Allah. Soon after dark, a firebomb was tossed at the storefront but did not ignite so the damage was only a broken window.

This brought the local police to investigate the incident and post a patrol near the store in case the perpetrators returned to complete the job. The racists had also planned to bomb the store but settled for throwing their own firebomb at some other store a few blocks further, this time owned by a Pakistani. Their handiwork was a little better than that of the Islamists and the store caught fire, but the quick response of the fire brigade prevented loss of life and limited the loss of property.

David gathered the Mossad team and told them to focus on Sayed's family and try and learn more about him. In a short while, they found out that he had lost one of his sons in a traffic accident and had a single son left, Ammer. They also discovered that Ammer was a successful businessman who lived in a large house in one of the better suburbs of Frankfurt.

Later that night, David sent the team to survey the house and they reported back there was one car in the two-car garage. One of the agents touched the car bonnet and found that the engine was warm, as if the driver had just returned from a long drive. The agent also said the lights in the house were still on and they could see through the partially drawn curtains that a man was sitting on the sofa, smoking a cigar and holding what looked like a late-night drink.

The description of the man fit their information about Ammer, Sayed's son. No other person was seen from the outside. David remembered the horrendous, yet effective, interrogation method he had deployed in Greece while chasing the Professor Modena, known as the *Alchemist*, and called the Mossad team to gather for a briefing.

By the time the team arrived at the safe house it was well past midnight. David was pleased to see that the force at his disposal was larger and more experienced than the small group of operatives he had in Athens, but on the other hand their target was not a Greek businessman or a scientist, but someone who understood Arabic and knew all about the Islamic State and their methods, so he decided to make some adaptations.

June 25, three in the morning, Frankfurt

The Mossad team used three nondescript cars and one van to carry out the plan. David knew they would not be able to draw Ammer away from his house and would have to gain entry quietly. Like most houses in that affluent neighborhood Ammer's house was equipped with a modern alarm system that was connected by landline to a security firm, so simply breaking and entering was not an option.

Fortunately, one of the agents had been trained exactly for such a situation and in less than five minutes found the telephone landline that was connected to the security firm. He knew that simply cutting it would instantly raise an alarm, as this would be the first thing even the most unsophisticated burglar would avoid doing. However, the technical division of Mossad had developed a device specifically for this purpose—all he had to do was place a special electromagnetic metallic ring around the wire and charge the circuit with the proper combination of DC and AC voltages. When this was in place, he signaled to David he was ready.

David guided two agents to the large glass door that led to the garden but saw that it was firmly latched and had an additional tamperproof device, so continued to the small wooden service door that led to the kitchen. The door was covered by several layers of paint but evidently was quite fragile. Although it was locked the hinges were almost exposed to the outside.

With a screwdriver that served as a chisel, the wood near the hinges was peeled away and the door was quietly removed from the frame. David motioned for the two agents to follow him up to the second floor where three bedrooms were located. The doors of two of them were ajar and David could see in one of them there was a double bed that had been recently occupied as the used sheets were still spread on the bed. David assumed that Nagib and Alia had probably slept there and whispered to one of the agents to take one of the pillowcases for DNA matching.

They could hear that someone was snoring in the bedroom with the closed door. One of the agents opened the door that did not even squeak and David stood at the foot of the bed while the two agents took positions right next to the heads of Ammer and his wife, Zenab.

At David's signal, each agent pulled the pillow from under the head of the sleeping couple and placed it on their faces denying them of air as well as keeping them silent. Ammer wriggled, twisted, and tried to turn his head while flailing with his hands but the Mossad agent held the pillow firmly until he stopped struggling.

Zenab was too weak and too surprised to put up a fight, so she was quiet after less than thirty seconds. The agents tied their hands and feet with strong, nylon cable ties. David checked them both and found a weak pulse, so he drew a small vial filled with a vile smelling liquid and brought it close to Ammer's nose, while holding his own breath. Within seconds Ammer opened his eyes, drew a deep breath and threw up.

David made sure that Ammer didn't choke on his own vomit and when he saw that Ammer realized his predicament, he smiled at him. In Arabic, he said that he had come to send him to the Gehinem (hell), but as he was a kind man, he would send his wife first, followed by Ammer's head and then the rest of his body, piece by piece. Ammer wet himself and stammered that he had a lot of money and would give it all if they let go of him and his wife.

David said that he was not interested in money only in information about his guests. Ammer was embarrassed by his loss of control of his bladder but gained a little confidence and said they had no guests and he was free to search the house.

David signaled to one of the agents to prod Zenab with a commando knife, making sure that Ammer saw it. When she gave a muffled scream, Ammer said that he would tell them everything they wanted to know. He proceeded to say that his cousin Alia and her husband visited his father's store and he offered to host them in his large house. He claimed they left in the morning and stole his wife's car and he had no idea where they went.

David was buying none of this and told the agent with the commando knife to cut off one of Zenab's fingers. Ammer immediately cried out that he would tell them everything and David told the agent to stop. Ammer said he had sent Nagib and Alia to his family cottage near Boppard and they were still there. He proceeded to say he'd had dinner with them the previous evening near the cottage. He gave them directions to the cottage and David threatened that they would be back if the information was not accurate.

As an afterthought, David asked him who they were running away from and Ammer said they only told him they were involved in a tax fraud scheme in the U.S. and were afraid Interpol and U.S. tax authorities were after them.

David said that if he continued with his lies, they would kill them both and stage it as a murder and suicide. Ammer then understood they were not going to believe his lies and came clean with a version of the truth—the CIA was after them for theft of classified information.

David was pretty sure that Ammer and Zenab would not call the police to report the incident because they would have a hard time to explain why they were sheltering a couple of fugitives. He, therefore, did not consider leaving one of his men to guard them until the address of the cottage was verified. David left a kitchen knife in the bathroom and told Ammer he could wriggle there and free himself and Zenab but once again threatened that he would return to finish the job if they told anyone about his uninvited visit.

Just before dawn the two Mossad agents and David headed

toward Boppard and the cottage. They reckoned they could get there before breakfast as they expected little traffic going out of Frankfurt that early in the morning. David thought about contacting Eugene in Washington to give him an update but decided to wait until he was sure that he had Nagib, Alia, and the information in his hands.

He had the pillowcase that was removed from the double bed in the spare bedroom of Ammer's house and wanted to send it to the forensic laboratory of the Israeli police to get the DNA profile but did not have the samples of Nagib and Alia for comparison, so despite his mistrust of the local American agents he knew he would need the cooperation of Greg, the Frankfurt CIA station chief and decided to call him later that morning. He dreaded having to explain how he got hold of it but that was the price of cooperation among friends...

June 25, four thirty in the morning, near Boppard

Alia and Nagib left the cottage after having a quick cup of coffee. They left the key that Ammer had given them in one of the flowerpots on the veranda and planned to call him later to thank him and tell him where they left the key.

The night before they had considered their options and took stock of their meager belongings. They had their passports that were in their own names and pretty much useless for crossing borders where they would be examined as they were sure that an international alert had been issued by U.S. authorities.

They had a few hundred Euros, some dollars in cash, and

credit cards that were probably also under surveillance, if not already cancelled. They had the car that Ammer had given them, that was used mainly by Zenab but registered to Ammer's company. This was an asset that afforded them mobility but could quickly become a liability if Ammer or others managed to trace it. They also had the supposedly untraceable cellphone that Ammer gave them but thought it best to shut it off and remove the SIM card until they absolutely had to use it.

Worst of all, they had no direct way of contacting people who could help them facilitate their plan of bartering the classified files for a means of taking revenge. They were afraid that Ammer had put them at a great risk by bringing the Korean and the Iranian to meet them. Nagib repeated his concerns about the Korean wielding a concealed gun and about the Iranian's interest in the price of the information rather than the content. He added that as a Sunni Muslim, although not an observant one, he did not like making deals with extreme Shiites represented by the Iranian or with heathens like the Koreans. They knew that agents of those two nations could not be trusted to make a fair deal.

After some pondering, they reached a decision to postpone meeting potential buyers until they could establish a safe hiding place for themselves. Anyway, the first order of the day was to get as far away as possible from Ammer's cottage. There were two main alternatives: either look for a remote place in the countryside or a small village where they would be noticed as strangers but could easily pose as hikers or tourists, or lose themselves in a big city where everyone minded their own business and didn't ask too many questions.

After weighing the pros and cons of each alternative, they opted for the second option. Frankfurt and Koln were about the same distance from Boppard but Nagib suggested they would be safer if they moved out of Germany, where people could already be looking for them. Another look at the map showed that Brussels was the best option—it was only about three hours' drive from Boppard, most of the time on busy highways.

It was especially attractive due to its large Muslim population constituting more than one quarter of the total population of the city. Although most of those were from Turkey or Morocco there was also a significant Arab population. Another advantage was the notoriously inefficient police force that adopted a liberal approach and didn't harass suspects.

Nagib had read somewhere that several of the European recruits of the Islamic State movement had come from Brussels, and these included not only youngsters from Muslim families but also some adventurous Christian youths who were attracted to Islam or just sought excitement and action. So, they were on their way and expected to reach Brussels at around seven thirty at the height of morning rush hour traffic, which would make it almost impossible for anyone to catch up with them.

***

David and the two Mossad agents followed the directions given to them by Ammer and reached the cottage just a couple of hours after Alia and Nagib had left. They parked their car on a small dirt road that led to another cottage about half a mile from Ammer's cottage and approached silently on foot. There was no car parked at the cottage and no lights were on nor were there any sounds of activity.

David motioned to one of the agents to circle the cottage while the other agent silently followed him up onto the veranda. They peeked through the windows and saw no signs of life inside. They tried the door handle and found that it was locked, looked under the doormat, the windowsill without success, but then it took them only another couple of minutes to find the key in the flowerpot. As expected, there was no one at home but they saw that the bedroom and bathroom had been in use and David collected another pillowcase from the bed while one of the agents asked him if he planned on opening a hotel. David was in no mood for jokes of this kind and gave the agent a forced smile and said they should head back to Frankfurt.

June 25, late morning, Frankfurt

On the way back from Boppard, David called Greg Dower and arranged to meet him at his office. Greg wanted to know why the sudden urgency, but David said it was best not discussed on an unsecure phone line. Because of the rush hour traffic, the drive back to Frankfurt was much slower than the drive to Boppard, so by the time David stepped into Greg's office it was close to ten in the morning.

Greg offered David coffee that was gratefully accepted.

Both men were reluctant to discuss the futile ambush outside Sayed's store the previous day, so they chatted a little about the failed firebombing of the store by Islamists and wondered if the incident at the nearby Pakistani store by German racists was related.

After these niceties, they got down to business. David presented Greg with the two pillowcases wrapped in plastic bags and told him the whole story, leaving out the details of the means used to extract the information from Ammer. Greg called in one of his assistants and directed her to send the pillowcases by courier to the FBI forensic laboratory and to make sure they also had DNA samples of Alia and Nagib from Los Alamos for comparison.

David said there was little doubt that a match would be found and added that this type of forensic evidence may be needed if the case was ever brought to court. He tried to gain more definitive information on the classified data that Nagib had downloaded but Greg refused to divulge anything specific, so David was left with his own speculations.

Greg wanted to know if David had any idea regarding the whereabouts of the couple and David said that although he had no concrete indication, he was assuming they would head to a city with a large population of Muslims, perhaps even there in Frankfurt.

However, Greg said it was unlikely they would return to Frankfurt and suggested hauling Ammer in for further questioning. David said that involving the German authorities would be counterproductive and formalities were unnecessary because he was sure Ammer would be in a very cooperative mood after the persuasive treatment he had received just a few hours earlier.

David invited Greg to accompany him on a return visit to Ammer's house. It turned out that, unsurprisingly, Ammer had called his office and said he wasn't feeling well and would take another day off. After all, he was the boss, so no one questioned his statement.

When David and Greg appeared at his doorstep and gently knocked on the door, they heard a woman sobbing and when the door opened they saw Zenab lying in a fetal position on the couch wrapped in a blanket and rocking herself back and forth with Ammer returning to her side and caressing her shoulders.

David said to Ammer and Zenab, "I hope you are feeling better, but you should have known that whoever aids and abets a criminal, may not be immune from punishment."

He then introduced his colleague. "This is Greg, a representative of the U.S. authorities, who has come to retrieve property of national security importance stolen from his country."

Ammer stared at his wife, stating, "I gave you all the information I had."

David told him about the fruitless trip to the cottage. Ammer said, "I didn't know about any stolen property and I had done nothing illegal. I only helped a family member who was in trouble."

David responded, "My colleague here is concerned with the laws of his country and of Germany, but I haven't got the slightest interest in legal matters, as you saw last night. I want to know what Nagib and Alia are up to."

Ammer said, "I swear to Allah that I have no idea about—"

Without a word David stood up, went into the kitchen and came back with a small paring knife, pretending to clean his fingernails.

Ammer demanded, "What are you doing?!"

David replied, "Just removing a little dirt from where it doesn't belong." He approached Zenab of the couch.

All blood drained away from Ammer's face and he held up his hand. "Stop, by God, I'll tell you everything."

Greg also turned pale but refrained from speaking, as Ammer continued, "Okay. Nagib told me in general terms what he had and asked me to arrange buyers for his information, but I told him I had no idea what to do and where to look..."

Once again, he stopped talking when he saw David grab Zenab's left hand and pretend to slice the tip of her finger with her wedding ring.

Zenab started shouting as some blood stained the blanket and Ammer couldn't quite see whether her fingertip was sliced off or if it was just a superficial cut. However, this got him going. "I took a couple of my friends to speak with Nagib yesterday evening."

"Who were they?"

"I don't really know them well."

"Cut the bullshit or you'll get your wedding ring back with the whole finger." David pulled on Zenab's left hand.

"Okay, Okay. One of them was an Iranian called Mahmoud and the other was a North Korean that goes by the name Kim."

Greg looked at David and nodded, implying he knew who Ammer was referring to.

Then David asked, "Do you know where they went?"

Ammer groaned truthfully for a change. "I have no idea, but they have my car and cell phone so you should be able to find them."

David stood up, motioned Greg to follow him and while departing said, "Ammer and Zenab, I hope never to see you two again, but if I do need to come back one more time you would curse the day you were born." As an afterthought, he added, "If Nagib and Alia contact you be sure to inform my colleague here immediately, or else…"

Greg left a business card with his phone number on the table and followed David to the car. He said he had learned a couple of lessons in a very short time. First, when time is short, the most convincing arguments are non-verbal, and second, when someone swears to tell the truth by God, Allah, or whoever, this is generally the beginning of a lie.

David shrugged and said that sometimes brute force solves problems, especially with amateurs, but a real professional would rather sacrifice his wife and his life than disclose vital secrets. David asked Greg to call Eugene on a secure line and update him on the events that took place during the last twenty-four hours.

CHAPTER 8

June 25, noon, Brussels

Nagib and Alia found a cheap hotel near the central train station of Brussels and checked in, paying cash that waived the formalities of presenting their passports and officially registering under their real names. The owner of the hotel, an Arab from some North African country, sat in his office and kept an eye on the young blonde girl that tended to the front desk and also served coffee at the four tables of the small café.

Nagib and Alia went up to their room on the second floor and were not surprised to see that it fulfilled their expectations—it was small, unclean not to say downright filthy, without air conditioning, and the sheets looked as if they had served many former customers. The toilet down the hall, shared by the occupants of the five rooms on the second floor was in no better shape. Being used to American standards, the hotel was not exactly their ideal place for a vacation but would be good enough as a place to hide for a short while.

Nagib considered calling Ammer and finding out whether he had other interested parties but was reluctant to tell him where they were. He felt a little uncomfortable about disappearing with Ammer's car but decided they may still need it as a getaway car, so they had best hang on to it for the time being. He even thought that if things got really bad, he could sell it to car thieves that would strip it down for spare parts or forge a license and resell it.

So, Nagib purchased another prepaid SIM card and called Ammer. Ammer saw an unidentified caller and guessed that it would be Nagib and hesitated before declining the call. However, the caller was unrelenting and called repeatedly until Ammer accepted the call and answered.

Nagib didn't want to say his name, once again fearing eavesdropping by authorities, and said, "Hello, it is me."

Ammer replied, "I was worried sick about you, I hope you are well and enjoying the cottage."

Nagib said, "We decided to leave the place because we didn't like the friends you brought last night."

"Where are you?" Ammer asked.

The answer was far away. Nagib didn't give any more details despite Ammer's enquiries.

Ammer was afraid of a return visit by David and Greg and refrained from even hinting that his life was threatened, so he continued talking in the hope of finding out where they were and what plans they had. He said, "Nagib, do you need anything?"

Nagib said that they were doing fine, and then his voice was drowned by a siren and he cut the connection. Ammer tried calling back Nagib's number but there was no answer. Still under the influence of David's intimidation he dialed the number on the card Greg had left him and told him about the call from Nagib.

Greg wanted to know exactly what was said and the number of the phone that Nagib used and Ammer supplied the information. Before hanging up Ammer added he had heard a siren in the background and thought that it sounded like a Belgian police car, but wasn't sure.

***

Nagib told Alia about his conversation and said, "Ammer sounded strange and unnatural as if he was under some extreme stress."

She answered, "How can you tell? We only met Ammer a few days ago and hardly know him. Perhaps he was just surprised we had left the cottage and disappeared with his car."

Nagib insisted, "I am sure that something is amiss and Ammer cannot be trusted."

Once again, they discussed their options. Alia said, "We have to get in touch with radical Islamists. They would be willing to support our cause in return for the classified blueprints. Let's try to contact Islamic State people. The whole world knows that they are very active in Brussels and have carried out several operations to prove that."

Nagib objected, "ISIS have no interest in advanced nuclear weapons, they don't have access to the fissile materials needed even for the most elementary designs. They are doing quite well, instilling terror in the hearts of the Crusaders with conventional means."

Then Nagib came up with a new idea. "The only truly Muslim state that has nuclear weapons is Pakistan. They probably have only primitive designs, if we can judge the tests they openly carried out in 1998. They see India as their dire enemy and probably fear they have fallen behind in the nuclear armament race. They would be extremely interested in obtaining our information."

Alia said, "But the Pakistani government is in cohorts with the Americans—"

Nagib intervened, "I am not talking about the government. I mean to contact Islamist opposition groups. I know that within the nuclear establishment there are many scientists who would gladly cooperate with any act against Israel and the United States. Remember the AQ Khan network that sold nuclear technology and equipment to Iran, Libya, North Korea, and probably half a dozen other countries. I am sure we can find these elements in Pakistan."

Alia was a bit reluctant but agreed with the plan as there seemed no better alternative.

Nagib and Alia entered a café that had free internet service and he switched on his computer. Then, just before he could sign in, Alia stretched her hand and in a very untypical move switched the computer off. He frowned, looked at her, and seeing the expression on her face, understood and nodded his approval, then he stood up and kissed her on her cheek.

They left the café and searched for an internet store where one could buy network time without having to use one's own username and password. They paid the teenager at the desk ten Euros and he gave them a small note with a password and directed them to a free position at the back of the store. They pulled up a couple of chairs and sat side by side.

Nagib logged on and then searched for, "Pakistani nuclear weapons" and was directed to Wikipedia. At a first glance, the website looked like an assortment of Khans that developed the Pakistani nuclear program—Munir Ahmad **Khan** who was Chairman of the Pakistani Atomic Energy Commission (PAEC), Abdul Qadeer **Khan,** the engineer who "brought" centrifuge enrichment technology from Europe and founded the "AQ **Khan** network," General Tikka **Khan** and Mr. Ghulam Ishaq **Khan** at the ministry of defense, and also many others, not only Khans.

Nagib saw the quote attributed to Zulfikar Ali Bhutto, the Pakistani Prime Minister. He said in 1965: "If India builds the bomb, we will eat grass and leaves for a thousand years, even go hungry, but we will get one of our own. The Christians have the bomb, the Jews have the bomb and now the Hindus have the bomb. Why not the Muslims too have the bomb?"

Nagib added that as a young undergraduate student in Palestine this, and the fact that Pakistan actually manufactured an atomic bomb, made him proud to be a Muslim. Nagib couldn't help himself from laughing when he saw that the biggest push to develop a Pakistani nuclear force came from the test India conducted in 1974, with the codename Smiling Buddha, because the Muslims had nothing to smile about.

More to the point, they read that Pakistani nuclear arsenal consisted, according to estimates, of about one hundred and twenty warheads. They continued reading and saw that Pakistan had produced compact plutonium bombs that could be carried by aircraft and missiles, and even nuclear weapons that had much higher yields as they were "spiked" with tritium.

The Pakistanis had also produced highly enriched uranium and were working on smaller nuclear weapons that could be used in the battlefield for tactical purposes. Nagib's face lit up when he read all this, and he told Alia that their blueprints would be of unsurpassed value to the Pakistanis and would give them a great advantage in their conflict with India.

So, now their dilemma was how to approach the Pakistanis and make sure they got what they wanted, and more importantly, that they got away safely. Simply presenting their goods could create such a temptation to the Pakistanis that they may just eliminate them and grab the classified information. They realized they needed to find an honest broker that would negotiate on their behalf, but before that they wanted to get a firsthand impression of the people they would be dealing with.

The address of the Embassy of the Islamic Republic of Pakistan was Avenue Delleur 57, 1170 Watermael-Boitsfort, and they saw it would be open for business in the afternoon between three and four. They decided to go to the consular section and enquire about tourist visas and also try to find out if there was a scientific attaché at the embassy, in the hope they could deal with him without having to go to Pakistan. They agreed not to divulge the fact the information they had would put them in the Pakistani national pantheon—if such a thing existed—side by side with AQ Khan, Zulfikar Ali Bhutto, and Abdus Salam, the—only—Pakistani Nobel laureate in physics.

June 25, noon, Frankfurt

Greg called David immediately and reported the conversation he'd had with Ammer. He added that his people had put a tap on Ammer's phone, so he also had a recording of the call and would receive a copy shortly. David said he would come over to listen to the recording.

By the time he arrived at Greg's office, the recordings of both calls were ready. First, they were convinced that Ammer had given Greg a full report of Nagib's call and did not try to hide any information or even hint that he had suffered a traumatic visit. They also realized Nagib was suspicious that Ammer may not be acting in his best interests and did not trust him. However, the most interesting part was the recording of the siren that the analysts said was indeed similar to that of the Belgian police cars, probably Opel Astra or Opel Vectra, but also similar to that of first responders in other European countries, so it wasn't conclusively in Belgium but did provide a clue.

David said this supported their supposition that Nagib and Alia would try to leave Germany and go underground in a big city that has a large Muslim community. They searched Google Earth maps and the closest place to Boppard that fit this description was Brussels. This could also explain the type of siren they heard in the background. Greg tried to put a trace on the phone from which Nagib had called but there was no active signal as it was shut off. However, the record showed the phone had last been used somewhere near Brussels center.

David knew the Americans were very anxious to catch

Nagib and recover the classified information before it was distributed to enemies of the United States. What was conceived as even a greater threat to national security was what would happen if the press and media became aware that highly sensitive and classified information had been stolen from one of the most well-guarded National Laboratories. Furthermore, to add insult to injury, that this was done by a person whose access to such material should never have been permitted.

David heard Greg referring to Nagib as "the dreadful renegade," when he talked to Eugene. When he enquired about this Greg told him that it was the codename given to Nagib, whose actions were obviously dreadful and he was considered as a renegade because he betrayed the country that gave him an education, a job, and a much better life than he could have possibly dreamed of in his home country. He added that this avoided mentioning his true name in the internal communications to help limit the number of people who knew Nagib and what he had done.

David offered to help Greg in the search for the couple, but Greg said he had no jurisdiction in Belgium and would have to hand over the case to the CIA station chief in Brussels. David said that Mossad had a strong presence in Brussels as it was the seat of several institutions of the European Community and to counteract the operations conducted by the Arab states and their many Muslim supporters.

These operations were not limited attacks on Israeli officials and tourists but also to attempts against the local Jewish community, like the 2014 shooting and murder at the Jewish Museum by a French jihadist. In addition to acts of terror against the residents of Brussels and tourists like using suicide bombers in the airport and Metro.

Greg said that he appreciated the offer and would introduce David to Herb Harden, the CIA station head in Brussels. David thanked Greg and wished him a successful career with the hope that the fact the couple was not apprehended while in Frankfurt, would not end it prematurely. Greg sighed and said if they were caught and the classified data retrieved then everybody would try to sweep the whole affair under the rug, but if the media got hold of the story then scapegoats would be sought, found, and sacrificed and he feared he would be on the short list.

David called the Mossad chief and brought Shimony up to date on the affair. Shimony told him to leave Frankfurt and focus on locating Nagib. David asked about the mission he had been assigned to concerning the Jewish community in Frankfurt that got him there in the first place and Shimony directed him to forget it as someone else would be sent from Tel Aviv to take over the job. He assured David he would receive full support from all Mossad agents in Europe and told him he would become a national hero, albeit only among the top leaders of the intelligence and security communities, if he could quietly obtain a copy of the information that would be considered as a national treasure in Israel.

David said he would be on his way to Brussels immediately and expected to arrive there in the early evening and asked Shimony to instruct all available Mossad agents to gather at one of the safe houses in Brussels for a meeting and briefing at ten that evening.

June 25, three in the afternoon, Brussels

Nagib and Alia took the metro train from Gare Centrale to Herrmann-Debroux station that was the last stop of Line five and then the short, number ninety-four, tram ride toward Louise getting off at Boitsfort Gare that was very close to the Embassy of the Islamic Republic of Pakistan.

As they approached the embassy on foot, they did not encounter any other tourists, and there appeared to be only a few Pakistanis who had business at the embassy. They were stopped first by the Belgian policeman outside the building who just asked them for some ID and when they showed him their U.S. passports they were allowed to continue. They were then directed to pass through a metal detector portal by the Pakistani security officer who also looked at their passports before waving them through to the receptionist.

When asked what business they had at the embassy they said they were considering a visit to Pakistan and Nagib added that he wanted to find out more about the level of chemical sciences there. The receptionist picked up the phone, muttered something in Urdu, and referred them to the person in charge of public relations.

A young woman dressed in a traditional shalwar kameez with embroidery on the front politely invited them to take a seat. Nagib was quite impressed by her good looks and lithe body that could be imagined beneath the colorful clothes. In lilting English, she said that her name was Junaid and asked how she could be of assistance.

They repeated that they were curious about Pakistan.

Junaid looked at their names in their passports and asked if they were Muslims, and both said that they were, but added that they did not practice the religion, and expected their visit to Pakistan to change that attitude. Junaid asked Nagib and Alia what kind of jobs they held in the U.S. and they answered that both were in government service until they recently quit, and that he was an analytical chemist and she was a secretary, refraining from mentioning Los Alamos National Laboratory.

Junaid who was, in fact, an agent of the Pakistan Intelligence Community (PIC), perceived that they were not completely forthcoming and when she saw that their home address was listed as Los Alamos, New Mexico, she decided to call the scientific attaché who was the senior member of PIC at the embassy.

She asked Nagib and Alia if they wanted some refreshments and when they said they would like mint tea she excused herself and went to arrange the refreshment and speak to the attaché. Before returning with the tea she quickly gave him an update on the unusual couple that had sauntered into the embassy.

She introduced the scientific attaché as Rahman Chenna and he told the couple that one of his responsibilities was to collect scientific data related to advanced projects that may be beneficial to Pakistan. At that stage, Nagib felt the conversation was being conducted with both sides revealing a little information and hiding a lot more, and again thought of how porcupines made love—very carefully.

Rahman asked them if they had ever visited the Bradbury Science Museum in Los Alamos or the National Museum of

Nuclear Science and History in Albuquerque. Nagib, who suspected where this supposedly innocent question was leading to, answered that as a scientist who lived in the area for some years he had done so on several occasions.

Rahman then said he had noticed that Nagib's birthplace was listed as Palestine and asked how he had an American passport and Nagib gave him a slightly modified version of the truth, only neglecting to mention he had worked at the lab. Rahman then decided to take another step forward and mentioned that his duties also involved gathering information related to military intelligence and technology, both conventional and unconventional.

Nagib, too, took another step forward and said they may have a commodity that could possibly interest the Pakistani government, but he was afraid it would be wasted and rendered worthless if it ended up in the wrong hands.

When Rahman asked what he meant by the wrong hands, Nagib said somewhat enigmatically that in the right hands the commodity would be fully utilized.

Rahman thought that before having a completely open discussion he should learn more about the couple and their motivation and looking at Junaid suggested the four of them meet for dinner.

Nagib said they were a bit short for cash and Rahman told them not to worry, it was his treat, and named a fancy restaurant near the center of town that was also within walking distance from their hotel. They parted and planned to meet at eight that evening for dinner.

Shortly before four in the afternoon, Alia and Nagib left

the embassy and she told him they were probably dealing with the right person. Although they had no experience with intelligence officers and secret agents, they were both convinced that the title of scientific attaché was only a façade for an operative of the Pakistani intelligence service.

Nagib felt elated that things had gone so smoothly, particularly after the dealings with the North Korean and Iranian agents, whom he suspected and feared.

Alia was slightly more reserved but also sensed they were on the verge of the breakthrough for their grand plan.

June 25, evening, Frankfurt

The day of June 25th is a day that Ammer and his wife, Zenab, would try to forget for the rest of their lives. As if the visits by David and Greg were not enough, as the evening set on Frankfurt, the North Korean Kim appeared at the front door of their home in what they had always regarded as a quiet suburb of Frankfurt.

Kim took one look at the couple and almost failed to recognize the frightened, traumatized man who opened the door as Ammer. He no longer looked like the successful, self-confident businessman who had driven him and the Iranian agent, Mahmoud, to Boppard the previous evening. Ammer was on the verge of weeping when Kim asked him where Nagib and Alia were, and without any prompting told Kim he thought they had moved to Brussels. He did warn Kim that other intelligence agencies were also trying to find the couple. Kim, who had intended to eliminate Ammer and whoever was unfortunate enough to be present in the house, decided that murder would just complicate things and have the German police and Interpol on his trail, so uncharacteristically disobeyed his orders and left the house quietly.

As he was leaving, he saw Mahmoud and a couple of bearded goons come up the pathway. He stopped in his tracks and pulled Mahmoud aside and briefly gave him an update on the situation. He suggested they combine their forces and search for Nagib together and then share the information. Mahmoud was not very enthusiastic about the idea of cooperation, especially in view of how North Koreans were regarded in Europe, but thought he would worry about sharing the data after they had it in their hands, thinking to himself, never sell the *bear's skin before* one has killed the beast. So, the Iranian and North Korean agreed to join forces in the hunt and made arrangement to meet in Brussels at noon the next day.

June 25, eight in the evening, Brussels

When Alia and Nagib entered the restaurant, they were guided to the table where Junaid and Rahman were already seated. They looked at the crowd in the restaurant and felt underdressed as all the men were wearing tailor made suits and the ladies fancy gowns.

Rahman was in a cashmere wool dark suit with a green tie, probably electing the color of Islam and Pakistan, and Junaid in a white dress that accentuated her lithe figure and smooth dark skin. Junaid noticed the couple's awkwardness and told them not to worry because there was no formal dress code and tourists often appeared in casual clothes like theirs.

Nagib noticed that both Pakistanis were drinking what appeared to be club soda with lemon rind but then got a whiff of gin and understood that appearances were not everything and that gin and tonic looked just like club soda.

Alia noticed that Junaid and Rahman were very much at ease with one another and was pretty sure they were sleeping together.

The conversation during dinner was about Brussels as a tourist attraction and the contrast between the big European city and small-town U.S. on the one hand and Islamabad, the bustling capital of Pakistan on the other hand.

After the main course had been served Rahman used that small talk as an opening to probe Nagib and Alia about their plans as well as about their beliefs and ideals. Nagib hesitantly said they were not sure what they wanted to do, beyond fighting for a better world. Rahman asked what they meant by that and Nagib talked about correcting historic evils, bringing justice to the Muslim people, and getting retribution for the deeds of the colonialist powers.

He mentioned the episode of the capturing of Saddam Hussein and the humiliation of a great Arab leader in the hands of the U.S. He also said he had left Palestine as a young man hoping to build a better life for himself far away from his homeland but events that occurred there—the destruction of his parents' house and the murder of his brother—did not let him forget where he had come from. He added that Alia had also suffered abuse and humiliation from the Israelis when she visited her family.

Rahman kept glancing at Junaid to see how she took this story and saw by the glitter in her eyes that she too was impressed by it. Nagib was a bit ashamed about his outburst and became very quiet.

Alia looked at him with admiring eyes and then asked Rahman and Junaid how they felt about the American involvement in Pakistan. Junaid looked at Rahman for approval and then said that like many Pakistani patriots they felt that the ruling class was only interested in its own self-preservation and ignored the common people.

The masses wanted revenge for the loss of territory and population to India in the war of 1971 and in several border skirmishes, and felt that the Americans were holding them back and supporting India while betraying Pakistan. They also didn't like the fact that U.S. intelligence agents were using Pakistan as the staging ground for their actions against the radical Islamic factions in Afghanistan with total disregard to the sovereignty of Pakistan.

Rahman added that there were many middle and low-ranking intelligence officers who shared similar views. Several leading scientists and engineers in the nuclear weapons establishment abhorred the treatment that AQ Khan, who was considered by all Pakistanis as a national hero, received from the government that was forced by the Americans to put him under house arrest.

Alia wondered whether Rahman and Junaid would not be considered by the mainstream government officials as traitors that are set on undermining the legitimate government of Pakistan. Wisely, she kept the thought to herself.

They had dessert and after it was served with coffee or tea, discussion focused on the real issue—what information Nagib and Alia had and what they wanted in return. Nagib admitted that he had worked at the Los Alamos National Laboratory as a research scientist and had been privy to classified information. He said that he could supply a sample of the blueprints he had obtained in order to prove their value and once the Pakistanis were convinced they were authentic, they could discuss the price.

He added that they were not interested in money—only enough to accomplish their plan—but they expected cooperation and logistical support. Upon hearing this statement, Rahman's interest grew because he was now convinced the information could be of real value.

He asked to be excused for a moment and motioned for Junaid to accompany him for a cigarette on the veranda outside the restaurant. When they left the table, Alia told Nagib what she had thought earlier that the two Pakistani agents were acting against the policy of their government.

Nagib countered by saying it was just what they needed as no sane government would dare to act directly against the United States and defy it and reminded her of what happened in Iraq and Afghanistan.

***

Meanwhile, on the veranda, Rahman asked Junaid what she thought about the couple and their proposition. Junaid said that in her opinion they were performing an act of treason against their adopted country and would be considered as renegades by the U.S. authorities.

Rahman, who was quite the cynic after years as an intelligence agent noted that they too would be judged by some people as traitors against their own government, so they should not worry too much about moral issues and focus on practical matters.

He said he was worried that they would be apprehended by U.S. authorities or local police and their blueprints would be lost forever. He suggested they secrete the couple in one of the apartments that served the Pakistani delegation for hosting visiting VIPs and doubled as a kind of "safe house." There was one comfortable two-bedroom apartment quite close to the Embassy on Dreve des Tumuli, that was not frequently used as the more important visitors considered it to be too modest and not respectful enough.

Junaid and Rahman returned to the table and Rahman told the couple that they would like to see a sample of the information they had for sale. Nagib interjected emphasizing that it was not a sale they wanted but cooperation. Rahman corrected himself and asked where they were staying. Nagib just said they were at a hotel near the central railway station without naming it but hastened to add that the information was in a safe place—neither on them nor in their hotel.

This was not true but Nagib started worrying the Pakistanis could arrange for an ambush, rob them of the data and dispose of their bodies. Rahman understood Nagib's concern and sought to assure him that as long as they had common interests—causing damage to the U.S. and Israel and strengthening the only Islamic state that had a demonstrated nuclear capability—there was nothing to fear.

The implied threat did not escape Alia or Nagib, so he repeated that the information was in safe hands and not with them, while subconsciously touching the pen with the embedded USB storage device in his shirt pocket.

Rahman saw the gesture but did not grasp its meaning. He then offered Nagib and Alia the free use of the residence reserved for visiting Pakistani VIPs and the couple said they would need to sleep on it. Rahman said they should keep away from the Pakistani embassy as too many questions may be raised by the consular staff members that were ever suspicious of the actions of the intelligence officers. He suggested they meet the next morning for breakfast at a café a few blocks away from the embassy.

At that time, he expected to be given the promised sample and hear more about what Nagib and Alia wanted in return. He added the offer of the apartment was still valid and he would expect their answer, and once again strongly recommended they leave their hotel as soon as possible.

Rahman called for the check and they all noticed they were the last customers left in the restaurant. When they exited the restaurant, Junaid quietly asked Rahman if they should covertly follow the couple to their hotel but he said the risk of scaring them away was too big and he believed they would meet at the café in the morning as arranged.

***

About a dozen Mossad operators were waiting for David in the Brussels apartment. The local chief resident, Kobi Shukrun, introduced the agents by their cover names, the real names were sometimes forgotten even by their owners. He gave a brief introduction and description of their fields of expertise. There were a couple of computer hackers and communication experts, another was an intelligence analyst, three were field agents with experience in surveillance and tracking as well as neutralizing security systems, and the others were in administrative positions with little field experience.

Kobi himself had been in one of the most sensitive positions in the Mossad's most secret section that dealt with termination of people who posed a clear and present danger to the state of Israel. He was offended when he was directed by Head of Mossad to follow the orders of a young upstart like David, who had little field experience.

David introduced himself, although that was quite unnecessary as he was a kind of legend in the Mossad after his pursuit of *the Alchemist*, a fact that further irritated Kobi. David briefed the gathering about Nagib and Alia and the stolen information and said they were probably in Brussels but there was a possibility they had already moved on. He added that Mossad was cooperating with the CIA, but the cooperation had its limits, and the Americans could be trusted only up to a point.

Kobi was not on good terms with the American agents in Brussels as a result of his participation a few years back in "taking down" a Palestinian Al Qaeda terrorist, who happened to be a U.S. citizen. After that he was kind of blacklisted by the American intelligence community, who had wanted to interrogate the terrorist in order to find out how he was enlisted by Al Qaeda and were not too happy the dead man could not talk.

David told the Mossad agents the latest communication by the couple was the phone call to Ammer earlier that day and it was traced to somewhere near the center of Brussels, probably in the vicinity of the Central Station. He then asked the local agents if they had any idea where the couple could be. One of the streetwise agents, Michelle, who was very familiar with the Muslim community of Brussels, said there were many cheap hotels in that area.

David noticed that Michelle was a dark-skinned, attractive, brunette who spoke Hebrew with a slight French accent and learned that her family was originally from Algiers. Michelle added that many of those cheap hotels were owned or operated by Muslims, mainly men who came from French speaking North African countries as they did not have a language barrier when looking for a job in Belgium, at least in the dominant French part.

David wondered out loud if a couple with American passports would not stand out in that area, but Michelle said the cheap hotels accommodated people from all over the world, and the fact that the couple were of Middle Eastern origins would help them blend in. Then David mentioned they had a car and asked where they could possibly find a place to park it for an extended period.

Michelle said that most parking lots in that area were expensive, but there was one large municipal lot that served the railway station and was reasonably priced. David asked Michelle to take one of the other agents and search that parking lot and gave her the details of the car that Ammer had loaned the couple. She was to report back to Kobi, the Mossad local chief. Meanwhile, the other agents should start checking the hotels in that area.

David thought it was too late at night to contact Herb Harden, the Brussels CIA station head, but considering it was only late afternoon in Washington, DC, he decided to call Eugene Powers. He dialed Eugene's private phone number and was immediately transferred to a voice message, so he said he was in Belgium and left his number with a request to be called back regardless of the time.

Thirty minutes later his phone rang and Eugene was on the line. David shared the information Mossad had and the conclusions, or rather the speculations, about the possible whereabouts of the couple. While still on the line he received a call-waiting ring and saw that it was from Kobi, so he apologized to Eugene and asked him to hang on while he took the call.

Kobi told him that Michelle and her buddy had indeed located the car in the parking lot and were setting up a watch to see if anyone came to pick it up. Kobi added they planted a miniature transmitter under the chassis, so they could track it from a distance if needed.

David thanked Kobi and told him they could call off the hotel search that was quite a formidable task and may alert Nagib they were homing in on him. David then switched back to the conversation with Eugene and updated him on this latest development.

Eugene said this new information justified waking up Herb Harden and he would do so himself and ask him to contact David. He added that although he was not a CIA field agent, only an NNSA administrator and scientist, he felt that he should be present at the site of the action.

David was pleased to hear this as he feared that rivalry between the CIA and Mossad could lead to a conflict unless some high-ranking government official, like Eugene, would supervise Harden and his people.

June 26, nine in the morning, Brussels

Alia and Nagib had discussed Rahman's offer of a safe apartment the previous night and had decided to accept the invitation, so they checked out of their small, smelly hotel. Nagib suggested that they take the car from the parking lot and drive over to the café, but Alia rejected the idea and said she had a premonition that Ammer may have reported the car stolen and it may have been located. She added that in all fairness they should inform him where the car was, because after all he was a family member who had tried to help them, and that would be the right thing to do.

Nagib was not really convinced by the ethical argument but thought that the car may be more of a liability than an asset, so agreed with her. Once again, they took the metro to Herrmann-Debroux station and then got on tram line ninety-four, getting off at Boitsfort Gare and walked with their light luggage to the café where they had arranged to meet

Rahman for breakfast.

Before they had left the hotel, Nagib had copied one small section of a blueprint on to a newly formatted disk-on-key, or thumb drive, that he kept in his pocket. Their laptop was placed in a shoulder bag that was part of their luggage.

They found the small café and saw that Rahman and Junaid were waiting for them. The Pakistani agents greeted the couple and Rahman said that judging by their luggage that his offer of a safe apartment was accepted.

Nagib and Alia smiled and confirmed that, so they all ordered cappuccino and croissants, and cut the small talk moving directly to the business on hand. Nagib took out his laptop, inserted the disk-on-key with the sample and loaded the blueprint. He then turned the screen around so that Rahman could see the schematic that was a section cut out from one of the advanced designs.

Junaid also stole a glance at the screen and her mouth opened and she softly exclaimed, "Bismillah."

Rahman frowned at her and silently asked Nagib if he had the complete design. Nagib assured him he had that as well as several other detailed blueprints. Rahman's dark skin turned red as blood rushed to his face. He realized the meaning of the information and its importance to his home country. He stammered and said they should continue the discussion in a safer environment and suggested they move to the apartment of Dreve des Tumuli.

They briskly walked over to the apartment building and when they reached it, Rahman drew out a set of keys from his pocket and let them in to the building. It was quite modest and there was no doorman or concierge, so they simply took the elevator up to the third floor and entered the apartment.

Junaid took Alia by the hand and led her to the bedrooms, kitchen, and bathroom. She opened the refrigerator and showed Alia there were some basic supplies in the kitchen, so they wouldn't have to go out for food.

Meanwhile, in the small cozy living-room Rahman briefed Nagib on the house rules, stressing the importance of keeping all windows and shutters or curtains shut and secured and not opening the door to anyone else. He also mentioned that the kitchen was supplied and cautioned Nagib about going out or even having take-away food delivered to the apartment.

Nagib, who by now was very conscious of security issues, listened and nodded in approval. Rahman took a SIM card out of his pocket and told Nagib it would be used to keep in touch with one another and then asked Nagib to give him his own phone and he exchanged the SIM cards.

Rahman said he would need to bring in his real boss, not the ambassador or anyone else from the embassy, but the Head of Pakistani intelligence, General Masood. He saw the expression of concern on Nagib's face and reassured him that Masood was to be fully trusted as he was a member of the clandestine council within the Pakistani administration that wanted to curtail the American dictate and advocated for an independent policy that would restore honor to Pakistan.

Rahman added that Masood was quite indifferent to the Americans influence in Pakistan until a team of U.S. Navy SEALs eliminated Osama Bin Laden on Pakistani soil with complete disregard of Pakistani sovereignty and without coordinating the attack with the Pakistani intelligence community.

Nagib was not really assured by this story and asked how long it would take Masood to get to Brussels. Rahman said he would be there that evening as he was on an informal visit to Berlin to organize intelligence sharing concerning Al-Qaida and IS terrorists with the German government and its intelligence services. Rahman said he was impressed by the sample Nagib had presented to him earlier, but it was way above his pay-grade to negotiate its price.

***

Meanwhile, the Mossad team that had been watching Ammer's car in the parking lot were becoming frustrated by the lack of action. Michelle called David and told him that no one even tried to approach the car and asked him how to proceed.

Kobi heard the conversation and said they could either start a door-to-door search of the hotels in the area or request assistance from the local police that had a network of surveillance cameras and had especially good coverage of the area near the central railway station where many illegal and criminal activities take place.

David asked if they had any automatic face-recognition software and Kobi said they had a sophisticated algorithm that could pick up facial features even in a crowd and match them with photographs of suspects. David decided to call Herb Harden, the CIA station chief and ask him to contact the Brussels police, after all the culprits were American citizens and it would not be easy to explain why Israeli agents are interested in them.

David called Harden and explained the situation and Harden acknowledged that he had received a phone call from Eugene and already had some ideas about how to proceed. Harden said that if they had to go through official channels to gain the cooperation of the local police they would have to give a reason for their request, but fortunately, he had an excellent relationship with the Belgian anti-terrorist police unit and its boss, Thierry Van Der Wals. Harden added that he would tell Thierry that Nagib and Alia were wanted by U.S. authorities in connection with their involvement with Islamic terror cells and were last seen in Brussels. David approved the plan, although he had hoped to be able to get to Nagib first and obtain the classified information he possessed before the Americans could recover it.

Harden called Thierry and requested his help in locating the couple. Thierry wondered why the CIA was involved, he thought that the Department of Homeland Security would be in charge of thwarting domestic terrorism, but agreed to search at the security cameras for a match with the photos that Harden had sent him electronically. He said that it could take several hours unless they could be more specific about the time and location. Harden replied that to the best of his knowledge, the couple arrived in Brussels around noon the previous day, left their car at a parking lot near the central railway station and probably found a cheap hotel in the same area. Thierry said this was very helpful and he would get his colleagues in the police to scan the surveillance photos taken by the cameras in the vicinity of the parking lot.

Within a couple of hours Harden received a call from Thierry inviting him to come over to the police headquarters. Harden asked if he could bring a foreign guest and was given permission to do so.

It was just after noon when David and Harden entered the police station and were escorted to the room where the photos were on display. There was no doubt that Nagib and Alia were photographed by a sequence of surveillance cameras from the moment they entered the parking lot and left their car until they reached the small hotel in which they spent the night. Harden asked for a short break and summoned two of his people to go to the hotel and interview the owner about the couple.

The camera nearest to the hotel recorded the couple leaving the hotel shortly after they checked in—the time was recorded as two twenty in the afternoon—and head to the Metro station. They were seen entering the station and buying Metro tickets and then waiting for the next train at a southbound platform, but it was not clear where they were heading.

The same camera recorded them returning to the hotel around six in the evening and then they were spotted on another camera leaving their hotel again just before eight. This time they didn't take a train but strolled on foot and Thierry said they were probably going somewhere for dinner, most likely at a restaurant in the vicinity of the hotel. They were captured on camera later that evening as they returned to the hotel. There was no one accompanying them.

They were next seen as they checked out of the hotel in the morning, just a few hours earlier, carrying their luggage to the central station and heading to the same metro platform they used the previous day. David asked if the photos from the cameras all along the line could be checked—the timing was easy to determine as they were seen boarding a south bound train at eight twenty in the morning. They were observed by the surveillance camera near the Gare de Boitsfort station as they were leaving the station before nine later that morning.

Unfortunately, there were only a few other surveillance cameras in that area so there was no trace of them after they left the station. David asked Thierry if he knew what points of interest were around the station, so he called for a map of Brussels and they looked at potential places in the vicinity. Harden was the first to notice that the Pakistani embassy was close to the station and wordlessly pointed his finger at it.

David looked at him and saw that his face took on a pale shade, practically blanched, as he understood the potential ramifications, and hastily offered Harden a glass of cold water. David asked Thierry if the embassy was under surveillance but was told that Belgium did not spy on diplomats, which David found hard to believe.

David thanked Thierry and apologized that he and Harden had to leave, and they were grateful for his cooperation. Once they were out of police headquarters, David asked Harden if his people could hack into the security cameras of the Pakistani embassy and see whether Nagib and Alia actually entered the embassy.

Harden, who slowly recovered from his shocked state, said

he would contact his NSA liaison officer and see if the footage was available. He then confided in David telling him that if the stolen blueprints were delivered to the Pakistanis then the balance of power between India and Pakistan in South Asia would be disturbed, and perhaps this could affect the Middle East and the whole world.

David had reached the same conclusions himself but played dumb asking Harden what information was contained in Nagib's possession, but Harden only kept repeating that it was potentially a major catastrophe without elaborating on the content of the stolen data.

David asked Harden if the CIA had additional information on the Pakistani embassy in Brussels and was told that many people in the U.S. administration, and especially in the intelligence community, were concerned that amongst the ruling class of Pakistan there was a strong resentment of the U.S. and its policy. Although there appeared to be a large degree of cooperation between the two countries on the official level—the U.S. supplied Pakistan with advanced weapon systems, aircraft, and technology, as well as financial aid—the undercurrents regarded the U.S. as an unreliable ally in times of crisis, giving as examples the role played by the U.S. during the skirmishes and wars with India.

The Pakistanis felt that the U.S. did not give them real support against India. Harden added that Pakistan had developed and tested nuclear devices despite attempts by the West to stop them from doing so and had produced a stock of several dozen warheads. The Americans found that to be particularly troublesome as the supervision of those warheads was in the hands of a special unit of Pakistani intelligence that was known to include sympathizers of fundamentalist Islamic movements. David was a bit surprised by the candid assessment of the U.S.-Pakistan relations and repeated his question, although from Harden's outburst he could guess that the answer was affirmative. Harden then said, that of course, all Pakistani official and especially unofficial institutions were watched by the U.S., and that included the large Pakistani mission in Brussels.

***

The embassy of the Islamic Republic of Iran in Brussels is located at 15 Avenue Franklin Roosevelt and that of the Democratic People's Republic of (North) Korea or DPRK was at Chaussee de la Hulpe 175, just a short way from the Pakistani embassy and quite close to the apartment in which Nagib and Alia sought refuge. However, the meeting between Kim and Mahmood took place near the central railway station from where Ammer had thought that Nagib's phone call originated.

Each participant brought with him an entourage of half a dozen goons but in a cosmopolitan city like Brussels neither the dark-skin of the Iranians nor the oriental appearance of the Koreans were out of place. Kim and Mahmoud were quite familiar with life in Western Europe and felt comfortably at home in Brussels. However, they did not know where to start the search and spent about an hour discussing this issue while the members of their entourages regarded each other with suspicion and kept a fair distance between them.

At the end of the discussion, they agreed that the most probable option for the couple to barter their goods would be either with the Islamic State people or the Pakistanis. Mahmoud said the Sunni IS Muslims were dire enemies of the Shiite Iranians so he proposed they divide the task: the Iranians will try to contact the Pakistanis while the DPRK contact IS operatives. Kim didn't like this idea but had nothing better to propose, so that was agreed upon.

PART 4. GETTING THE DEAL

CHAPTER 9

June 26, evening, Brussels

Nagib and Alia settled down in the apartment and he watched some sports on TV while she prepared a light meal from the items in the kitchen. As they were finishing their meal Nagib's phone with the SIM card given to him by Rahman rang and he saw that it was Rahman on the caller ID. He answered and was told, without mentioning any names, to expect a visit an hour later.

An hour later there was a quiet rap on the door and after looking through the peephole Nagib opened the door to let in Rahman, Junaid, and an older man who was introduced as General Masood, Head of Intelligence.

Alia offered everyone coffee or tea and they all opted for herbal tea. Masood took the lead and said he had been briefed by Rahman and understood that Nagib had something very valuable for sale. Nagib reiterated that he was not interested in money for himself and really was interested in cooperation to strike a blow at the enemies of Islam, especially the Americans and Israelis.

Masood said they had a common cause and common enemies and, therefore, cooperation should be forthcoming. He then asked what Nagib had to offer and when Nagib gave an overview of the blueprints he had downloaded describing the wide range of warheads that included tactical, extremely small "suitcase bombs" as well as the "super high yield (SHY) device."

Naturally he didn't use the word stolen blueprints, and while talking he became aware of Masood's jaw dropping open. It was such a hilarious sight, he barely managed to keep a straight face. Masood excused himself and beckoned Rahman and Junaid to follow him to the bedroom.

***

In Urdu, he quietly asked them if they were sure this was not some kind of sting operation by the intelligence services of America, Israel, or India and was assured by Rahman that the sample he was given in the morning was indeed the real thing. Masood remained skeptical and said that such a cornucopia must be a gift of Allah and saw nods of approval by his younger colleagues.

***

When the Pakistanis returned to the living room, Nagib could easily read their expressions and knew that he could make any demands he wanted.

Masood tried to play it cool but could not refrain from smiling when he asked Nagib what he wanted in return. Nagib and Alia held hands and repeated they wanted revenge and justice, and they thought the punishment should equal the crimes committed by the Americans and Israelis against the Muslims.

When asked what exactly they had in mind they said they were thinking on a scale of tens of thousands of casualties. Masood said that could only be achieved by a war or a long series of terrorist operations. Nagib said that for these types of operations he could contact any Muslim country in the world or jihadist organization, but for unconventional options he needed cooperation from Pakistan.

General Masood appeared thoughtful and said that if Nagib was referring to nuclear weapons he should know that none had been used against populations since World War II in 1945.

Nagib said that he was aware of that and he would settle for a couple of tactical warheads, preferably the size of the "suitcase bombs," with yields of a few kilotons—one for use against the Americans and one for the Israelis.

Masood said the risks were too great because if word of Pakistani involvement got out then the total destruction of his homeland was assured—if not by the Americans then by the Israelis who were believed to have a large arsenal of nuclear weapons.

Nagib said that with the information he had in his possession Pakistan could build its own arsenal of advanced weapons would ensure that no one would mess with them—in other words create a balance of mutual nuclear terror even with the U.S.

Masood noted that the timeline was not right—if Nagib insisted on receiving the tactical warheads when he delivered the blueprints the Pakistanis would not have enough time to produce the advanced designs.

Nagib said frankly that if he handed over the blueprints and waited for the warheads, there was no guarantee the Pakistanis would not renege from carrying out their part of the deal. Nagib added that he had a solution. He would firsthand over only the blueprints for the smaller warheads. The Pakistanis could either supply him with two of their own tactical warheads or, if their performance was not satisfactory—meaning yields of less than ten kilotons—then they could quickly use the blueprints to manufacture a couple of devices with advanced designs and hand them over to Nagib. Once these were received, he would release the designs of the larger, strategic warheads. Nagib said that he would not use the warheads until the Pakistanis had time to produce these advanced designs.

Rahman intervened and asked whether the blueprints were in a safe place and Nagib assured him that they were. The general who was still concerned with the whole deal asked if his country would be guaranteed exclusivity and Nagib promised him he did not intend to share the designs with any other country or organization.

Masood then asked how Nagib intended to transport the nuclear devices and deliver them to the target area and was told that Nagib and Alia already had preliminary plans for this, but he preferred to not to share them at this stage.

Junaid, who was a lot more practical although with less field experience than the men, asked Nagib where he intended to go in to hiding with the warheads until the Pakistani scientists and engineers were ready with the modernized weapons.

Nagib and Alia exchanged a long look and had to admit they had not considered they would need to find a safe haven, probably for several months if not for a few years. Masood, who understood the problem, told them that hiding in Pakistan would be an option but he would need approval of the council for the deal in general and specifically for offering them asylum, as their very presence in Pakistan would lead to extreme pressure from the U.S. to extradite them.

Nagib said he thought they would be safe under the auspices of the Islamic State in parts of Iraq and Syria that were under IS control. Rahman looked at him as if he had just escaped from a mental institution and said there was no way he would be able to live there and stay in possession of a nuclear warhead, let alone of his own head.

Alia, too, didn't like this wild idea her husband had just come up with and said they could possibly approach the Saudis who were desperately trying to get their hands on a nuclear weapon of their own in response to Iran's efforts to develop the Shiite bomb. There were no foolproof solutions to this problem so Nagib asked for some extra time to sleep on it. They parted and agreed to meet the next day at noon and Masood promised to return with an answer about the deal and the asylum in Pakistan.

***

Once outside the apartment, the three Pakistanis quietly discussed the matter. The senior man, Masood, said that possession of the blueprints would turn Pakistan from a second-rate nuclear power in to a leading one, superior to all but the Americans, Russians, and Chinese, provided the information was accurate and reliable.

Rahman agreed and added that he was not qualified to professionally judge of the value of the data, but he was convinced that Nagib believed they were the genuine blueprints. Junaid, once again being the practical person, said that she was worried the Americans as well as other intelligence agencies were trying to hunt down the couple and recover the files, and added that she felt they were not safe enough in Brussels.

Masood then wondered out loud if there was a way to get the files without paying the requested price, but Rahman said Nagib was probably too clever to fall for such a ploy. He commented that if he would be in such a delicate position, he would make sure the access to the files was encoded in such a way that any unauthenticated attempts to open them would lead to their total self—destruction.

He added that they could go through the motions of complying with Nagib's conditions and later find a way to renege of their part of the deal.

Junaid asked what he had in mind and Rahman said they could supply inoperable or fake warheads, or even deliver genuine products but forcibly recover them.

***

While this was taking place in the small apartment, David wondered how he could enlist the assets of the American intelligence community to locate the couple and seize the classified data for the benefit of his country.

The most productive approach would be to cooperate with Harden and make a joint effort to find the couple either by hacking into the Belgian surveillance cameras or through the Pakistanis. He knew that Mossad kept a close watch on Pakistanis with ties to Al Qaeda fearing that a rogue nuclear weapon would end in the hands of the ruthless terrorist organization. He was also aware of the fact that Al Qaeda was losing favor among radical Islamists to the more extreme and callous Islamic State movement.

He decided to consult with Haim Shimony, the head of Mossad, and see if there was any specific information on personnel at the Pakistani embassy in Brussels with ties to these two organizations. He returned to the offices of the Israeli delegation to the European Community and used a secure line to call Shimony.

He was surprised to learn that Mossad was actively tracking a general in Pakistani intelligence and one of the most senior operatives suspected of being a sympathizer of Islamic radicals who was on a visit to Europe. Shimony added that the general, Masood Azzam, was on an official visit to Berlin when he told his German hosts that some urgent matter had come up and he had to skip the dinner party that had been arranged in honor of the newly-formed German-Pakistani intelligence cooperation agreement.

He excused himself and said he had to go to Brussels to tend to a relative that had fallen sick. The Mossad team managed to place one of the agents on the same flight and called ahead to alert the agents in Brussels. David asked if they knew where the general was going and Shimony said he would patch him into the team in Brussels.

David immediately recognized Kobi's voice and asked him what was going on. Kobi said that he received the sudden call from the Mossad office in Berlin and didn't have time to update David as he had to deploy his agents on the pressing mission.

David was angry that he wasn't informed immediately but suppressed his rage and asked Kobi for an update. Kobi told him that the general was met by Rahman Chenna, who was the senior member of Pakistani intelligence in Brussels operating under the guise of the scientific attaché. Rahman was accompanied by a young woman, obviously also Pakistani that was not known to the Mossad operatives.

David asked where they all went and Kobi apologetically told him that Rahman had taken aggressive evasive action and the Mossad agents lost track of him. Shimony followed the conversation and reprimanded Kobi for unprofessional behavior—first, on account of failing to update David in real time and keep him in the loop, and secondly, for losing track of the Pakistanis.

Kobi apologized and begged for another chance to prove himself worthy of his position and Shimony consented on condition he obeyed David's orders.

David told the peevish, but repentant, Kobi to meet him immediately at the offices of the Israeli delegation that were practically empty at this time in the evening and bring his agent Michelle who seemed to be the best acquainted with Brussels.

Within half an hour the three of them were closely studying a map of Brussels using Google Earth and Street View options. They were surprised to see that the embassies of Pakistan, North Korea, and Iran were located along the same thoroughfare, Chaussee de Hulpe that merges into Franklin Rooseveltlaan, and that the former two were quite close to each other.

Michelle commented that it looked as if these three members of the New Evil Empire, evil at least from Israel's viewpoint, stuck close together. Anyway, they started a survey of the area close to the Pakistani embassy and saw that off the thoroughfare there were a few apartment buildings.

Considering it was quite late, they expected there would be very little regular traffic in the area and David decided it would be a waste of time to post an agent near the Pakistani embassy at night, but told Kobi to have two of his agents in position to follow whichever employees left the embassy in the morning.

***

Herb Harden assembled his agents at the American embassy where the CIA had half of the basement and a small conference room that was built like a Faraday cage preventing the transmission and reception of electronic signals other than those that were fed into the room through optical fibers.

Harden asked one of the technicians on his team to present the latest photos from the ground-based cameras and satellite images of the Pakistani embassy in Brussels. He was disappointed there was not full around-the-clock video coverage but only snapshots taken at intervals by a camera positioned opposite the gates of the embassy.

The CIA had a list of the Pakistani staff members and knew which diplomats were actually agents of Pakistani intelligence and had photographs of the "scientific attaché" Rahman Chenna and his assistant Junaid.

Face matching software was applied to the snapshots, but the two "diplomats" were not identified in any of them. As an afterthought, Harden called for the photos of Nagib and Alia and the software program came up with a hit. The two of them were seen exiting the embassy just before four in the afternoon on the 25th of June. Although they could not tell from the photos what the couple was doing in the embassy, it confirmed their suspicion that they had contacted the Pakistanis.

Harden asked the technician to enlarge and process the part of the photo in which the face of Nagib could clearly be seen, although Alia's features were partly obscured by her scarf.

A close look at Nagib's expression showed that he was

concerned about something and deep in thought. The excited CIA station chief called Eugene on a secure line and told him that one of their biggest fears was substantiated.

Eugene asked for a copy of the snapshot and it was sent to him immediately. Eugene studied Nagib's worried facial expression and said his impression was that no deal had been finalized or else Nagib would look more relieved and less concerned.

Harden agreed with the interpretation and asked Eugene for further instructions. Eugene said he would make arrangements to fly to Brussels as soon as possible and suggested that Harden should call the Israeli team and update David about the identification of Nagib and Alia at the Pakistani embassy. Harden said that to contact a foreign agent and share the information he would need a direct order from his CIA boss in Langley, and Eugene said that he would arrange for the necessary confirmation and asked Harden to call his boss after thirty minutes.

Harden called his boss in Langley and received a direct order to cooperate and then called David in Brussels. Although this call was made on an open line, he conveyed the information.

David told him that his team had arrived at the same conclusion, even without photographic evidence, and had already surveyed the vicinity of the Pakistani embassy and searched for possible safe houses in which the couple could be hiding. David said that he would have agents posted near the Pakistani embassy in order to track embassy personnel that participated in suspect activities, and Harden said that the CIA had two leading suspects—Rahman and Junaid.

David asked for their photographs and when he received them, he thanked Harden and said that his agents would keep a close watch on those two "diplomats."

Harden then said he had informed Eugene of these developments and that he would be arriving in Brussels the following afternoon.

***

While these events were taking place at the Pakistani safe house, the Israeli delegation and U.S. embassy, the odd couple—Kim the North Korean and Mahmoud the Iranian, were also in session trying to determine where Nagib and Alia could be.

Their thought processes were quite similar to those of the Israelis and Americans, leading to the same logical conclusion that the culprits must have contacted, or intended to contact, the Pakistanis. Kim had disqualified the notion they had earlier that the Islamic State may be a viable alternative reasoning that the ISIS was not in a position to pursue nuclear weapons in view of the setbacks their forces have suffered in northern Syria, close to the Turkish border.

They were also in trouble in the quagmire of what used to be Iraq where the U.S. and its allies kept unleashing aerial strikes from unmanned drones and fighter jets flown by Jordanians, Saudis, and even Iranians. Mahmoud agreed that the last thing the Shiite regime in Iran wanted was an atomic bomb in the hands of the most radical Sunni movement that executed fellow Shiites on a daily basis. So, at Kim's suggestion, they posted two teams of agents, a North Korean team and an Iranian team across the road from the Pakistani embassy.

June 27, morning, Brussels

Rahman and Junaid arrived together at the Pakistani embassy and entered the building's parking lot from the side of Dreve de Duc. They noticed that there appeared to be a few vans parked on the quiet side street, something that was quite unusual in this residential area. Although the official address of the embassy was on Avenue Delleur, the staff generally used the Dreve de Duc entrance to access the parking lot.

Rahman told Junaid to behave normally and not stare at the vans and pretend to go about their business as if everything was in order. Once inside the embassy they summoned the security guards and told them the embassy was being watched by unknown entities and they should be exceptionally alert.

Rahman then entered the ambassador's office and informed him that General Masood was in town and they were involved in a special operation that concerned national security.

The ambassador was a political appointee and totally loyal to the government, so was not pleased to learn that the Head of Intelligence, General Masood Azzam, was on his turf without even giving him a courtesy call. He knew, of course, that Rahman really worked for the General and guessed that they were carrying out a clandestine operation.

When Rahman asked him to call the local police and get them to chase away the watchers in the vans on Dreve de Duc he became very unhappy but had to cooperate with the powerful intelligence chief's request. As he finished talking to the ambassador, Rahman's cell phone rang and when he answered it, he recognized General Masood's voice.

The General simply said the deal was on and Nagib and Alia must be brought to safety in Pakistan as quickly as possible, or at least to a secure place that was under Pakistani control.

***

The Israeli agents in the van across the street from the embassy saw the Belgian police patrol car drive down the street and pull up right behind them. They knew what was coming and before the policeman could get out of the patrol car the driver of the van started it and drove away in order to avoid being questioned.

***

The policeman noted the van's license plate and quickly learned that it was rented by a local businessman. He didn't see that the passenger got out of the van as soon as it turned the corner on to Avenue Emile Van Becelaere, and returned on foot to take a position outside the embassy.

***

The driver of the black van with the CIA agents didn't wait for the patrol car to approach and drove away in a hurry. Further down the small narrow street the economy size car with the Iranians and the motorcycle with a North Korean agent noticed the commotion and they too preferred to avoid confrontation with the police so they took off in a hurry.

***

Rahman had watched the scene play out from the window of his office and laughed to himself how one patrol car got agents from several countries fleeing in a hurry. However, he now realized there were at least four forces with a great interest in the Pakistani embassy and it would not be easy to get to the safe house and move Nagib and Alia to a safer place without being followed. He didn't want to scare Nagib and Alia, so he called Nagib and informed him that the General gave his approval and deal was on. He added they should be prepared to leave the apartment in a hurry, although he couldn't say exactly when they would have to move.

Rahman summoned Junaid to his office and told her that the situation was becoming more and more complicated and they were ordered by General Masood to transport the couple to a safe place without being followed.

Junaid asked what he had in mind and he answered that the safest place would be in Pakistan, but not in a large population center where people loyal to the government may suspect them and inform the officials about a strange couple of tourists.

Junaid said that she had relatives in Gandaf that was about seventy-five miles north of Islamabad, the capital of Pakistani. These relatives were in the opposition to the government and its pro-American policy and lived near the Tarbele Dam. She said she thought they owned a couple of houseboats moored on the banks of one of the beautiful lakes in the area.

Rahman liked the idea, but they still had to solve the problem of getting Alia and Nagib there without being detected by opposing intelligence services and by their own government's bureaucrats. Rahman looked at the Google Earth map to see where this lake was and suddenly realized it was not too far from Abbottabad, where Osama Bin Laden had sought refuge until he was eliminated by a team of U.S. Navy SEALs.

He pointed this out to Junaid and said he wasn't sure the Americans wouldn't try to do the same thing in Gandaf, but she said that lightning doesn't strike twice at the same spot.

Junaid checked the flights of PIA, the Pakistani airline, to Islamabad. She knew there were no PIA flights or from Brussels, but she saw that there was an afternoon flight from Paris, via Milan to Islamabad. By car it would take a little over three hours to get to the center of Paris from Brussels if there was no heavy traffic and she figured with Rahman driving they could probably make the trip to the Charles De Gaulle airport that was much closer than Paris center in two and a half hours or less.

This meant that in order to catch the PIA afternoon flight they would have to leave Brussels before noon. She told Rahman they would have to really hurry if they were to get out of Europe that day. Alternately, they could also catch a flight to

London, or any other European city serviced by PIA and then get to Pakistan with a different PIA flight.

Rahman said that he preferred the Paris option as he was sure that Brussels airport was under surveillance. He realized they had to shake off the agents that would be following them before going to the apartment and then hustle Nagib and Alia to Paris.

Alia said she had a plan: they should dress up as Pakistani women and leave the embassy with a crowd of similarly dressed women—either as employees of the embassy or as Pakistani women who had business there. The foreign agents would not know who to follow as all the women would have veils.

Rahman liked the plan and asked her to book four tickets on the PIA flight from Paris to Islamabad and also warn Nagib and Alia to be ready for departure in fifteen minutes, while he made arrangements that a Pakistani intelligence agent from the Paris embassy would wait for them at the airport to pick up the car they would use to get from Brussels to the Paris Charles De Gaulle airport.

***

The Mossad agent posted on Dreve De Duc road opposite the back entrance to the embassy was pretending to be reading a newspaper saw a drove of some twenty women all dressed in Pakistani garments and veiled faces leave the building, get into the dozen or so cars parked there and drive out and turn on to Chaussee de la Hulpe.

He phoned his partner in the van that was parked around the corner, but they didn't know which car to follow. The CIA team, the North Koreans, and the Iranians, were in an identical conundrum and had to make a choice which car to follow based on instincts alone.

Two of the cars from the Pakistani embassy turned off the thoroughfare at the first junction, three more at the second junction, and then split in to three smaller streets, and the rest also turned off at different intersections.

***

The agents in the two vans, the economy size car, and the motorcycle blindly guessed which car to follow. Rahman and Junaid saw the commotion and were pleased no one had followed them. They reached the apartment building and Junaid ran up the stairs to get the American couple, while Rahman removed the Pakistani female garb and veil and turned the car around.

Junaid directed Alia to sit in the front passenger seat while she and Nagib got in the back and Rahman took off slowly to avoid drawing attention to the car.

The drive along the E19 and A1 to Paris was fast because they left Brussels after the morning rush hour. On the way, Rahman explained the game plan in detail. First, he described the events that took place outside the embassy earlier that day and emphasized that there were several parties showing unwelcome attention to the comings and goings at the Pakistani embassy. He mentioned that he had spotted two vans, a small car, and a motorcycle parked across the road from the embassy's back entrance and they all took off in a hurry when a local police patrol car pulled up behind the first van.

Nagib asked him if he could see the people in these vehicles and Rahman said when the guy on the motorcycle removed his helmet and goggles, he could see that he had a round head and slanted eyes and was probably from the Far East, possibly Korean. He added that there were two people in the front seat of the small car, and they looked Arab or oriental. Nagib said those were probably Iranians that had already shown an interest in his merchandize.

Junaid then took over and explained the rationale of moving as quickly as possible out of Europe and to the safety afforded in Pakistan. She gave a brief review of the internal politics of Pakistan and the forces behind them, saying that General Masood was one of the leaders of the movement, so far in secret, that believed that Pakistan had been shortchanged by the West.

The Americans, in particular, had humiliated Pakistan time and again and in order to restore national honor the Pakistanis had to avenge the indiscretions brought upon them by the West. To do this with impunity required the possession of an arsenal of nuclear weapons that would serve as an insurance policy and repel attempts to intervene and disarm Pakistan.

She gave the example of North Korea, that was treated with respect only after demonstrating it had nuclear weapons. She added that the ruling government in Pakistan was controlled by corrupt politicians that were more interested in acquiring a personal fortune, in Swiss banks of course, than in the welfare of the Pakistani people and in the national pride. Therefore, the blueprints and information that Nagib and Alia were going to deliver to General Masood and his cohorts must not fall into the hands of the government officials who would probably sell them back to the Americans rather than use them to build the formidable nuclear force that Pakistan so desperately needed and deserved.

Furthermore, she said, the government may directly extradite them to the Americans, or even eliminate them on Pakistani soil at the request of the CIA. Nagib wondered how their presence in Pakistan could be concealed from the authorities and Rahman said that the supporters of the movement were everywhere.

In Islamabad, and mainly in the countryside, they would make sure the two American tourists did not raise any suspicion. Junaid then told them about her relatives in Gandaf and said they could have a safe and quiet vacation in a beautiful setting while the scientists and engineers of the Pakistani nuclear establishment studied the design of the small portable nuclear device and manufactured two of them, as agreed upon.

Once these two were handed over to Nagib and Alia the Pakistani intelligence community would help them leave Pakistan with the devices and transport them to wherever they wished to use them.

Nagib asked how long it would take to complete these two devices and Rahman said he was not qualified to answer that, but a meeting would be arranged with the top weapon designer who was privy to their movement and he would give his assessment of that.

They reached the Charles De Gaulle airport in less than two and a half hours and met a Pakistani intelligence agent from the Paris office outside the departures section of the terminal and Rahman handed over the car.

They went to the PIA counter, picked up the first-class airline tickets ready for them, and as they only had carry-on luggage, they proceeded to go through airport security and passport control. The Pakistani couple were a few steps in front of the American couple in order not to arouse suspicion.

The four waited a very short time in the first-class lounge before their flight was called, but the two couples kept their distance from each other until they boarded the PIA plane. The first leg of the flight from Paris to Milan was very short but the four travelers were all worried they might be taken off the plane in Milan, if the agents that had been following them would manage to track them and have them stopped.

Once the plane took off from Malpensa airport in Milan and was on its way to Pakistan, they relaxed as they were certain that no force could stop them now from reaching Pakistan, barring, of course, an act of Force Majeure.

***

The NSA network monitoring system picked up the fact that the four passengers had gone through the passport control checkpoint at Charles De Gaulle airport. However, by the time the information was relayed to the CIA station chiefs in Brussels and Paris, the PIA flight with the foursome on board had already departed from Milan on the nonstop leg to Islamabad.

When Harden tried to discover why the warning had been delayed, the NSA investigated the case and found that the four first class tickets on the PIA were booked earlier that morning under assumed names and, therefore, were not flagged before.

The PIA reservation system had been instructed that the four tickets would be picked up by someone from Pakistani intelligence and ordered not to ask any questions. Harden informed David of this development and told him that Eugene's flight from Washington was scheduled to land in Brussels shortly and invited David to come meet with the two of them at the U.S. embassy.

David called off the Mossad team that had been used in Brussels and told Kobi that they should return to their regular duties. He also called Shimony at the Tel Aviv headquarters and updated him. Shimony said that if Nagib and Alia were not stopped before reaching Pakistan, there was little that Mossad could do until they emerged again in Europe or the U.S., and instructed David to return to Israel after meeting with Eugene.

David was met at the gate of the U.S. embassy and escorted by one of Harden's agents to a small conference room. Eugene was drinking coffee and rubbing his red eyes after the long overnight flight from the U.S. but rose to greet David with a firm handshake.

Harden reviewed the situation and said he had contacted

George—Blakey—Blakemore, the CIA station chief in Islamabad, and asked him to try and follow Nagib and Alia.

David wondered if the U.S. could not ask the Pakistani authorities to arrest the couple and extradite them to the U.S. but Eugene said that would not be possible given the short time they had, and in any case they had to assume the Pakistanis would not be cooperative in view of the potential benefit they hoped to gain. David said that Israel had no real assets in Pakistan, which was not completely true because Mossad had enlisted a highly placed scientist in Pakistan's nuclear industry.

This gentleman was caught on camera in a delicate situation with the bellboy at a hotel in a major European city in which he attended a conference. He didn't know that bellboy had been recruited by Mossad specifically for this purpose when it became known that this was his weakness.

Mossad offered the scientist a large sum of money for his cooperation to sweeten the deal and so far the arrangement worked well for both sides. On the other hand, the U.S. had a lot of influence in Pakistan and officially the two countries were close allies, at least theoretically. They all knew that there were some parts of Pakistan, even in the major cities like Islamabad, Peshawar, and Karachi where any American was not safe if unaccompanied by bodyguards or local police.

***

Kim and Mahmoud did not know where Nagib and Alia were but suspected they had been spirited out of Brussels and possibly even out of Belgium. They saw that life at the Pakistani embassy had returned to normal and when Kim innocently asked for a meeting with the scientific attaché, he was told the man had gone on vacation.

This confirmed their suspicions that the couple had fled the coop. Mahmoud said that there was a good chance they had been moved to Pakistan where Iran had the support of the small Shiite minority. He hoped he could enlist their help to search for the American couple.

Kim said that North Korea also had good ties with Pakistan and that he could enquire through official channels if the American couple had showed up in Pakistan.

CHAPTER 10

June 28, early morning, Islamabad

They landed in the renovated Benazir Bhutto airport serving Islamabad that was actually in the Chaklala area of Rawalpindi, just before dawn. Thanks to the help of Rahman and the Pakistani intelligence service the Americans cleared passport control and customs without delay and without being registered.

A chauffeur driven car belonging to the intelligence service waited for them at the exit from the terminal. The driver said he had orders to take them wherever they wanted to go, and they set out for the two hour drive to Gandaf.

Nagib was impressed by the modernized airport and the contrast between it and the roads they travelled on, the further away they got from Islamabad the narrower they became and in need of urgent repair.

They turned off Swabi road toward Gandaf, that turned out to be a fairly large village in a valley with a single narrow road climbing slowly through the valley and ending in the hills to the east of the village.

Junaid directed the driver to the house of her relatives in the village. She asked them to wait in the car while she went in and explained that she needed to borrow one of their house-boats for a few days.

Nagib said he had to stretch his legs after the long flight and uncomfortable drive and despite Rahman's protests opened the door and got out of the car. The first thing that struck him was the smell of goats but despite the heat, the air was clear with a light breeze from the west, the visibility was good and he enjoyed stretching his legs.

After a few minutes Junaid returned with a strange expression on her face. She got back in the car and said she had been completely wrong—her relatives had a small shack near the river and not a houseboat, as she had imagined from her childhood days. She directed the driver to a minimarket near the center of the village and invited Alia to accompany her to buy food for a few days. They entered the store and Alia gasped when she saw the merchandise—there was almost nothing there, and certainly no real selection, so she just told Junaid to buy whatever she thought would be edible.

There were no plastic bags, or for that matter no paper bags either, so the shopkeeper gave them a used cloth bag in which Junaid stuffed the meager food supplies she had bought. They returned to the car and headed to the shack that was nicely situated near the shore of the artificial lake that was created by the Tarbela Dam.

When they reached the shack Nagib and Alia realized it was almost empty of furniture—there were a couple of thin mattresses on the floor, no electricity, and no running water. The toilet was an old-fashioned smelly outhouse and the kitchen included a roughhewn wood table, a couple of wooden stools, and instead of a sink there was a copper pot and an earthenware jar with a piece of cloth to keep out flies and other bugs.

Alia announced that there was no way in the world that she would stay in a place like this and Nagib supported her. Even Rahman was speechless when he saw the living conditions in the shack and told Junaid that they would have to find somewhere else.

They first drove back to Junaid's relatives in Gandaf and returned the key to the shack. Her relatives were a bit offended their hospitality was not well received but Junaid said they were dealing with spoiled Americans who could not survive without some of their home comforts like electricity and a toilet with running water.

After some discussion the relatives said they had heard the best hotel in the area was the Melmastun Hotel and restaurant in Swabi, but of course they had never actually stayed there or even seen it with their eyes.

Rahman took no chances and checked it on the internet and saw that it opened in 2014 and on its homepage was described as "a beautiful resort along the River Indus offering delicious Pakistani food. Hotel rooms are also available for staying."

Rahman checked the map and didn't quite understand how anything in Swabi could be on the shore of the Indus River but decided not to mention that. So, they headed to the hotel and were glad to see that two rooms were available.

Nagib and Alia were settled in one room while the other was taken by Junaid, and Rahman pretended to be sleeping in the car. Of course, they all knew exactly where he would be spending the night. Junaid found some poor peasants near the hotel and made them very happy when she gave them the food they had bought in Gandaf.

The hotel's restaurant turned out to be everything it claimed—serving delicious Pakistani food typical of the Khyber Pakhtunkhwa region. When they ordered their mutton Karahi, the waiter asked if they wanted it mild, medium, or spicy hot. Nagib said that he liked very spicy food, but Junaid tried to tell him that in Pakistan spicy hot was like rocket fuel. However, Nagib prided himself on being a Palestinian man and someone who was used to spicy food. Rahman intervened and warned him that spicy in Pakistan was something else but Nagib, who by now, could not back out of it said that he insisted on having the spiciest flavored dish of mutton.

Rahman told the waiter what Nagib wanted and in Urdu told him to bring a large jug of cold water and some yogurt. The food arrived and Nagib took one bite and beads of perspiration broke out on his forehead, his face was covered with a patina of sweat, and he reached out to the glass of cold water and gulped it down, refilled it, and repeated the action.

Rahman and Junaid giggled quietly while Alia looked at his red face with deep concern until Nagib managed to say that he was fine, and perspiration was the natural reaction of his body when he consumed hot, spicy food. He didn't eat any more mutton and asked for some more yogurt to cool his throbbing mouth.

June 28, evening, Islamabad

The CIA station in Islamabad was one of the largest the United States maintained in Asia, or for that matter in any country. The reasons were evident to anyone who had studied recent historical events—in Pakistan there was a large following of radical Islamist movements, including Al Qaeda, and the highly permeable border between Afghanistan and Pakistan through which supplies, weapons, and terrorists moved freely caused a constant headache to the forces of the U.S. and its allies in Afghanistan.

The position taken by the Pakistani government was ambivalent—they liked U.S. economic aid but hated Americans. The raid to eliminate Bin Laden that took place on Pakistani soil without notifying the local authorities also added to the inherent tension between the two countries. The station chief, George—Blakey—Blakemore, an experienced CIA veteran who had seen real military and antiterrorist action in Iraq and Afghanistan, was in his office when he was summoned by the Director of the CIA, Admiral John J. Johnson, III, to participate in a video conference call on a secure line.

The Admiral told Blakey, as the station chief was known by one and all, that Dr. Eugene Powers from the NNSA was on his way to Islamabad and that he expected full cooperation to try and contain the dire situation that was developing in Pakistan and threatened the national security of the U.S.A. Blakey was not too thrilled with the directive he had received but said that he would do his best. The Admiral signed off without another word, leaving Blakey with a puzzled look on his face.

Eugene's flight landed late at night and he was met by Blakey himself, who was curious to know what caused all this excitement. When he heard Eugene's description of the missing classified information and what was at stake, he was speechless.

After some contemplation, he realized this was his chance to excel and get a promotion that would send him to a comfortable job in Langley until his retirement, much to the delight of his wife. Blakey told Eugene he had some good contacts inside the Pakistani intelligence community but then continued to say there were two main factions within that organization—one faction thought that closer relations with the West and strengthening democracy in Pakistan was the pathway for better life in Pakistan, and the other faction judged everything in terms of national pride.

Any event that appeared to infringe on the honor of Pakistan as they perceived it, be it a defeat in a cricket match or a military skirmish with India was regarded as an insult to Pakistani manhood. Eugene said he was familiar with this attitude as he had seen it in the Middle East and even in parts of Europe where tribal wars of old, between religions, families, and people who had been neighbors for centuries, still erupted at the sight of a minor provocation. Once these started there was no telling how they would end, although a bloody massacre was the usual outcome.

Blakey wanted to move on to more practical matters and asked Eugene how he intended to find the renegade couple amid a population that was not friendly, if not outright hostile to the United States.

Eugene said that according to his analysis of the situation, the Pakistani Atomic Energy Commission (PAEC) would have to be involved in utilizing the information Nagib had.

Blakey said there was a scientist, codenamed Jairo, after J. Robert Oppenheimer, the legendary director of the Manhattan Project, with whom the CIA had an indirect connection. Jairo was in a close relationship with one of his co-workers, Alma, a young woman with whom he apparently had a romantic affair and she would get word to her American contact.

The CIA agent who was responsible for retaining contact with Alma was a glamorous female agent, Linda Katz, whom no one suspected as being anything but an empty-headed blonde, while in fact she was a very intelligent and well trained operative. Blakey said that several men had tried to hit on Linda, but all were rejected out of hand and the rumor was that she was more interested in women, especially local liberated Pakistani women.

Eugene said he was not interested in rumors or in anyone's sex life and sexual preferences, and that as long as Linda maintained contact with Jairo through her relationship with Alma he was happy.

June 29, Swabi, Pakistan

After a sleepless night in the uncomfortable narrow bed, Nagib and Alia met with Rahman and Junaid for breakfast that consisted of coffee, if one could call the dark fluid that was served in cracked cups coffee, and of tea that had a nice minty aroma, and some sweet pastries. In a deviation from their morning routine, Nagib and Alia declined the doubtful coffee and preferred tea that tasted good and refreshing.

Rahman said that he had to go to Islamabad to meet with General Masood who had returned there from Europe and had to take the sample blueprints that included the detailed design of the small nukes. He added that a meeting had been arranged with the leading scientists of the Pakistani atomic energy commission and did not mention that only sympathizers of their nationalistic cause were selected.

Nagib asked if they would be told about the source of the blueprints and Rahman assured him that sharing sensitive information would be, as it always was, on "a need to know" basis. In other words, the scientists would see the Los Alamos National Laboratory logo and the fact that it was highly classified information but would not be told how Pakistani intelligence got hold of it and who brought it, and certainly not about their presence in Pakistan.

Nagib asked how much longer they would have to stay in Swabi, and Rahman said that he would make arrangements to have them transferred to a better residence at a safe place, and that they would only need to spend one more night at the Melmastun Hotel.

Alia said the quality difference between dinner that was really good, and the mediocre breakfast was something she could not understand. Junaid told her that in the evening the chef did the cooking himself while in the morning one of the waiters was in charge of the kitchen and they were used to having local people who did not usually care about breakfast.

Rahman took off with the car and the chauffer while Junaid did her best to entertain Alia and Nagib with stories about the history of Pakistan and about the political upheaval since terrorist organizations made a point of attacking government institutions and especially targeted hotels, restaurants and bars frequented by foreigners.

She said that in the 1971 War with India that ended in a shameful defeat for Pakistani forces, the Americans supported Pakistan with old and outdated weapon systems while India received massive military aid from the Soviet Union. The situation worsened after a shift in the Indian government toward a Western orientation that severed the strong ties with the USSR.

The Pakistanis felt as if the West and the U.S. had betrayed them and favored relationship with India that was much larger than Pakistan and therefore presented a potentially larger market for Western goods and was also a source of cheap labor. At present, India was a major source of skilled engineers and scientists that were tempted to leave their homeland and work in the U.S.

The U.S. selected the best and brightest, promised them citizenship and high salaries, and boosted their economy at the expense of the poor Indian government that educated and trained them. Pakistani scientists were not welcome in the U.S., mainly because after 9/11 all Muslims were suspected of being terrorists and supporters of Al Qaeda, although some European countries, especially the United Kingdom, did reluctantly accept them.

Alia wanted to mention AQ Khan, who managed to copy—not to say steal—the uranium enrichment technology from his employers in Germany and build a similar plant in Pakistan. This made him a national hero but was a case in point that exemplified the risks of employing untrustworthy foreigners in sensitive installations. Then Alia considered what she and Nagib were up to—doing practically the same thing, or even worse—wisely refrained from saying what was on her mind.

When the two women had a moment alone, while Nagib went out for a walk to stretch his legs, Alia asked Junaid if she and Rahman intended to get married. Junaid blushed and said that Rahman already had a wife and a three-year-old son but according to Islamic customs he could take another wife, or three more for that matter, but she, as a liberated modern woman, could not put up with the idea of being wife number two, so marriage was out of the question although they did enjoy each other's company without any formal commitment.

Alia was impressed by that and said she admired Junaid's levelheaded approach and added that living in America had spared her from having a similar fate. When Nagib returned he noted that the two women were feeling much more comfortable with each other and wondered what brought this about.

June 29, Islamabad, Pakistan

Employees at the American embassy in the Diplomatic Enclave of Islamabad noticed that things were not as usual.

The U.S. ambassador to Pakistan was nominated to the office in recognition of his financial contributions to the President's election campaign and knew very little about Pakistan and even less about clandestine operations.

When Blakey, the CIA station chief, asked for a meeting the ambassador was flattered because during his whole two-year term as ambassador he was treated as a figurehead and practically ignored, even ridiculed behind his back, by the professional diplomats and intelligence agents. Blakey introduced Dr. Eugene Powers as a senior NNSA scientist sent on a secret mission by the President himself.

He added that all he was allowed to say about the mission was that it concerned U.S. national security and that Pakistan was the focal point, but he could not reveal any details except to say that it involved recovery of highly classified information that was illicitly stolen from a national laboratory that was overseen by the NNSA.

The ambassador was taken aback by this introduction and asked Blakey what he was required to do with this, and Blakey said he wanted the ambassador to arrange an informal, personal meeting with the Pakistani defense minister without the presence of any member from the Pakistani intelligence agency.

The ambassador said this was not according to protocol, but he would try to comply with the request. He added that very little happened in Pakistan that the intelligence agency didn't know about, but he would try to arrange a cocktail party, the Fourth of July was just around the corner, and during the reception try to get a word in private with the defense minister.

Blakey was a bit surprised the ambassador came up with this good idea although he had to wait almost a whole week but realized that any other arrangement was bound to be intercepted by Pakistani intelligence. Eugene also approved of the plan.

The ambassador said that invitations would be sent out to the A list that included some ministers of the Pakistani government, some members of parliament, several other ambassadors, as well as some high-ranking officers in the air force, army, and intelligence service. He promised to have the invitation to the defense minister delivered personally and make sure he confirmed it.

As soon as they left the ambassador's office Blakey said that after knowing the ambassador for two years this was the first time he was impressed by him and believed he may have some substance beneath the façade of a rich lightweight friend of the President.

Eugene asked Blakey if there was anything they could do before the Fourth of July party and Blakey said they could get the NSA to monitor telephones and e-mail addresses that were registered to key Pakistani personnel and try to find out whether there were any contacts with Nagib and Alia. He added the best thing would be to contact their man at the Pakistan Atomic Energy Commission and find out if there was any word of blueprints of advanced designs turning up.

Eugene commented he had heard that when cell phones were invented, no one could wipe the smile off the faces of the NSA director. He believed that even the tiniest bit of communication would be recorded on the agency's powerful computers and analyzed by human experts or sophisticated software so the "bad guys"—and countless innocents—would have nowhere to hide.

This had been confirmed by Edward Snowden who was considered by some as a whistleblower and by others as a renegade. The nightmare of the NSA director was soon to become a common reality—cheap, unregistered pre-paid SIM cards and single-use SIM chips or "burn-phones" as they were called. These devices combined with terrorists, or other people who were up to no good according to the NSA hit-list, who were reasonably intelligent enough not to use words that would obviously trigger the automatic monitoring system, made the task of randomly following the "bad guys" practically a futile exercise.

Blakey agreed that the chances of the NSA striking gold were slim and did what old agents liked to do—rely on HUMINT or human intelligence provided by flesh and blood agents and not by computers or machines. So, he summoned Linda Katz to his office and when the young woman walked in Eugene saw the intelligent look in her eyes and her athletic body that was honed on the soccer field of her college and had a feeling that she could be trusted.

After the brief introductions Eugene outlined the situation. Linda asked some astute questions about the form in which the information would be handed over to the Pakistanis and what it contained. Eugene said it would probably be electronic files as no hardcopies were taken from the lab although they could have been printed since the disappearance of the couple. The files contained classified designs and blueprints that were highly sensitive.

Linda said she could imagine what kind of designs but a warning look from Blakey stopped her in mid-sentence before she could elaborate. She asked about the timeframe and Blakey told her the couple had arrived in Islamabad less than two days earlier but there was no trace of their whereabouts.

Eugene said the data would probably be given to the PAEC scientists within a day or two. Linda said she would contact Alma and make sure she met with her scientist lover, Jairo, within a couple of days. Linda said she would discretely guide Alma how to obtain the information, but she emphasized that Alma was not consciously working for the CIA.

***

Rahman arrived at the headquarters of the Pakistani intelligence service and went straight to General Masood's office. Rahman saw that there were two other men in the spacious room. The general was expecting him and as soon as he entered the office the general and the other two men stood up and gave him a quiet applause.

Masood introduced the older man as Professor Abdul Malick, a physicist and senior research scientist with PAEC, and the younger man as Dr. Khadim Ansari, an engineer with the Kahuta Project. Masood said he had already given the two gentlemen a brief description of the classified material that was now in their possession without specifying who brought it to the Pakistan intelligence service and where it had come from, although the logo of Los Alamos National Laboratory attested to its source.

Masood explained that the blueprints they now had were the most advanced designs of small, tactical warheads, but the "treasure chest," as he called the asset, had detailed designs for many more nuclear devices more powerful than anything in Pakistan's arsenal.

Rahman inserted the San Disk flash memory with the schematics of the small nuclear device in Masood's computer and switched on the overhead projector. Meanwhile, the general pressed a button on his desk and the window shutters closed, so as soon as the projector's lamp reached its full luminosity even the most minor details could be clearly seen.

The two scientists took a few minutes to study the images of the completed weapons that were displayed and then went over the detailed cross-sections of the components. The scientists talked to one another, completely ignoring the general and Rahman, and from the looks on their faces it was obvious they were taken by surprise by the innovative design.

After a few minutes Professor Malick said they were impressed by the simplicity and sophistication of the weapon and added that although the Pakistani arsenal had a weapon of similar geometrical dimensions the yield of the U.S. design they were watching was probably higher by a factor of ten or twenty, making it equivalent to the large first generation atomic bombs like those used against Japan.

Masood was extremely pleased with the response and asked Dr. Ansari how long it would take PAEC to produce two of these warheads. Here the scientists went into a short conference, once again ignoring the general and Rahman, and said all the mechanical parts were easily copied. They had the proper machinery and construction materials on hand, but they were concerned the core of the device that contained the fissionable material was made of an alloy of plutonium they were not familiar with.

In addition, they said, the quality of the plutonium used in the core, super-weapon grade plutonium that contained over ninety-nine percent of the fissionable plutonium-239, was something that Pakistan had never produced.

Seeing the question forming of General Masood's lips, the Professor went into his teaching mode and gave a short lecture on the production of plutonium. He explained that plutonium was produced in a nuclear reactor fueled with uranium. When uranium-238 captured a neutron, it could be transmuted into plutonium-239, the fissionable atom used in nuclear weapons.

The amount of plutonium produced in a reactor depended on the burn-up of the uranium fuel—more irradiation produced more plutonium. However, there was a catch—if irradiation continued some of the plutonium-239 also captured a neutron and was converted to the undesirable plutonium-240, and with further neutron captures even heavier isotopes of plutonium would be formed. Each of these complicated the construction of an efficient nuclear weapon. Plutonium-240 tended to spontaneously emit neutrons that could lead to a premature ignition of a chain-reaction and result in a low yield or even a fizzle of the weapon. Plutonium-241 decayed to form americium-241 that emitted powerful gamma radiation that could deleteriously affect the conventional explosives used to compress the plutonium to a critical mass that enabled the chain-reaction to proceed.

Rahman and Masood looked at each other for a moment and then asked why that concerned the scientists, so the Professor explained that Pakistan had needed a lot of bombs quickly that required a lot of plutonium, and, therefore, the burn-up of fuel in Pakistani reactors was higher, leading to larger fractions of plutonium-240 and plutonium-241 and only about ninety-three percent plutonium-239.

Thus, the plutonium that Pakistan possessed may not be suitable for the advanced design brought to them. The general said that as far as he understood plutonium was plutonium and the whole lecture was just a waste of his time. The scientists protested but the now furious general said if they couldn't deliver the advanced bombs, he would find other scientists who could. Rahman was taken aback by the general's blatant reaction and tried to get everybody to calm down and discuss the matter in terms of scientific and engineering principles and see what could be done. He suggested that they convene a board of scientists to see how to overcome the concerns raised by the professor.

The general's rage cooled down and he said that he would indeed form a committee to address the issue and nominated Rahman to be his representative there. Professor Malick would be appointed as chairman and he was asked to invite five top experts on nuclear physics in Pakistan, provided that they could be trusted to keep the secret. The professor said it would be of the highest priority and he expected the first meeting to take place the following day.

***

David Avivi returned to Mossad headquarters in Tel Aviv and briefed Haim Shimony, the Mossad chief, on the events that had taken place in Germany and in Brussels. He said that they were ahead of the other intelligence agencies that took an interest in Nagib and Alia and in the information they had acquired, but always a step or two behind the couple. He also added there was not much Mossad could do inside Pakistan and they had to wait until the couple left that country and hopefully it wouldn't be too late. Shimony told him that the Israeli Security Agency, the ISA, had interrogated Nagib's parents and all the relatives they could locate, but none seemed to have any idea about Nagib's plans.

They were surprised to learn he had left the United States as they were convinced he was enjoying his life there and was prospering professionally and financially. Alia's relatives were also questioned but the last they had heard about her, from her parents, was that she had married a Palestinian and both were gainfully employed by the U.S. federal government.

David asked Shimony about contacting the cooperative scientist in the Pakistani nuclear establishment but was told he would contact them if anything relevant came his way.

***

The North Korean embassy in Pakistan was situated at House No. 9, on Street No. 18, F-8/2 in Islamabad, far from the U.S. embassy and Diplomatic Enclave where many of the foreign institutions and embassies were located. Apparently, the North Korean didn't feel threatened in Pakistan, after all the two countries cooperated in the fields of missile development and nuclear technology, although there was practically very little exchange of commercial goods between these two poor countries.

Kim arrived at the embassy the previous night and convened with the ambassador and the military attaché and briefed them about the invaluable information that Nagib intended to hand over to the Pakistanis. He asked them if they had connections within the intelligence service and the PAEC that could inform them if the classified data was transferred and more to the point if the DPRK could also get a copy of the blueprints.

The attaché was skeptical if the Pakistanis would share such information with anyone but believed that for the proper price a copy could be obtained. The ambassador was even less optimistic and said that the cooperation between the two countries had its limits. Kim said he would stay in Islamabad for a few days to see how the situation developed.

***

The embassy of Iran in Islamabad was also in the Diplomatic Enclave as the Shiite Muslims didn't feel very much at home amidst the mostly Sunni Pakistanis. Mahmoud arrived at the embassy when it opened in the morning and asked for a meeting with the ambassador who was an appointee of the Revolutionary Guards to which he also belonged. The ambassador was pleased to see Mahmoud and listened attentively to his story about Nagib and Alia and the classified information they possessed.

He said that the blueprints and advanced designs were exactly what Iran needed to deter the Big Satan, America, and the Little Satan, Israel, from attacking the nuclear facilities in Iran. They both knew that Iran was a threshold nuclear power—it had the technology to produce fissile materials, had done testing to simulate real atomic bombs and had delivery systems in the form of missiles of various ranges and capabilities—but as yet Iran had not crossed this threshold mainly because it feared the reaction from both the Big Satan and the Little Satan.

The cooperation between Pakistan and Iran had its ups and downs but as a testament to the close relations was the fact that Iran had the embassy in Islamabad as well as three consulates in Lahore, Peshawar, and Quetta, while Pakistan had its embassy in Tehran and consulates in Mashad and Zahedan. Pakistan provided great assistance to Iran when it started working on uranium enrichment centrifuge technology. Part of the help was through official government channels and part was through the AQ Khan network. The countries also shared some aspects of missile technology.

The ambassador said he would reach out to his contacts in the Pakistani nuclear industry and the military but was doubtful they would share the information with Iran unless promised something big in return.

Mahmoud said he would hang around for a few days in case something came up.

CHAPTER 11

July 1st, Islamabad, Pakistan

Professor Malick called the committee meeting to order. Rahman looked at the nuclear physicists that were gathered around the table and felt like the village idiot. Here were five of the most talented and intelligent people that lived in Pakistan, in addition to the professor and Dr. Ansari, and he, who had a bachelor's degree in engineering, was supposed to follow their discussion and report to General Masood.

Before the professor could start the scientific part of the debate Rahman asked for permission to speak. He said they had all been vetted by the Pakistani Intelligence service and were cleared to share the state's most sensitive information, but what they were about to see was much more sensitive as it could reflect on Pakistan's international relations, and potentially could even lead to the annihilation of the country.

He glanced around the table again and saw the skeptical looks and the curiosity on the faces of the five physicists, so he added that Professor Malick would explain what he was referring to but it was his duty to caution them that this was far beyond the usual top-secret material they had all dealt with before.

Professor Malick gave an abbreviated version of the events that led to possession of the advanced designs for the small warheads they were about to see on the screen and turned on the projector.

The scientists were not initially impressed as they had seen designs that superficially looked like the one displayed on the screen. They were all familiar with the "football design" that included two subcritical masses of plutonium each shaped like half an American football—or a rugby ball in the rest of the world—that were placed inside a metal pipe. When compressed by detonating conventional explosives at both ends, they were joined to reach a critical density and configuration. This was much simpler and lighter than the classical implosion device that required precisely timed detonation of several dozen shaped explosives to compress a sphere of plutonium into the high density required for criticality.

The professor reminded the scientists, not that they really needed it, that the committee headed by Rep. Dan Burton—R-Indiana, who was also one of the few supporters of Pakistan against India in the U.S. Congress, displayed a mock-up hypothetical "suitcase nuke" at a press conference in the year 2000. This was supposed to demonstrate a model of the devices that General Lebed reported as missing after the dismemberment of the USSR.

However, when they saw that the calculated yield of the small nuke was as large as the bombs dropped on Hiroshima and Nagasaki, but its weight was in the range of fifty-five pounds and not several tons they fell silent. Each one silently contemplated the implications of having such a weapon, or

224 | Charlie Wolfe

the repercussions, if such a device fell into the wrong hands recalling that Pakistan had many enemies.

As more detailed schematics of the small nuke were shown, one of the physicists interrupted the presentation pointing out the requirements of the plutonium core and saying that Pakistan had never produced such a high grade of plutonium-239, with less than one percent of all other plutonium isotopes. The professor was pleased with the comment and said that one of the objectives of this respectable committee was to assess what would happen if the super-grade plutonium in the design was replaced by the type of material they had produced for Pakistan's nuclear arsenal.

One of the physicists said they should also discuss how the performance of the device would be affected if high enriched uranium would be used instead of plutonium, but this suggestion was immediately discounted by all other members of the committee from basic physical considerations. Another member asked if they could use uranium-233 that had relevant nuclear properties that were quite similar to plutonium but Dr. Ansari said Pakistan had not produced this material and only half-jokingly added that perhaps India could test that hypothesis as it was known they had experimented with uranium-233 that was produced in thorium fueled reactors.

Rahman did his best to follow the discussion but was soon lost in a quagmire of physical data, arguments about cross-sections, implosion velocity, critical mass, initiators, assembly speed, and other things he could only vaguely understand. The debate became heated and he noticed there were two factions—those that believed that even lower-grade plutonium would work and those that claimed the super-grade material was essential. There was a consensus all the other components of the small nuke could be manufactured in-house or were even part of the stockpile of the Pakistani nuclear arsenal.

The discussion went on and on with no side convincing the other side and Rahman felt that even after three hours the committee could not reach a unanimous agreement, so he suggested they break for lunch and continue afterwards. Professor Malick supported the motion and a light lunch was brought into the conference room.

Rahman noticed that after the appetites were sated and tea was served with some sweet pastries, the discussion continued in a more relaxed atmosphere. One of the physicists suggested the debate could be settled by a field test of a device that would be constructed according to the blueprints with the highest-grade Pakistani plutonium that could be made available for the test.

Rahman said this was a political issue and would involve matters of national security as Pakistan had agreed not to carry out any further nuclear tests unless India did so first. He didn't add that even if a small-scale test could go undetected by satellites, seismographs, the International Monitoring System that used gamma-detection stations and all foreign intelligence services it could not hide from the government of Pakistan.

The officials would probably understand there was a strong faction amid the Pakistani administration that was undermining the legally elected government for reasons of national pride. He knew all the scientists on the committee were members of that faction but felt that some things were best not mentioned. To his surprise, all the members of the committee nodded in approval that a clandestine nuclear test was out of the question.

Professor Malick concluded the meeting by saying he would present both points of view to General Masood and thanked the members of the committee for their time and repeated the warning they were not to discuss the matter with anyone outside the committee and certainly not communicate by phone, e-mail, or other electronic media with any other committee member. Before departing, the professor said they should all contemplate the problem, and should all meet again three days later on July 4.

Dr. Anwar Usman was one of the physicists that participated in the meeting. They did not know that Anwar was targeted by the CIA as a source of information and was given the codename Jairo. Anwar himself was also blissfully unaware of that. He was only in his mid-thirties but was considered as a brilliant scientist with great potential both in carrying out groundbreaking research and even as a future director of Pakistan Institute of Nuclear Science & Technology (PIN-STECH). He was tall, thin, and clean shaven, that in Pakistan made a statement he was not a follower of radical Islam, and had been a supporter of the movement that believed Pakistan deserved respect from the world as a nuclear power and should not be treated as another backward third world country.

He had graduated from Pakistan's top university at the top of his class and had published several scientific articles in leading journals that received hundreds of citations. He spent a couple of years as a post-doctoral fellow at Trinity College, at Cambridge University in the UK—not to be confused with Dublin's Trinity College—and was offered a position there as a Senior Research Fellow that he declined saying his country needed him.

Upon his return to Pakistan he joined PINSTECH and soon became a leading figure in the research community. It was not surprising he was summoned by Professor Malick to join the committee. As a young reasonably attractive man, he had many admirers among his female co-workers, but his scientific career left him little time for personal life. When Alma, a good-looking female engineer who was working with him on a classified project, invited him for dinner he was glad because it was very convenient for him and saved him the trouble of dating.

The relationship developed quickly and before long they became lovers, but as both were focused on their work they did not meet openly and kept the affair from their colleagues. They usually met only on weekends and spent the night together, in what for him was exciting sex, and for her nice and satisfying but not enough to fulfill her secret fantasies.

Six months earlier, Islamabad

That changed when Alma met Linda, whom she considered to be a secretary at the U.S. embassy. They literally met by accident when Alma failed to stop in time as a traffic light turned red, while Linda who all her life was used to respect traffic regulations, stopped promptly. The front of Alma's car suffered more damage than Linda's back fender, but they only saw that after they got out of their cars.

Alma was very embarrassed about the accident because she always considered herself as an excellent driver, but Linda saw that the damage to her car was minor and gently tried to get her to calm down. When she saw how distressed Alma still was, she felt sorry for her and invited her for tea at a nearby café. Alma kept apologizing again and again until Linda told her to relax and enjoy her tea. They exchanged details of car insurance and cell phone numbers.

A few days later, Alma called Linda and said she still felt guilty about the accident and invited her for dinner. Linda said the insurance covered the cost of the minor repair and Alma needn't feel bad about it, but Alma insisted the least she could do was to cook dinner for her.

Linda, who as a CIA agent was encouraged to try and enlist local people, gladly accepted the invitation.

The next evening Linda went over to Alma's apartment and brought Swiss chocolates and a bottle of French red wine. Alma opened the door wearing a colorful shalwar kameez and as Linda entered the modest lounge and saw the dining table set for two. She noticed there were candles and a couple wine glasses on the table, so without hesitation presented Alma with the chocolates saying they were for dessert and took out the bottle of wine saying she hoped Alma liked red wine.

Alma stated she hadn't expected these gifts and had a bottle of chilled white wine ready, so Linda said two bottles were better than one and the night was still young and asked Alma to uncork the red wine and allow it to "breathe."

Alma turned off the bright overhead lights saying the food she had cooked was best consumed slowly in a relaxed atmosphere and filled their glasses with white wine. They toasted each other and drank the first glass of wine before eating the lentil soup Alma had prepared.

Linda refilled the glasses and they sipped the wine looking at each other for a long moment without saying a word. Alma got up from the table and brought the main course while Linda refilled their glasses once again emptying the bottle of white wine. They drank the last of the white wine while eating slowly and talked a little about themselves. Linda asked Alma if she had been married and Alma answered that educated women in Pakistan who pursued a professional career were not regarded as good wives because most Pakistani men preferred to have their woman at home to take care of their needs and raise the family.

She shyly admitted she was having a relationship with one of her co-workers, a physicist at PINSTECH where she too worked as an engineer. She added that he was not the typical Pakistani chauvinist male as he had spent some time living in England and was an exceptionally gifted scientist. Linda smiled and said she understood perfectly what Alma was talking about and said in her college days she had tried having relationships with men but found them to be self-centered and childish without any understanding of her own needs.

She surprised Alma by saying the attitude of most American men toward independent career women was not that different. She added she felt more comfortable in the company of strong-willed women than with men. By then the bottle of red wine was also empty and the two women were a bit tipsy.

Linda stood up and said she had to leave as it was getting late and Alma also rose from the table and walked over to Linda and said she enjoyed the evening tremendously. Linda gave her a short perfunctory hug that turned in to a close, full-bodied embrace.

Linda, who was a couple of inches taller gently kissed the top of Alma's head and when Alma turned her head up to look into Linda's eyes their lips met for an instant.

Alma had never kissed a woman before and stood motion-less for a minute before responding to Linda's delicate lips and their kiss became passionate. Linda who had some experience with women pulled back slightly and looked directly in Alma's eyes, and said she'd better leave now but they should meet again and the next time she would cook dinner for Alma.

One last hug and she was gone. Alma stood staring at the door wanting to call Linda to return but feeling strange and embarrassed at the way her body responded to Linda's kisses. Linda also had an urge to return to the apartment but thought there was potential for a long-term relationship that she did not want to spoil by being overly aggressive.

The following week Linda called Alma and invited her to dinner. She thought that having a relationship, she did not re-gard this as an affair, with a lovely woman who worked for PINSTECH would allow her to combine business and pleasure. She was sure that Alma would be in big trouble if word got out she was involved with an American woman, even a CIA operative.

Alma hesitated before accepting the dinner invitation as she was aware of the potential complications with her employer and the Pakistani counter-intelligence service, but she was intrigued and attracted by the very thought of having a relationship with another woman. She felt this could be the excitement she found lacking in her affair with Anwar. Finally, she reached a decision and called Linda saying she would be delighted to see her again.

Linda answered the doorbell with a smile and as soon as the door closed behind Alma, she embraced her in her powerful arms. Alma gasped from excitement as well as from the strong squeeze and clung onto Linda's shoulders and neck. Linda pulled back slightly and hand in hand led Alma to the dining table upon which as assortment of salads was laid out.

She poured two glasses of wine and pointed at the chicken salad, egg salad, Waldorf salad, some cold cuts, and other salads and said she was not really a great cook. Alma sipped her wine and smiled saying no one was perfect and she was glad they were together. After eating a little and drinking a lot of wine the two women sat close to each other on the narrow sofa and Linda told Alma that in the U.S. this type of sofa was called a "love seat."

Alma laughed and said that the name was perfect and cuddled up to Linda leaning her head on Linda's shoulder. Linda caressed her gently and patted her on the head while Alma purred quietly like a cat and put her arms around Linda. They exchanged long, deep kisses on the sofa until Linda stood up, helped Alma to her feet and gently led her to the bedroom. The scented candle that was lit there spread a delicate aroma that was intoxicating.

Linda slowly undressed Alma, kissing every inch of bare

brown skin that came in to view while remaining fully dressed. Alma moaned softly at first and then more and more loudly as Linda bent down and kissed her exposed breasts and erect dark nipples, working her way down her tight stomach and to the curly black hair between her thighs.

Alma pulled Linda back up and started to remove her clothes. The sight of Linda's ivory white breasts with the dark aura around her nipples made her catch her breath before continuing to remove the designer jeans and underwear from Linda's supple body.

Linda sat on the bed and lay down inviting Alma to join her. Alma said she had never been intimate with a woman and didn't know what to do but Linda told her not to worry about that and just behave naturally—and she would lead the way. Linda started gently caressing Alma's taut body moving slowly from her head, to her face and neck and then further down staying longer in regions where she felt Alma respond strongly. Her hands and lips, and especially her tongue, drew groans as Alma wriggled and started shaking in rhythmic undulating motions.

Suddenly, Linda stopped moving and Alma's writhing grew stronger and her moaning grew louder and as soon as Linda moved again Alma's body shook in an orgasm that left her breathless. Linda started caressing herself and when she saw that Alma recovered, took her hand and guided it to the short blond hair at the pit of her abdomen.

Alma's fingers found the wet opening between Linda's thighs and automatically massaged the enlarged clitoris bringing tears of joy and pleasure to Linda's eyes. Linda clasped Alma's hand

and held it tight while she reached an orgasm. After that, the two women kissed each other very gently and cuddled on the bed. The sight of Alma's limbs with their dark skin mingled with Linda's white limbs would have sent every photographer or artist into a frenzy, had anyone been around to record the sight.

Linda invited Alma to spend the night with her and the two women fell into a sound sleep hugging each other. In the morning, after going to the bathroom and having a cup of coffee, they shyly looked at one another, kissed for a while and then made love again.

Alma said she had to go home because she invited Anwar to lunch and an afternoon tryst, saying she had never experienced with him what they had together.

Linda, now reverting to her job as a CIA operative, said she was not jealous or even bothered by Alma's affair with Anwar because no man could ever feel what they had just shared. She added that they would have to hide their relationship even from their colleagues and friends or else both would get in to trouble.

After Alma left, Linda went to the drawer in the dresser opposite the bed and removed the memory chip from the camera she had installed there. She inserted it in her laptop and watched the whole bedroom scene again—enjoying every moment—and then removed it and stored it among her lingerie. She hoped she would never have to use it for blackmailing Alma, whom she really liked, but her ingrained training took over and she made sure she could always gain the upper hand in her relationship with Alma.

July 3, Islamabad

Dr. Anwar Usman was still feeling the burden of the great responsibility thrust upon his shoulders by Professor Malick, or for that matter, by his country. Although he was the youngest member of the committee, he knew that his colleagues respected his opinion and waited to hear his viewpoint at the next meeting of the committee that was set for the following day.

Anwar thought he would be able to think more clearly after a date, a close encounter as he defined it in his mind, with Alma. On the way to his office, he entered the laboratory in which Alma was making precise measurements of a finely shaped object and called her aside for a moment supposedly to ask her what the object was for.

Her co-workers suspected that the relationship between Alma and Anwar extended beyond work hours and pretended not to notice his unexpected appearance in the lab. Anwar said he wanted to arrange a date for that evening, and although she was a bit surprised as that was not on their normal schedule, she smiled and said she was looking forward to it.

Anwar arrived in the evening and the moment Alma saw him she knew something was bothering him. She didn't say anything about it until they had finished the fine dinner she had prepared, and then she commented he looked distracted and asked if she could help.

Anwar had enlisted her help several times previously as a sounding board for his ideas and admired her practical approach to problems and her agile mind. That had been the main reason he was attracted to her in the first place, and her good looks did nothing to daunt his enthusiasm about her. What he didn't know was that most of the things he told her she shared with her lover, Linda, who said she wanted to know her better by understanding more about her work.

As yet, the information that Alma passed on was interesting from a scientific or technical point of view and was not really classified, and certainly not of a sensitive nature with regard to Pakistan's national security.

After dinner they went to bed as was their custom. It was evident to Alma that Anwar's mind was not where his body was. His body went through the motions and Alma did her best to demonstrate how satisfying it was by groaning and moaning until the act was completed.

When they lay quietly in her bed with her hand caressing his chest gently and her head nestled on his shoulder, she asked him what was going on in his mind.

Anwar was a bit embarrassed by his distracted love-making and told her he couldn't disclose what was really bothering him because he had been sworn to secrecy. He said he would like to discuss a hypothetical question that troubled him, and she said she liked hypothetical problems.

Anwar said, "What would do if you had information that could affect the security and future of Pakistan?"

Alma didn't know what he was referring to, so she said, "Would sharing this information change the situation?"

Anwar answered, "Yes, but it could be viewed as treason."

She asked, "Who would be betrayed?"

His response was ambiguous, "If I go to the administration,

I would be betraying my friends and colleagues and perhaps the national security, because exposure may lead to a blood bath. If I don't do anything, a potential catastrophe may befall us, and I would feel like the ultimate traitor to my country."

She thought about this for a few moments and asked, "What if you do nothing?"

He pondered this and after some time said, "Then I would not be able to live with myself."

Alma wondered what this poor man was going through and said, "Then you have to take action. Without knowing any details, I assume the security of our country must come first and putting it in danger is out of the question."

"I am not sure that the pathways I mentioned are absolute. There is a chance that going to the administration would lead to the same result as betraying it, and a chance that a foreign power would cause as much damage to Pakistan as if it did not receive the information."

Alma did not know what to say so she continued to rub his head and hug him tightly.

They made love one more time before falling asleep. In the morning, he said he had to leave early because he had come to a decision. She tried to enquire which option he had selected but he evaded answering.

CHAPTER 12

July 3, Karachi, Pakistan

While these events were taking place in Islamabad, Nagib and Alia were transferred from the rustic Melmastun Hotel in Swabi to Karachi, where they were lodged in one of the nicest hotels in that cosmopolitan city.

The bustling city of Karachi with its thirteen million inhabitants was the largest city in Pakistan and considered as one of the five most populated cities in the world. The city was the main seaport and financial center of Pakistan and had several first-class hotels.

Although Karachi was called "the city that never sleeps," because of its night life, Alia and Nagib slept very well in the comfortable bed after enjoying a long soak in the hot tub that was in the suite Junaid had arranged for them, courtesy of General Masood and the Pakistani intelligence service.

The suite was large and contained two bedrooms—one for the couple and one for Junaid who was appointed as their "babysitter" and instructed to watch over them and make sure that they were happy.

Apparently, after the first meeting with Professor Malick and the nuclear physicists, General Masood realized that abiding by his part of the deal, namely constructing two small nukes according to the Los Alamos blueprints and handing them over to Nagib, in exchange for the rest of the stolen diagrams would take much longer than initially estimated.

He heard from Rahman they were very unhappy about the living conditions in the Swabi region and even hinted they would like to reconsider the whole agreement. Masood was sure they were bluffing—there was no way that they could manage on their own to get out of Pakistan without being stopped and he believed they certainly couldn't go the U.S. embassy and ask for asylum.

On second thought, he had to consider the lenient approach the Americans adopted when it came to criminals who confessed all and were forgiven if no actual damage to U.S. interests was evident.

Rahman reported to him that Nagib mentioned the fact that while they were in Germany, Iranian and North Korean agents had tried to strike a deal with the couple and the general thought that in desperation they may go to one of these embassies for shelter. His conclusion was that it was easier to keep them happy and satisfied than worry about what they would do if they felt disgruntled.

Rahman flew over to Karachi from Islamabad to pay them a visit and update them on the progress of the deal, without informing them of the debate about the plutonium quality that took place in the committee. He told them the scientists and engineers were studying the blueprints and checking them in order to devise a schedule for producing the two small warheads.

When Rahman saw the hotel in which they were staying and heard from Junaid about the suite she was sharing with the couple he wanted to stay in Karachi for a few nights, but the general only allowed him to spend one night there before returning to the committee's meetings. Rahman and Junaid made the most of that night, first having a small party with Nagib and Alia in the hot tub, then each couple retired to their respective bedrooms for further partying.

The next morning, while having breakfast in their suite, the foursome felt as if they had a lot in common, mainly that they were all working toward a joint successful operation.

Nagib asked Rahman, "May I speak frankly with you?"

Rahman said, "Of course, what's bothering you?"

Nagib hesitated a little and said, "You must realize the risks to your country involved in assisting us. If the Americans find out that Pakistan had helped us produce and detonate a nuclear device on U.S. soil, the retaliation may be an all-out attack on Pakistan and in the very least annihilation of major cities and the infrastructure. Who knows, India may seize the opportunity and subjugate Pakistan to Indian rule."

Rahman, who had considered all this before, said, "Let me give you an explanation about the way Pakistanis view the United States. In the 1950s and 1960s. Pakistan and the U.S. were on very friendly terms. The U.S. even supplied Pakistan with a nuclear research reactor, PARR-1, that went critical in 1965. Pakistan joined the South East Asia Treaty Organization, SEATO, and the "Baghdad Pact" while the U.S. assisted Pakistan economically and militarily and saw Pakistan as "the most allied ally." Later, especially after Pakistan's defeat by India in the 1971 Bangladesh war it became "the ignored ally," especially after Pakistan tried to respond to India's 1974 "peaceful" nuclear test by developing its own nuclear industry. This changed again in 1980 when the USSR invaded Afghanistan and the U.S. used Pakistan as a staging ground to support the anti-Soviet forces, including Bin Laden and the Mujahidin. After the Soviets were forced out of Afghanistan the U.S. lost interest in Pakistan and their policy shifted strongly toward India. Throughout the 1990s, Pakistan felt that the U.S. used a double-standard by condemning Pakistan while ignoring India's nuclear efforts. The U.S. stopped supplying PARR-1 with highly enriched uranium used to fuel the reactor and Pakistan switched to low-enriched uranium supplied by China. However, after 9/11 the U.S. once again needed Pakistan to help it chase Bin Laden and his supporters in Afghanistan in what the Americans termed "the global war on terrorism" but Pakistanis, and other Muslims, saw this as "the global war on Islam." This reached a high point when U.S. commandos trespassed brutally on Pakistani territory and killed Bin Laden. So, Nagib, you must understand that despite the dependence of Pakistan on U.S. economic support and military aid the people of Pakistan resent the United States and see it as a "fair weather friend" that cannot be trusted in time of stress and as a hypocrite that treats Pakistan with duplicity."

Nagib and Alia were surprised by this diatribe and remained silent for a moment or two, before Alia said, "I had never known that there were such strong feelings toward the United States among the Pakistani people."

Junaid contributed her opinion to the conversation, "This is also the sentiment in large parts of the military, government, intelligence services, and the nuclear community. The deep animosity of Pakistanis toward the United States and its policy in the region, or against Muslims in general, was expressed by many attacks on the American embassy and consulates in Pakistan. As early as 1979, a false rumor was spread charging the U.S. of bombing the Grand Mosque in Mecca. Students stormed the U.S. embassy in Islamabad and burned it to the ground. After 9/11 and the response of the U.S., a series of attacks was launched against the American consulate in Karachi between 2002 and 2006. In 2010, an attack on the U.S. consulate in Peshawar took place resulting in the death of a handful of U.S. Marines and citizens."

Rahman added, "The Americans in their diplomatic enclave are not aware of these strong emotions. They do not know that there are many high-ranking Pakistani officials who refrain from having anything to do with U.S. representatives. Nagib, this is the reason that you are getting so much help from General Masood and his faction in the administration. Someone else may have regarded you two as a valuable prize and would have handed you over to the Americans for personal gain or in order to receive a reward for Pakistan."

Alia and Nagib looked at each other and she said, "Thanks for the lesson. We now understand that we can count on you and General Masood."

July 4, Islamabad

The Fourth of July party at the American embassy in Islamabad was a great success socially. It was attended by the high and mighty of the Pakistani administration, including three government ministers, many high ranking civil servants, the top echelon of the military, and intelligence services, and most of the top officials of the Corps Diplomatique—or diplomatic corps as commoners addressed it.

Eugene almost felt as if he had been transported to the days of the Raj, as the British government in that part of the world was remembered. The military men, there were no women of high enough rank, were dressed in their formal uniforms adorned with ribbons and medals.

The civilian administrators were in their best suits and some of the diplomats even wore tuxedos. Some of the women at this gathering were dressed in long silk gowns, and some of the younger ones displayed a fair amount of bare skin, which was quite unusual in public affairs in Pakistan but none of the men seemed to complain. In these Fourth of July celebrations, the U.S. embassy served hot dogs and hamburgers—no pork, of course—cooked in the best American tradition but also some local dishes and gourmet foods for those who appreciated a good, free treat. The drinks were served in two separate areas—one served soft drinks according to the restrictions imposed by Islam, and in the other area you had to push your way through the throng to get to the counter and order your cocktail or real booze.

In one corner, a small band played jazz and a blues singer

provided light entertainment. At one stage the ambassador asked the band to stop playing and stepped on to the small podium. He delivered a short speech about the excellent relations and cooperation between Pakistan and the U.S. and added that although Pakistan was a young country, officially founded in 1947, it had a great tradition and has been the home to many ancient and modern civilizations while the United States was founded over two centuries earlier but was still a young country. He concluded by thanking the guests for attending the Independence Day celebrations and called for a toast to continued friendship.

The ambassador introduced Eugene to some of the more important patrons, presenting him as a scientist and administrator from the NNSA who was on a private visit to Pakistan. When Eugene was asked by some guests, who wanted to make polite small talk, what he was looking for in Pakistan, he answered he was on a comparative study mission visiting the closest U.S. allies in Asia and this was his first stop. The only local person he recognized was Professor Malick, whom he had met at scientific conferences and he was surprised the professor appeared to be ignoring him and avoiding getting in a conversation with him.

As the atmosphere warmed and the guests were having a good time brought upon by the food and drinks, the CIA station chief, Blakey, cornered Eugene and told him the ambassador wanted to see him on the veranda and led him there. When they got there, Eugene saw that the ambassador was engrossed in a conversation with a distinguished looking Pakistani who was introduced earlier as the minister of defense.

They were talking in low voices and stopped for a moment when Eugene approached. The ambassador asked Eugene to describe the classified information stolen from the Los Alamos Laboratory, and Eugene said these were blueprints and schematic designs of the most advanced nuclear devices in the U.S. arsenal. He added that in the wrong hands they could pose a threat to world peace, especially if they fell into the hands of radical terrorists. He also emphasized that the U.S. administration viewed this very seriously and would do anything, barring nothing, to retrieve the stolen files.

The ambassador then interjected that the people responsible for stealing the files were American citizens and according to the latest surveillance information were in Pakistan at present. The defense minister turned pale and beads of perspiration appeared on his high forehead and said that he knew nothing about this.

The ambassador implied there may be elements in the Pakistani government that would like to acquire these blueprints in order to improve their nuclear arsenal and do so clandestinely. The minister admitted there was a strong pro-Islamist and anti-American faction that may be involved in such a plot and promised to try and find out what was going on.

Blakey knocked on the door and told the ambassador he was needed at the reception, so the ambassador left first, and the minister and Eugene waited a minute before following.

Eugene pulled Blakey aside and told him the ambassador had informed the minister of defense about the stolen blueprints and that the culprits were in Pakistan. Blakey asked how the minister reacted and Eugene said that the revelation shocked him and that he understood the extent of aggravation to the U.S. administration and the implications to Pakistan, if the stolen diagrams were not recovered.

Eugene also mentioned the strange behavior of Professor Malick, who clearly avoided him. Blakey said the professor was regarded as the leading scientific authority by Pakistan's nuclear community, and although he had never spoken out publicly in support of Pakistan's right to build its nuclear arsenal and use it if necessary, he was known as a member of the nationalistic hard line faction within the government.

***

Linda was not invited to attend the Fourth of July reception at the embassy because officially she was just a low rank secretary. She knew that her presence there could blow her cover as people in similar positions did not participate in the formal event and usually held a small party of their own. Sometimes they invited friends and acquaintances from the local community.

Linda wanted to arrange an invitation for Alma, but when they discussed the matter Alma declined saying that as an employee in PINSTECH she would need special permission to attend a social event in a foreign embassy and she didn't want to attract attention to their relationship.

She told Linda she missed her and invited her to come over to her apartment after the party. Linda had quite a few drinks at the unofficial embassy party before driving over to Alma's apartment. So, when Alma opened the door she stepped in, kicked the door shut with the heel of her foot, and gave Alma a deep passionate kiss.

Alma pulled back, laughed quietly, told Linda to slow down a little. She led her to the sofa in her living room and pointed to a chilled bottle of bubbly wine and the two glasses set on the coffee table. She told Linda to open the bottle and pour the wine while she went in the kitchen to grab some snacks. They toasted each other and the Fourth of July and sipped the bubbly wine.

Although Linda was not a great wine connoisseur, bubbly wine was not high on her list of favorite drinks, but Alma's company made up for that. They cuddled on the sofa and then Alma took Linda's hand and led her to the bedroom saying it was her mission to make Linda enjoy Independence Day.

Over the last six months since their relationship had begun, Alma had come a long way and under Linda's tutoring had learned a lot about the ways to pleasure her own body and that of her lovers. Strangely enough, she also put this new knowledge to good practice in her affair with Anwar, who appreciated the new sexual advances she made.

Alma made sure that Linda would never forget this particular Fourth of July celebration by performing the things Linda liked most. Alma proved that she was a keen student, who enjoyed learning theoretically and practicing experimentally what her tutor showed her. Linda reciprocated and added a few new tricks to their expanding play book.

After a while, the two young women lay in each other's arms. Linda knew that Alma had seen Anwar the previous evening—after all Alma told her about her affair with the brilliant physicist—and asked if all was well with the other part of her love life. Alma said she noted that Anwar was under a lot of pressure and Linda waited to hear some details, but these were not forthcoming, so she decided to take a more active approach.

She said the trouble with men was they cannot express their feelings or share their problems as opposed to women. Alma sighed and said that was indeed the case with men but in a very uncharacteristic manner Anwar raised a strange dilemma, which really seemed to bother him. Alma added that he presented a hypothetical question that concerned national security, potential catastrophe, and loyalty, but she could not fathom the reason for this question and could only guess it related to some decision he had to make and present it to a top-secret committee.

Linda felt she had heard enough to confirm her suspicion that Alma's other lover held a pivotal position in the Pakistani nuclear establishment to which the classified data was presented. She didn't want to appear to be too inquisitive, so she said these hypothetical matters were way above her head and leaned over to kiss Alma gently on her soft earlobe. One thing led to another and soon they had fallen asleep after making love slowly and gently.

July 5, Islamabad

Despite the holiday in the U.S. and its official sites worldwide, a meeting was held at the embassy at noon. The ambassador, Blakey and Eugene listened to Linda's report. She did not go into any details about her relationship with Alma, although they all understood it wasn't a casual fling, and focused on the information she had gleaned about Anwar.

They all inferred that Anwar was a key player in the Pakistani nuclear establishment and that he was entrusted with a difficult decision. Evidently, he understood the implications of acting on the data that had been handed over by Nagib and the alternatives—doing nothing or informing the authorities.

Blakey suggested putting a tail on Anwar but Eugene said there was no point in doing so because whatever he was involved in would take place either at PINSTECH or at the offices of the intelligence services and unless they could record the meeting they would not learn anything new. Their main objectives were to find the couple and retrieve the data before it was passed on and following Anwar would get them no closer to that.

Blakey thanked Linda for her performance and achievement and asked her to stay in touch with Alma and try to learn more about Anwar and the committee. Linda said she intended to do so anyway and asked if there was any specific information they wanted.

Eugene stated that they would like to know what Nagib had already handed over to the Pakistanis and added that he didn't expect Anwar to know where the couple was staying.

After Linda left, the ambassador repeated he had issued a terse warning to the Pakistani minister of defense and wondered what effect that would have on the plans of the nationalist faction, who were sure to get word of this. While they were discussing this question, the duty officer entered the conference room with a printed message and gave it to Blakey.

The CIA station chief read it and said the show had begun and announced he had just been informed the minister of defense had been placed under house arrest by the Pakistani intelligence service and was facing an investigation of corruption in the department that dealt with purchasing armament for the military. He added that he was sure it was not a coincidence and was probably a countermove by the nationalist faction to prevent a probe the minister had initiated that morning.

A couple of hours later an official announcement by the Pakistani government mourned the tragic death of the minister of defense, who had left a suicide note pleading guilty to the accusations of corruption and took his own life by shooting himself.

The government spokesman also stated a forensic investigation would not be necessary because in his suicide note the minister clearly expressed the reasons for his final act. When the U.S. ambassador heard the news from Blakey, he called for an urgent meeting to discuss the severity of the situation, but there was not much they could do about it.

***

General Masood was not pleased with the way the experts of the Pakistani nuclear establishment were handling the blueprints for the small nuke. He was frustrated that the committee had not reached a unanimous decision and no scientist was willing to guarantee that copying the design and building it with their lower-grade plutonium would work as advertised. What was even worse they had no constructive suggestions how to fix the problem and give him assurances that it would work at all.

He realized that Professor Malick could not provide the scientific leadership he had hoped for and decided to disband the committee and summon Dr. Anwar Usman for a private meeting and ask him for his frank opinion. He was tired of receiving from the scientists answers like those given by lawyers—"on the one hand… and on the other hand…"—and looked for a decisive trustworthy opinion.

When Anwar arrived at work, he was surprised to see the PINSTECH chief security officer waiting for him. He was instructed to accompany the officer and was driven to the headquarters of the Pakistani intelligence service where he was escorted to General Masood's office. The general welcomed him warmly and invited him to sit down in a comfortable recliner at the coffee table in the corner of his office while he took the recliner on the other side of the table. With a small smile, he told his secretary he was not to be disturbed unless a nuclear war with India broke out. Anwar had never seen the general behaving like this and expected a truly unconventional meeting.

The general started by flattering Anwar. "I wish to commend you for being an outstanding scientist and a true patriot." In a menacing voice he added, "Your personal life is none of the business of the intelligence service, but of course we know about your affair with gorgeous little Alma."

Anwar paled a little but waited for the general to continue. Masood said, "You have probably deduced that you and the other committee members were given only a sample of the information on the advanced designs of nuclear weapons that were copied from the Americans."

Anwar nodded and the general continued, "The American scientist who brought us these designs is undoubtedly considered as a renegade by his people, although he does have a good reason for handing these secrets to us. Actually, two good reasons. One, because he views Pakistan as the only Muslim country that can supply him with what he wants, and second, he can understand that we are not great fans of the U.S. and its policy in Asia."

Anwar started seriously worrying what the general was implying—a nuclear weapon in the hands of a fanatic, so he timidly asked, "What did we promise him?"

Masood said, "Only two small nukes, and after he receives these, he would hand over the schematics of much more powerful weapons, the top of the line in the American arsenal."

Anwar was shocked. "General Masood, you are aware that the origin of the small nukes could be traced back to us. Modern nuclear forensics is bound to be able to prove that the plutonium comes from Pakistan, not to mention other pieces of evidence that would point to us. And Allah knows how they would respond—look what they did after 9/11 when only three thousand people were killed on U.S. soil—they invaded Iraq, intensified their war in Afghanistan, chased and persecuted Muslims everywhere, and increased their support of corrupt Arab regimes and Israel."

The general smiled bitterly and said, "Yes, yes, of course, they did these things against countries that had weak armies and some conventional weapons but no nuclear weapons. Look at the American intervention, or actually fear of intervening, in what used to be Syria. They threatened war because the Assad's forces used chemical weapons but only after the Russians threw their weight around did Syria disband its chemical weapons, or at least convince the West that they were all destroyed. We know that some of these weapons had been smuggled out of Syria to Lebanon, Iraq, Iran, and even Turkey for future use. No, my dear Anwar, the mighty Americans wouldn't dare to mess with a nuclear power."

Anwar said, "General, I have a suggestion that would allow us to obtain the rest of the blueprints without risking the wrath of the U.S. Why don't we simply arrest the American renegade and take the blueprints without giving him the nukes?"

Masood looked up, surprised, and said, "I have given him my word of honor and so far, he has kept his part of the deal."

Anwar had his response ready. "Of course, we'll give him nukes, but we'll make sure they do not work properly. Alternatively, we could force him to reveal all the information, by force and torture if necessary. After all, it is our national security that is involved here and perhaps even our country's very existence."

The general said, "Naturally, we also considered using force to extract the information but decided against it because we believed that an act against American assets is also in our interest, and having it done by an American citizen would exonerate Pakistan. We were not aware of the possibility that it would be traced to us and the ramifications if we are put to blame. Thank you for your insights. I see no point in continuing the committee's work but would like you to serve as my special advisor for nuclear and scientific matters."

The general summoned Rahman, who escorted Anwar back to PINSTECH to collect his personal belongings and relocate to the headquarters of the intelligence services.

Rahman helped Anwar settle down in his new office that was down the hall from General Masood's office and was then called to the general's office. The general told him to assemble the committee one last time and thank them for their time and effort and then dismiss them.

He also told Rahman about the conversation he had had with Dr. Anwar Usman and about Anwar's insights, which were the reason he decided to move him to the headquarters.

Rahman asked if the couple, Nagib and Alia, should be informed about these developments but the general said they should only be told that work was in progress and hopefully they would receive the two devices soon, without specifying a date.

Rahman suggested he should fly to Karachi to tell them in person, and the general who was no fool and knew about his affair grinned and said he must make sure to give Junaid his warm regards. Rahman saw that the general actually winked when he said this, and blushed.

***

Before leaving his office in PINSTECH, Anwar called Alma and told her he had been posted temporarily elsewhere and he would tell her about it in the evening, if she was free.

Alma saw that he looked slightly relieved and the worried expression was gone and said she would love to see him and would prepare something special for him.

In the evening, after dinner he told her he had been transferred to the headquarters of the intelligence services and would serve as a special assistant to General Masood.

She told him she was glad that whatever had been bothering him before seemed to have gone away.

Anwar smiled and said he had found a way out of the dilemma that had troubled him before, a solution that would prevent the danger he feared would sweep his country into a catastrophe without having to betray anything or anyone that mattered.

CHAPTER 13

July 5, Karachi

Nagib and Alia were getting used to the lifestyle of the rich and famous, enjoying the amenities of the hotel and their suite.

Junaid did not complain either and started to get attached to the couple. From time to time, Nagib asked her what was happening in Islamabad and she told him what Rahman had informed her, that work was in progress.

As they were planning another night on the town, there was a knock on the suite's door and Rahman entered with a big smile. First, he reassured Nagib that everything was going according to plan and the two "gifts" would be ready soon.

Afterwards, he asked Junaid what they had planned for the evening and she said they intended to go out to the top-ranking restaurant in Karachi for dinner.

Rahman said it was a very bad idea and a breach of security could put them at risk because this particular restaurant was a favorite among foreign businesspeople and many Americans ate there regularly, including members of the CIA. He proposed they order food from the same restaurant, but have it delivered to their suite. Everyone agreed it was a good plan.

Rahman spent a couple of nights in Karachi and made sure the couple didn't take any more excursions in to town. The four young people grew quite close together during their stay in the hotel suite and found they had a lot in common with regard to their views on the way the West, headed by the U.S.A treated the "natives" in Asia and Africa.

They all thought the "natives" had every right to get even, or realizing it was impossible to correct all historical injustices with one deed, at least contribute to this end.

However, Rahman said the plan might backfire if Pakistan was held accountable for the detonation of a nuclear device in the heart of Western democratic states including Israel, and the retribution may lead to a total destruction of his country.

Nagib tried to reassure him it would be impossible to trace the devices back to Pakistan but Rahman said he had heard a lecture about the wonders of nuclear forensics and feared the origin of the plutonium may be determined by advanced analytical methods that were practiced by a handful of laboratories in the West.

Nagib couldn't argue with that as he knew that one of those laboratories was at Los Alamos. Nagib suggested that the Pakistanis could claim that some of their plutonium had disappeared and was probably stolen by sympathizers of some radical Islamic faction, perhaps by supporters of the Islamic State.

In that case, Pakistan could only be blamed for failing to implement appropriate security measures to guard the strategic nuclear materials.

Rahman said he would present this suggestion to the

experts when he returned to Islamabad in a couple of days.

***

The Iranians got word that special activity concerning Pakistan's nuclear program was taking place and that General Masood from the intelligence service was involved. Their informer in PINSTECH was a mid-level technician that worked in the same department as

Dr. Anwar Usman and was surprised to see him collect his personal items and carry them out while being escorted by another young man. The technician's curiosity drove him to ask his co-worker where Anwar was going and who his escort was.

His colleague said it was a secret, but that she had recognized his escort as an operative of the intelligence services because she had seen him before. The technician, who was ordered by his Iranian contact to watch out for any irregularities arranged a meeting with his contact and told him that Anwar was transferred temporarily to an undisclosed position, but he found out it involved the intelligence services.

The Iranian commended him on a job well done and rewarded him with a bonus, he said he would receive another fat bonus if he could find out the name of the person who escorted Dr. Usman.

The technician managed to discover that the escort's name was Rahman Chenna, and he, indeed, received the fat bonus as promised.

Rahman's name was well known to the Iranians as an

operative of Pakistani intelligence and they also knew about his cover as a science attaché in Brussels and his involvement in bringing Nagib and Alia to Pakistan.

Their hackers managed to penetrate the airline ticketing system and saw he had been booked on a flight from Islamabad to Karachi. The Iranians didn't have an official consulate in Karachi, which was surprising considering the importance of that harbor town and its proximity to Iran, but did have several commercial offices that served as a front to the Iranian Revolutionary Guards (IRG), and minded their substantial business assets in Pakistan.

A phone call from Islamabad and a description of Rahman were enough to have two agents of the IRG at the arrivals gate in Karachi airport. They had no trouble picking up Rahman, who felt totally safe in Pakistan and following him to the hotel in which the American couple was enjoying their suite.

However, they did not know in which room Rahman was staying and were afraid to raise suspicion by asking too many questions, so they sat in the hotel lobby and sipped tea waiting for Rahman to emerge again. They noticed there quite a few Americans at the hotel but as they had not been briefed on Nagib and Alia didn't know what to look for.

July 6, Islamabad

Linda and Alma spent the evening in Linda's apartment. Their relationship had now reached a phase where they spent most of their free time together. The sex continued to be formidable and even better as Alma took on a more active role, but their relationship had deepened and extended beyond pure atavistic satisfaction.

In a liberal society, they would have probably moved in together to share an apartment and become a couple but in the conservative Pakistani society, that was out of the question.

Alma's affair with Anwar didn't interfere with the way the two women regarded each other just as the fact that both worked in organizations that frowned upon significant relationships with people of foreign nations.

One of the advantages for Linda was that from Alma she learned to cook Pakistani dishes and was also driven to extend her repertoire of fast food beyond salads, pasta, and hamburgers. One could say that in her own way she was becoming domesticated. Her boss, Blakey, knew about her affair with Alma and encouraged it because of the access to PINSTECH in general and to Dr. Anwar Usman in particular.

The tall athletic blonde American girl, who was nothing less than an operative of the CIA and the attractive dark-skinned young woman, who was an engineer in one of Pakistan's classified institutions, may have looked like an odd couple to an observer. But in fact, they had a lot in common—both were highly intelligent, independent, and strong-willed women, who did not receive the credit they deserved from the mainly male society in which they operated.

The discussions they had were philosophical and concerned the world situation in general, but they also talked a lot about the radical Islamic movements and the threat they posed to the current world order.

With great difficulty, Alma managed to convey to Linda

the feeling of a large part of Pakistani society about the roughshod meddling of America and the West in the affairs of the rest of the world.

This was particularly troublesome in the Asian sub-continent that included India, Pakistan, Bangladesh, Afghanistan, and some of the smaller countries like Sri Lanka, Bhutan, and Tibet. She said that democracy may be the best type of government for the U.S., Australia, and parts of Europe but was unsuitable for most societies in Asia and Africa.

This was especially true in countries that were artificially created by drawing straight lines on a map by representatives of colonial powers with total disregard of ethnic, religious, cultural, and traditional features of the population. Notable examples were Iraq, Syria, and Lebanon, or more accurately what used to be Iraq and Syria, where Shiites, Sunnis, Kurds, Christians of various sorts, and many other minorities were forced to share a geographical region and a formal government.

As long as a strong dictator held power and kept this mélange together, the country seemed to be unified and stable. This could be done in a society that knew no better and was kept in an ignorant state. However, the advent of television and the increase in the level of literacy and especially after the dissemination of the internet, Facebook, Twitter, cell phones, and other information and communication channels things changed.

People could see that in other countries the standard of living was higher and wanted a better life for themselves and a better future for their children. Everyone could see demonstrations against the rulers, masses in the streets throwing stones, tossing burning flares at police forces, mass murders carried out by members of one tribe, or religion, against people who were their good neighbors for centuries and wondered if they were next in line.

Linda said these things had occurred throughout human history and mentioned well-known historical precedents like tribal wars in the ancient world, the empires founded by the Egyptians, Assyrians, Babylonians, Persians, Greeks, and Romans, the conquests of the Americas by the Spanish, Portuguese, French, and British, not to mention incidents such as the massacre of the French Huguenots by the French Catholics or the mutual genocide of Hutu and Tutsi in Burundi.

Alma argued that all these examples were irrelevant because of two things: first, the scale of the potential conflict was unprecedented and included one and half a billion Muslims, and second, the availability of weapons of mass destruction that could lead to mutual annihilation of civilization.

She said that if radical, fanatic factions like the Islamic State could not be stopped dead in their-tracks a world conflict was inevitable because that movement was not ready for a compromise or even negotiations. ISIS had a totalitarian approach –you are either one of us and accept the teachings of Muhammad and the law of Shariya or you are no more.

Linda saw an opening and asked Alma if she believed in the goals of ISIS and was not surprised to hear that Alma opposed their approach, although there were anti-American elements in Pakistan that thought they could use ISIS to settle the score with the West.

Linda said she was relieved to hear that Alma herself was against ISIS and wondered how strong was the support for it inside the Pakistani administration. Alma said there was a faction that had inroads with the intelligence services and the nuclear community, and they could be persuaded to participate in dangerous and adventurous actions against the U.S.

Linda innocently asked if Anwar was one of these and Alma said he was opposed to these factions but had to keep quiet about it because if he were suspected as not being patriotic enough, he would surely lose his privileged top-secret status and his job.

Linda now realized that Alma and Anwar wouldn't knowingly give her classified information and she would have to either resort to blackmail and use the video she recorded during her first intimate encounter with Alma or use subterfuge and try to get her to inadvertently reveal the items that interested her most—where Nagib and Alia were being kept and what classified information they had passed on to the Pakistanis.

So, she asked Alma, "How is your affair with Anwar progressing?"

Alma's answer surprised her, "We no longer work together as he has suddenly been transferred from PINSTECH, but we will remain in contact as before because he was still in Islamabad area."

Linda didn't want to appear to be too inquisitive about Anwar's new posting and asked, "Will Anwar's new job affect our own relationship?"

Alma replied, "It should not have any effect because I'll

still be spending time with Anwar, as before."

Linda said, "Have you seen Anwar recently?"

Alma nodded. "We spent some time together last night and he behaved as if the great burden that had troubled him lately had been removed. I think it has something to do with a decision that had been made and with his new job as an advisor."

Linda asked, "Whose advisor?"

Alma recognized her indiscretion and said she didn't know. Linda realized that the atmosphere had changed and patted the seat next to her and motioned for Alma to join her.

After holding each other and some tender kisses they moved to Linda's bed and made love. Alma felt that their relationship had gone through another stage and the level of intimacy and mutual trust had risen while Linda felt torn between her lover and her job.

Alma didn't sleep over claiming she had to tidy her apartment. Linda was glad because she wanted to report the news about Anwar's new posting, to what she was now sure was as an advisor to General Masood in the intelligence services. She knew it must be significant and related to Nagib and his information although she was uncertain in what way.

July 23, Islamabad

Rahman had presented Nagib's suggestion that Pakistan should announce that some of its plutonium was missing.

General Masood asked Anwar what he thought about this idea, and the physicist replied it had certain merits, even if the statement was not believed by anyone. He added that the Pakistani government should first deny this, and state no material was really missing, and it was only an error of accounting, and after a couple of days admit that some plutonium had been stolen and inside cooperation was suspected.

They knew Pakistan had a bad track record after the way the government handled the case of the AQ Khan network a few years previously but agreed as long as denial was plausible it would do no harm to announce that some plutonium was missing.

The timing of this announcement was to coincide with the transfer of the devices to the hands of Nagib.

Two small nukes were manufactured by PINSTECH according to the blueprints supplied by Nagib. Testing them was out of the question because the global networks for monitoring nuclear tests were sure to detect such a test.

These systems were operated officially by an organization called Comprehensive Test Ban Treaty Organization (CTBTO), but there were other informal monitoring networks operated by different intelligence gathering entities like the American NNSA, the Russians, Chinese, and of course, by India that was watching what Pakistan was doing with a hawk's eye.

Under Anwar's guidance, the core of the devices consisted of plutonium as described in the blueprints, but it was of a lower grade because there was no super high grade material in Pakistan.

General Masood asked Anwar if Nagib wouldn't discover the switch and Anwar told him the famous anecdote about the first atomic bomb of the Soviet Union.

He said, "Stalin appointed Lavrenti *Beria, the head of the NKVD (a predecessor of the KGB),* to oversee the production of plutonium in the USSR. When the first batch had been produced and purified, Beria visited the laboratory and was shown a metallic sphere. He was told it was plutonium but being ever suspicious he asked how he could verify it. The chief scientist who was head of the project, Igor Kurchatov, told him plutonium emitted radiation that caused its temperature to rise, and told Beria to touch it and feel the heat. Beria felt the metallic sphere and found it was indeed hot. He thought for a moment and asked how he could be sure it wasn't heated in an oven before his visit but was later convinced it was genuine plutonium."

The general laughed and said it was a nice story but wondered if it was relevant so Anwar told him that when they presented Nagib with the device the only test he would be able to perform without an analytical laboratory would be to feel the temperature of the plutonium core and promised it would be naturally hot regardless of the quality of the plutonium.

When he saw that the general was in a good mood, he told him another anecdote. "After Beria was convinced that the plutonium was genuine, he consulted Stalin and asked him which scientists and engineers should be awarded medals for the success of the project. Stalin's simple answer was to give medals to those he would have executed if the project failed."

The general said that as much as he hated communism and Stalin, he had to admit that he was a very practical man.

Anwar didn't like to be away from his research and his

laboratory but had started to enjoy the proximity to the corridors of power and being in the nerve center where important decisions were made. He called Alma and arranged to see her in the evening telling her he had to go to Karachi on an important mission the following day.

Alma, as usual said she would be delighted because they had barely seen each other during the last week. She then called Linda and said she had to cancel their date because Anwar wanted to see her. Linda asked if there was any special reason and Alma blurted that he told her he had to go to Karachi.

Linda said she understood, and they could meet the following evening. She immediately called Blakey and informed him of this development. Blakey realized this could be the best chance to find Nagib and Alia in Pakistan and told all his agents to head to Karachi and wait for him there.

July 24, Karachi

Nagib and Alia were excited when Junaid told them that Rahman would arrive with one of the leading physicists from PINSTECH and assured them they would have some good news concerning the delivery of the two "gifts."

The past few days had been very peaceful—they were not aware of the presence of the Iranians or the North Koreans that were desperately trying to find them. Nagib was relieved that the memory stick, or thumb drive, in his pen had not been discovered. He noticed that someone had gone through his laptop in search of the files with the blueprints and knew the hidden files had not been copied because attempts to do so without the correct sequence of passwords would cause the laptop to shut down.

When Junaid was taking a shower he whispered to Alia he had expected such an attempt and was grateful to the pimpled youngster in Pasadena for the software protection he had installed, in what seemed to be ages ago, but was in fact a little more than one month. His pen was in public display in his shirt pocket, as it was always , and he used it to write notes or sign for hotel deliveries.

***

Linda arrived in Karachi on a morning flight from Islamabad and joined the meeting of the American agents, not only from the CIA but from all the agencies, that was held in the Karachi office of the largest U.S. trade partner in Pakistan.

Naturally it belonged to a defense contractor whose main line of business was to sell American-made armaments and spare parts to the Pakistani military. All in all, there were about a dozen men and two women chatting and having coffee or sodas when the CIA station chief, George Blakemore, entered the room.

Blakey proceeded to explain that their mission was to follow Dr. Anwar Usman and Rahman Chenna when they landed in Karachi later in the afternoon and see if they met with two American citizens, Nagib and Alia Jaber, and if the opportunity presented itself to snatch the Americans and bring them to a safe location.

In the old days he would have handed out photographs

of all the people concerned but he simply sent the photos to their cell phones. He then divided the agents in to two task forces—one section consisting of eight people in four cars was responsible for following the Pakistani scientist and intelligence agent from the airport to wherever they were going, and the second group was put in charge of forcibly snatching the couple and included only agents that had diplomatic immunity in case the kidnapping attempt failed and the operatives were arrested.

Blakey said the CIA had received an unconfirmed message that the renegade couple could be in one of the most expensive hotels, enjoying life at the expense of the Pakistani taxpayer, or more probably thanks to the U.S. financial aid to Pakistan the American taxpayer was footing the bill. Blakey added that in case the couple could not be captured alive the fallback position would be to eliminate them—what used to be called "terminate with extreme prejudice" in the good old days—and retrieve the files.

One of the more intelligent agents asked what would happen if there were copies of these files they could not recover. All Blakey could say was they thought it would be counterproductive for Nagib to make copies. The meeting dispersed and Linda found herself in the car with Blakey and another embassy official who drove the car. They headed toward the best hotel in Karachi, expecting the trail would end there or at one of the other upper-class hotels on the same street.

Anwar and Rahman were on board a small private jet that belonged to the Pakistani intelligence services. Once the plane landed at Karachi airport, they were met by an escort of three jeeps packed with heavily armed members of the elite unit of the Pakistani Special Forces. The drivers turned on their flashing lights and sirens and headed to the hotel in which Junaid and the couple were staying. The small convoy made so much noise and the flashing lights could be seen from miles away so the American agents in charge of following them had no difficulty in doing their job with their eyes closed.

On the other hand, the second task force reached the hotel and realized there was not a chance in hell they would be able to snatch Nagib and Alia in view of the heavily armed guards. Blakey called off the force, thanked them for their efforts and told them to return to their routine jobs.

Nagib and Alia were waiting restlessly in the suite when Anwar and Rahman arrived with an armed escort. After a brief introduction Anwar, Rahman and Nagib retired to a corner of the suite and held a quiet conversation. Anwar told Nagib the two small nukes had been constructed according to the blueprints and they were now in Islamabad waiting for his approval.

Rahman said shipping arrangements were made and added that the Pakistanis expected to receive the other designs after Nagib's inspection. Nagib smiled broadly and said he appreciated the fact that the agreement had been honored by the Pakistanis and he would fulfill his part as soon as the devices were in his custody.

Meanwhile, Alia and Junaid packed all their clothes and were ready to leave as soon as the men finished their little conference.

The entourage left the suite in which the American couple

and Junaid had spent a very enjoyable time. For the couple, this was a period of relief that afforded them a feeling of security they had not had since they left Los Alamos over a month earlier, and both of them realized that once they left Pakistan with or without the devices, they would have to constantly look over their shoulder because a myriad of intelligence services would be after them.

As they made their way through the hotel's lobby they were observed by Linda and Blakey, who were having coffee in the corner and by the Iranian agents, who were sipping tea in the opposite corner. The North Koreans were not in the lobby although one of their agents was parked about fifty feet behind the three jeeps. None of the agents bothered to follow the entourage because they had all figured out they were on the way to the airport for a flight back to Islamabad.

The group got into the middle jeep and the convoy of three vehicles made its way back to the airport where the private jet was parked with its engines turning. Nagib and Alia accompanied by Rahman and Junaid as well as Anwar and two armed bodyguards boarded the waiting jet.

Rahman told the couple they would be taken to a safe house that belonged to the Pakistani intelligence services and would be discreetly taken to see the devices at a hangar in PINSTECH. He said the dimensions of the devices were small enough so they could comfortably fit in a standard twenty-nine-inch suitcase of the type that had a rugged hard-sided shell.

Rahman said two such suitcases were ready, but the devices would be placed inside them only after being inspected and approved by Nagib.

CHAPTER 14

July 25, Islamabad

Nagib and Alia spent a sleepless night in the safe house they were taken to the previous evening. They were on the second floor of the building. Armed guards were placed on the roof of the building, on the lower floor, and outside the front and back doors.

The reason they had so little sleep was obvious—they now reached the most dangerous stage of their journey to Pakistan, because once they handed over all the designs there was absolutely nothing to prevent the Pakistanis from reneging on the deal and arresting them, or more likely making them disappear.

Alia suggested they hand over the thumb drive with the files protected by a password and send the password only after they felt safe with the devices on European soil, or far away from Pakistan.

Nagib liked the idea but was not sure the Pakistanis would accept this last minute change because of two reasons—they might fear that he would not keep his word and hand over the password and in addition they would feel offended because he didn't trust them and that would be a sign of disrespect.

Furthermore, the Pakistanis could be justly worried about the couple's safety since quite a few intelligence organizations were after them, and especially the Americans would not hesitate to eliminate them on sight, so they wouldn't be able to deliver the passwords.

In the morning, Rahman came to the safe house to take Nagib and Alia to inspect the devices. Once again, a convoy of three jeeps, manned by armed soldiers, was waiting to take them to PINSTECH.

Nagib realized the institute was located in Nilore, which was on the outskirts of Islamabad. On the way to the site, Rahman proudly told him that most of PINSTECH's former directors had obtained their doctorates in the West, mainly the UK, U.S., Canada, and Japan, but the current director got his doctorate in nuclear engineering from Peshawar University.

They used one of PINSTECH's side entrances and once Rahman showed his ID, they were waved through with no further checks. The two escorting jeeps parked near the gate and the jeep with Rahman, Nagib, Alia, and the driver who was obviously also from the intelligence services, drove up to a small hangar.

As they approached the hangar, its doors opened and they drove in and parked by a small cubicle that served as the temporary office. Anwar was already waiting for them there and when they got out of the car, he came forward to welcome them.

Alia noted two standard twenty-nine-inch suitcases in the middle of the hangar and saw that the agent who had driven their jeep was now holding a video camera and recording everything that took place in the hangar.

Anwar, who was holding a radiation detector, led them toward the suitcase. He opened it just as one would open a suitcase with clothes and placed the detector close to the metal pipe strapped to one side of the suitcase. The detector's clicking sound increased a little in volume and in frequency, indicating the presence of some type of gamma emitting material.

When Anwar stepped back a few feet, the clicking ceased. Anwar showed Nagib that the reading from the detector was around one count per second—1 cps in scientific jargon— that was pretty much the background level in that hangar. He closed the suitcase and placed the detector so that it touched the suitcase and the reading increased very slightly to 2 cps.

Anwar looked at Nagib's reaction and said, "Okay. So, you know there is something radioactive in the suitcase, and you know that external radiation is very low, but you probably want to know if there is any plutonium here, don't you?"

Nagib nodded and replied, "Yes, can you convince me that this is the real thing?"

Anwar said, "As a scientist from Los Alamos National Laboratory you have probably heard the story about Beria's visit to the laboratory that produced plutonium."

Nagib smiled. "Of course, I know it. Can I touch the device to feel if it is hot?"

Anwar said, "By all means. Please put on the polyethylene gloves and touch the metal pipe." Nagib adorned the gloves and hesitantly touched the pipe, feeling that it was slightly warmer than the surrounding objects.

He said, "Well, I am sure you did not heat this pipe before we got here and believe the heat comes from the decay of some radioactive material. How do I know it is plutonium and not something else?"

Anwar, who had anticipated a degree of skepticism, signaled to Rahman to bring his laptop from the small office. When the laptop was switched on, Anwar searched the files and displayed a spectrum. He explained this was a display of the intensity of the signal from alpha-particles as a function of the particle energy and pointed to distinct peaks he said arose from alpha-decay of plutonium atoms.

Nagib studied the spectrum and said, "I am now convinced the material from which the spectrum was recorded was indeed plutonium. I take your word this material is inside these pipes."

In a formal tone Rahman, looking at the video camera, said, "Dr. Nagib Jaber, do you formally acknowledge these two suitcases contain a small nuclear device?"

Nagib faced the camera and said, "I do, and I hope they were constructed according to the blueprints I gave you."

Anwar said, "I solemnly testify they were, but with a small caveat—they have not been tested. I would be grateful if you now fulfill your part of the deal and hand over the other blueprints."

Anwar then explained to Nagib how to detonate the suitcase bombs and said it was very simple because the devices did not have a sophisticated Permissive Action Link (PAL) installed to prevent unauthorized arming or detonation of a nuclear weapon. Anwar said all they needed to do was to make sure the battery pack was fully charged and set the digital timer, much like the type used on microwave ovens in every modern household.

Now came the tricky part Nagib and Alia had discussed the previous evening. He said, "I am fully ready to complete the deal as soon as we are out of Pakistan with the two suitcases." He waited for Rahman's reaction.

As expected, Rahman barely controlled the anger in his voice, "The agreement was that as soon as you inspected the devices and approved them you would deliver the rest of the schematics."

Nagib protested, "But if I give you the blueprints while still in Pakistan you can simply arrest me and take back the two devices and there is nothing I can do about it. I need insurance, or at least strong assurances that this won't happen."

Rahman looked flabbergasted and said he needed permission from General Masood to alter the agreement and left them standing in the middle of the hanger while he stepped into the small office to call the general.

Meanwhile, Anwar looked at the situation rationally and said to Nagib, "I understand your apprehension and am sure we can find a viable solution. As one scientist to another I can say if the Pakistani authorities had any intention to renege on the deal, they could have done so any moment after you stepped on Pakistani soil. Remember, that officially you never entered the country and no one who cares about you knows where you are, and you are certainly in no position to go to the American embassy—they would probably shoot you first and carry out an investigation later."

Nagib replied, "So, what do you propose?"

Anwar said, "The best solution for everyone is that you turn in your American passports and Rahman will issue you with original Pakistani passports and allow you to leave the country. The two suitcases can be sent as part of a "diplomatic pouch," that is immune from being searched to any Pakistani embassy of your choice. You will go there and collect the suitcases that will be handed to you as soon as you deliver the rest of the blueprints. What do you think of this?"

Nagib consulted Alia and after a few minutes said, "This sounds reasonable, but we need to retain our American passports to enter the U.S. freely."

Rahman returned all worked up with a red face and ready for an outburst, but Anwar said, "Before you say anything, we have another idea." He reiterated the discussion.

Rahman nodded and said it was a good solution although the general had other ideas about how to terminate the negotiations, and then laughed and said, "Nagib and Alia you must be dreaming of being able to use your U.S. passports ever again. The minute they will be used for buying an airline ticket, presented at a passport control booth at any border crossing in the world or used in a hotel, car rental agency, or anywhere else, the NSA will know about it instantly and within minutes you'll be arrested, if not worse."

Nagib thought about this for a minute but held on to the American passports saying he would feel better with them. Rahman said it would take twenty-four hours to issue Pakistani passports and asked them if they wanted any particular names on them.

Alia said she always liked the name Fatima and suggested that for her husband Munir would be nice. Nagib agreed and said their last name should be something symbolic that represented their objective and suggested "Abu Jihad."

Everyone smiled and Rahman invited Munir and Fatima Abu Jihad to accompany him back to the safe house. They left the hangar after making sure that the suitcases were stored in a locker and a guard was posted at its door. The convoy made its way back to the safe house.

***

In the evening, Anwar arranged a date with his girlfriend after calling her and telling her he wanted something special to celebrate a breakthrough. Alma did not know what to expect but his jovial mood was contagious, and she sang to herself softly while cooking his favorite dishes. She was surprised when he turned up on her doorstep at the appointed time and took a bottle of wine out of his bag and presented it to her with a big smile.

This was quite unusual as they seldom drank alcohol together. Of course, he had no idea she and Linda regularly consumed a couple of wine bottles whenever they spent an evening with each other. She opened the wine bottle and filled a couple of glasses and asked him what they were celebrating. Once again, he smiled and said he wished to make a toast.

She looked at him as he said, "Alma, it is time we got married"

Before he could continue, she burst out laughing, and said, "Yes, but who will take us?" When she saw the astonished look on his face, she added, "Of course, I agree. I love you."

Anwar suddenly felt relieved because for a moment he thought she was serious, and said, "There is something else I wish to celebrate. You must have noticed that I had been distraught recently, and you know that I was away from my laboratory at PINSTECH on a special assignment. Well, now this problem has been solved and I'll return to the laboratory in a couple of days."

Alma suggested they drink another glass to commemorate that and before long the bottle was empty. She went in the kitchen and brought out another bottle. He was a bit surprised to see she had wine in the house and when she saw his inquisitive look she said a girl friend had given it to her and told her to open it if there was a very special reason, so his marriage proposal was indeed a good reason.

Anwar didn't ask who the friend was and that was just as well because Alma didn't want to tell him about her relationship with Linda.

Once they had consumed dinner and the two bottles of wine, they retired to the bedroom to seal the deal in the most pleasurable way. Anwar had noted that their lovemaking had become much more intense and enjoyable during the last few months and attributed it to his own improved technique. This contributed to his ego and he felt elated he had made her an active partner in their love life, not realizing that Alma guided him every step of the way.

Alma was glad to see him in such a good mood and said, "I

would love for you to share this problem and its solution with me, if you can without breaching any security issues."

He said, "You know I cannot tell you all about it, but as the problem is solved, I can tell you about something that happened today that concerns plutonium. In your work at PINSTECH, you have come across this material and you know that the grade of plutonium cannot be determined by alpha spectrometry because the two important isotopes, plutonium-239 and plutonium-240 are practically indistinguishable. Today, I managed to convince another scientist that lower-grade plutonium was high-grade material."

She asked who the scientist was, and he said, "Someone who now calls himself Munir Abu Jihad and he will be very famous soon, so remember the name."

Both fell asleep with a satiated smile on their faces.

***

Blakey and his staff at the American embassy were frustrated because they failed to stop Nagib and Alia. What was even worse from their point of view was the fact the couple had been no more than a few feet from them in the hotel lobby in Karachi and there was nothing they could do about it because of the heavily armed entourage that accompanied them.

Blakey's informers reported the special jet had landed in Islamabad and another armed convoy escorted the passengers to an undisclosed location. Blakey felt that the horses were about to leave the stable and there was no way to bring them back. None of his contacts could provide any useful information except to say the big project overseen by General Masood, whatever it was, appeared to be coming to an end.

Blakey turned to Linda and asked her if she could use her own contact to figure out what was happening, and Linda said she would try to arrange a meeting with Alma.

***

The Iranians and North Koreans were no better off than the Americans. They knew that something big was afoot in Islamabad and deduced that it concerned PINSTECH but none of their agents and collaborators could supply any useful details. The Iranians heard from one of the guards of the side gate that a small convoy headed by an operative of the Pakistani intelligence services entered the site and one jeep drove to a small hangar while the other two remained at the gate.

The jeep's windows were shaded, and he couldn't see who was inside but noted there were silhouettes of a man and a woman seated in the back seat. He added that the small hangar was well guarded, and this was quite irregular because it was usually empty.

The Iranian agent who received this report told the guard to keep an eye on the hangar and report any activity. He also called his North Korean colleague and, in an unusual gesture, shared the information with him.

***

The official announcement by the Pakistani Atomic Energy Commission (PAEC) was extremely out of character. It said that the Head of PAEC initiated a formal investigation into the disappearance of an undisclosed amount of plutonium from the stores of PINSTECH.

This was unusual because these things were generally kept far away from the public eye. The announcement was received by all foreign intelligence agencies as a ruse and not as a credible fact.

CHAPTER 15

July 26, Islamabad

At noon, Rahman entered the safe house in which Alia and Nagib were staying and waving a wad of American dollars and two Pakistani passports greeted them by their new names Fatima and Munir Abu Jihad.

Nagib looked through the passports and was glad to see they appeared to be used with several entry and exit stamps in the first five pages. Rahman then asked them if they had decided where they wanted to go, and more importantly what was their chosen destination for the suitcases.

Considering their prime targets were Israel and the United States, that was a very complicated issue. First, because holders of Pakistani passports could not enter Israel at all and there was no embassy or even a Pakistani delegation in Israel. Second, going to the United States with Pakistani passports required a visa which they had no chance of obtaining and in addition it would also be very risky for the couple to set foot on American soil. Even if the suitcase could be shipped there with immunity and impunity as a "diplomatic pouch," they wouldn't be able to legally enter either country.

Nagib said they wanted to detonate the devices simultaneously in Israel and the U.S., and, therefore, each of them would have to travel alone to their separate destinations. Their plan was for Alia to travel to Mexico and infiltrate into southern California with the multitude of illegal aliens that crossed the porous border every day or night.

So, they requested that one suitcase should be sent to the consulate general of Pakistan in Los Angeles, either directly or via the embassy in Washington, DC. Alia would identify herself to the representative of the Pakistani intelligence service and he would hand over the suitcase. He would also hire some regular criminals to assist her if that was needed but in no way would directly involve Pakistan in the final act of planting the bomb.

Getting a device in to Israel would be much more challenging. There would be no problem sending the suitcase to the Pakistani embassy in Jordan, Lebanon, or Syria that bordered on Israel, but getting it across the border through the official check points was something else, especially as Syria and Lebanon had no regular border-crossing arrangements with Israel.

The only viable alternative would be to smuggle the suitcase and Nagib, of course, with other terrorists but the chance of success was low because those borders were closely watched by the Israeli Defense Force. Nagib then came up with the idea of the Sinai Peninsula that belonged to Egypt had lately become an unruly place. Islamic State supporters freely launched attacks on posts of the Egyptian Army and police forces. They attacked roadblocks, camps, vehicle depots, population centers, and inflicted severe damage and death.

They adopted the heinous practice of making video

recordings of mass executions of Egyptian soldiers and public beheadings of their officers. In addition, there were other factions that tried to take advantage of the situation and smuggle drugs and refugees or work-seekers into Israeli territory or across the border into Israel or right through the southern part of Israel into Jordan.

There were also tunnels dug from the Gaza strip that were prepared by Hamas and its supporters to carry out armed raids in Israel. Any of those could be used to get Nagib with his suitcase into Israel. Once inside, he could count on the assistance of Palestinian radical factions to take him to the population centers in Tel Aviv, Haifa, or Jerusalem, where the bomb would have the biggest effect.

Rahman said that although Pakistan wanted to maintain its good relations with Egypt, the opportunities of getting across the border in Sinai was the most promising and said he would see what could be done about it, with the obvious solution of sending the suitcase to the Pakistani embassy in Cairo.

Nagib should encounter no problem flying from Islamabad to Cairo and using his Pakistani passport to enter Egypt.

This plan was in contradiction to Alia's original statement that she did not want to do anything against the U.S. that afforded her family a chance for a better life, but Nagib was the one who would have to cross Sinai into Israel because a woman didn't stand a chance of surviving the expected hardships in the company of a bunch of wild men.

The plan also called for some coordinated timing so that the two events would take place simultaneously. Alia started to have second thoughts and then came up with a new idea that depended on the good will and ability of the Pakistani intelligence services.

She asked Rahman if his service could equip them with fake passports from European countries, like Greece or Turkey where their darker skin color would be the norm, or even from Scandinavian countries in which many immigrants from North Africa and the Arab world now resided legally.

Rahman said it would take time and could be done but wondered how that would solve the problem of getting the suitcase bombs through airport security and customs without diplomatic immunity. After some further discussion, they decided to continue with the original plan. Rahman was pleased the details for their departure from Pakistan were finalized because he feared their plan would be discovered by the official government who would terminate it.

In addition, he feared the "suicide" of the former defense minister would alert the authorities to open a real investigation regarding the circumstances of his death and that may foil the whole plan.

***

Linda had arrived in time for dinner but as soon as she entered Alma's apartment and they exchanged their usual loving and tender kisses, Alma pulled Linda to sofa and said that she had some exciting news and proceeded to tell her about the upcoming wedding.

Linda was not totally surprised because she knew that deep

down Alma was not a rebel and would follow the norm in Pakistan and stick to the standard lifestyle and raise a family.

Same-sex marriages were nonexistent in Pakistan and even having an open affair with a member of the same sex could get both members of the couple in serious trouble with the law. Linda was truly glad that her close friend and lover was so happy and although she knew she would really miss her relationship with Alma, she felt no resentment.

After dinner that was consumed quickly to allow them to spend more time in an intimate fashion, they moved to the bedroom. Their lovemaking was extremely slow and gentle as they both knew this would have to be the last time in view of Anwar's marriage proposition.

After feeling fully satiated, Linda cuddled with Alma and asked her how Anwar had proposed—wondering if there was any dramatic gesture that she deemed as pathetic—and was glad to hear that Anwar had been very civil and straightforward because, based on what Alma had told her about him, she had come to respect his intellect.

Alma excitedly related everything that happened the previous night with Anwar and even told Linda about the low-grade plutonium he presented as high-grade material to a foreign scientist with a funny name. Linda said she had no interest in stuff like plutonium but asked what she meant by a funny name and Alma said that it was Munir Abu Jihad.

When Linda enquired what was so funny about the name, Alma said that Abu Jihad meant "father of the holy war," which she considered as hilarious. They made love once more and Linda wished Alma all the happiness in the world with

Anwar and left with tears in her eyes while Alma stood sobbing at the door.

As soon as Linda was in her car, she called Blakey and asked him to meet her immediately. By the time she reached the embassy, Blakey was there and he led her to the safe conference room where she told him about Anwar, the plutonium, and Munir Abu Jihad.

Both realized this was the new name Nagib Jaber would be using and that plutonium was involved although they were not quite sure what low-grade material meant. It was late afternoon in Washington, DC, so Blakey called Eugene on a secure line and updated him on these recent developments.

He also said he had a gut feeling the elimination of the minister of defense a few hours after they spoke to him at the embassy was related. Eugene said he had talked to a professor at Georgetown University, who was an expert on Pakistani politics and got a long lecture about the two factions in the Pakistani administration and the rivalry between them, in particular about national pride and the country's nuclear arsenal.

Eugene deliberated whether to call his Mossad colleague David Avivi and share the shocking news with him and decided that due to the fact that special nuclear materials, SNMs as fissile materials were called, were involved it would be beneficial to alert Mossad and get its experienced agents to help track the culprits and plutonium.

David was woken up by Eugene's call and when Eugene said he had news of extreme importance and urgency that he could not divulge on the phone, he agreed to fly to Washington and meet in person as soon as possible.

July 27, Islamabad

Alia and Nagib, now holders of Pakistani passports with the names of Fatima and Munir Abu Jihad, spent what they realistically considered as their last night together. Alia asked Nagib if he had any second thoughts about the plan that would most likely lead to their deaths and he looked at her and said it was their historical role, their historical duty, to avenge the crimes committed by Israel and its American ally against the Palestinian people and Islam.

Alia noted a new resolve in his eyes that were staring into empty space and avoiding eye contact with her. She asked him once more if he did not prefer to start a family and leave the business of taking revenge to others, but he insisted it was their responsibility. She tried once again and said they could make a major contribution to the strength of Islam by delivering the advanced blueprints to Pakistan, but he said that they would probably never use them against the West for fear of retaliation. Alia looked at him once again and wiped a tear from the corner of her eyes and said that history would remember him as a true champion of the Palestinian cause and as the person who made the biggest contribution ever to the Ummah, an Arabic word representing the entire nation of Islam.

They decided the most appropriate day for unleashing their attack on the Jewish infidels in Israel and on the Christian followers of the false Messiah, Jesus, in the United States would be during the month of Ramadan, when Muslims practice *sawm* fasting from dawn to dusk. Even more significantly, they set the date at the festival of Eid al-Fitr that ends the month of Ramadan and is a cause for celebration during which Muslims wear their finest clothes and decorate their homes.

Nagib said the gift they would give to Islam by carrying out their attacks would be the ultimate sign of devotion, spiritual and physical, that will never be forgotten by fellow believers. As the Muslims adhere to a lunar calendar the exact date of Eid al-Fitr shifts by eleven days every year relative to the solar year of three hundred and sixty-five days. This year it coincided with the American celebration of Labor Day, on Monday, September 2nd.

For a moment, a fleeting thought passed through Alia's mind that perhaps they should wait a few more days until 9/11 but when she expressed this, Nagib objected saying the Americans would be more alert on that date and it had no religious significance to Muslims, unlike Eid al-Fitr. He added that Labor Day special sales would assure large crowds of shoppers in shopping centers and malls and that would be a perfect target for Alia's suitcase bomb.

They then discussed the exact time for the attack, considering there was a ten-hour time difference between Israel and California. Nagib suggested the best time would be noon time in Los Angeles when shopping would be at its peak and Eid al-Fitr festivities in Israel and Palestine would be under way at ten in the evening, local time.

As the target in Israel was Tel Aviv, a city that never stops, the exact number of casualties was not expected to change much during the day or night.

They expected the five weeks until their intended D-Day would allow them ample time to get to their targets and yet the date was close enough to reduce the probability of unveiling the plot. They decided they would tell Rahman and the Pakistanis about their plans with regard to the date but not the exact time nor the intended targets. They knew that the fewer people who knew their plans the better the chance of evading capture.

July 28, Islamabad

Rahman had overseen the arrangements made by the Pakistani intelligence services and when he arrived at the apartment to escort Nagib and Alia, now Munir and Fatima, to the airport he was not surprised to see they were very quiet and introverted. They appeared to be in a contemplative mood, each with their own thoughts about the future.

Nagib, somewhat formal and stiff, informed Rahman about their decision to carry out strikes at the same time in Israel and the U.S. and to do it on Eid al-Fitr. When Rahman tried to learn more about the exact time and location of the targets, Nagib answered these details were not relevant.

When they reached the airport, Alia boarded a flight to Mexico City and Nagib a flight to Cairo. Rahman assured them the special suitcases would be sent to Los Angeles and Cairo by diplomatic pouch and gave them the contact details of the people in the Pakistani embassies in both cities.

They agreed the code phrase to verify their identities and those of the contacts would be: "Do you remember my cousin

Junaid?" The answer would be: "She just married, Rahman."

Rahman smiled and said this indeed was his intention once the task was successfully completed. Rahman again raised the question of handing over the complete blueprints and Nagib answered that both he and Alia would have a copy that would be delivered at the two embassies in return for the suitcases.

***

At the American embassy in Islamabad, the information supplied by Linda effectively meant that their role in the pursuit of Nagib and Alia Jaber had ended as the couple was ready to leave Pakistan.

Blakey felt like he had failed miserably in his attempts to apprehend the couple or even get the Pakistanis to arrest them. He started to feel the undercurrents in the Pakistani administration that became evident with the "suicide" of the minister of defense shortly after being briefed by the ambassador about the sensitive information in the possession of Nagib.

He also understood that his best source in the Pakistani nuclear establishment had dried out when Linda and Alma curtailed their affair. He was not really surprised when he was summoned back to Langley for an indefinite period.

***

The Iranian intelligence service was alerted by their man at PINSTECH the two suitcases were removed from the small hangar and taken to the airport. The IRG agent, Mahmoud, tried to trace their destination and succeeded in discovering that one was sent to Cairo and the other one to Los Angeles. He presumed that Cairo was probably a convenient transitional place for moving it further and he guessed that it would be smuggled to Israel.

He had consulted with his chief at the Iranian Revolutionary Guards and was told the main interest of Iran was in the blueprints of the advanced designs. No one worried about the fate of Nagib and Alia, and as far as the Islamic Republic of Iran was concerned, they could become martyrs, national heroes of Sunni infidels.

So, Mahmoud was now facing a bigger problem—getting a copy of the schematics. When he tried to understand the rationale of this directive, his boss who was not usually inclined to explaining his orders, simply said that within the provisions of the 2015 agreement between Iran and the P5+1— U.S., Russia, UK, France, China, and Germany—Iran was prohibited from carrying out nuclear weapon research and, therefore, acquiring designs of approved advanced weapons represented a real windfall.

If Iran ever decided to clandestinely produce, or somehow obtain, fissile materials it could take the next step to constructing powerful nuclear weapons in a very short time without the need to perform tests or experiments.

Mahmoud asked his boss how he was supposed to get hold of the schematics and was told in no uncertain terms it was now his problem and he was to take whatever measures he found fit. He would receive any assistance he requested but was to be held responsible and accountable. He understood that by accountability his dear life was on the line, while success would be attributed to his boss. He realized that neither Cairo nor Los Angeles were teeming with supporters of the Islamic Republic of Iran so snatching Nagib, Alia, or the blueprints wouldn't be easy.

July 28, Washington, DC

David arrived at Newark airport on a nonstop flight from Tel Aviv and after rushing through immigration and customs boarded the short flight to Reagan National airport in Washington, DC. Eugene was waiting for him at the Arrivals exit and whisked him into a waiting limousine that was driven by an employee of the NNSA. They entered the office building in which Eugene was stationed and got down to business immediately.

Eugene said, "Nagib and Alia had been issued Pakistani passports in the names of Munir and Fatima Abu Jihad and were scheduled to leave Pakistan separately. We managed to find out that Nagib was to fly to Cairo and Alia to Mexico City."

David raised an eyebrow when he heard these destinations and asked Eugene. "What do you think the purpose of flying to Cairo and Mexico City could be?"

Eugene said, "I am pretty sure that Cairo is just for transition into Israel and Mexico City would probably be a stopover on the way into the United States."

David concurred and asked, "Is the U.S. intending to do

anything about this? Is it possible to get the Mexican government to arrest Alia on some trumped-up charges?"

Eugene said, "In view of the current relations between the two countries I doubt whether this is feasible."

David asked, "Could you get some third party to issue a "contract" on Alia in Mexico?"

Eugene replied, "Sadly, the days of "termination with extreme prejudice" are long gone and the present administration is reluctant to get involved in the elimination of a U.S. citizen in a foreign country without a court order and a directive signed by the President."

David suggested, "Maybe Mossad can be enlisted for the task."

Eugene shuddered at the thought and said, "This is out of the question."

David then asked, "Does the U.S. have any idea what Nagib and Alia are up to?"

Eugene gave him all the details related by Alma to Linda and onwards to the CIA and NNSA. He told David about the switch to low-grade plutonium and David wondered if that would affect the performance of the devices; assuming there were devices. He said he had to ask a frank and indiscreet question, and Eugene said he would provide an answer if he could.

So, David asked, "Are there blueprints of portable, small nukes among the copied designs?"

Eugene wriggled visibly before answering, "Hey, I never admitted that the stolen, sensitive material included weapon designs. But let's say that hypothetically there could be such things among the classified files that were downloaded."

Eugene and David were both physicists with advanced degrees and training in nuclear physics, so David asked, "Hypothetically of course, could such devices be transported in a suitcase?"

Eugene said, "You must be familiar with the "football" configuration. Let's say, again hypothetically, that we have improved it by cutting down the size and weight of the plutonium core and have achieved this by using super-grade material."

David thought about this and asked, "Do you think low-grade plutonium would work?"

Eugene replied, "Without knowing exactly what the device consists of, it would be impossible to predict this."

David asked, "What do you think of the statement issued by the Head of PAEC about missing plutonium."

Eugene smiled bitterly and said, "We believe this is just the Pakistani's version for "plausible deniability" in case the plutonium is traced back to them."

David thanked him and said he had to catch a flight back to Tel Aviv and promised to stay in touch.

July 30, Tel Aviv

In Tel Aviv the news forwarded by Eugene and delivered verbally by David was analyzed carefully and received with a mixture of some consternation and some hope. Mossad's ability to operate in Pakistan was somewhere between severely limited to non-existent while in Cairo, and certainly in Los

Angeles there were ample opportunities.

The meeting was held in Haim Shimony's office, and the Mossad chief asked David what he thought about the situation that was now developing. David said that in view of the information supplied by the Israeli Security Agency, the ISA was quite sure Nagib would try to avenge the death of his terrorist brother, Yassir, and the demolition of his parents' house, by detonating a nuclear device somewhere in Israel.

The fact that the device was sent to Cairo indicated it would have to be smuggled across the border into Israel. David suggested that Mossad deploy all its assets in Egypt to keep an eye on the Pakistani embassy there with instructions to spot Nagib and eliminate him if capturing him is not possible. In parallel, patrols along the border between Egypt and Israel should be doubled, with special attention given to locating cross-border tunnels that are dug by smugglers of drugs and humans.

The "Fish," the ISA senior representative at the meeting, said close surveillance would be placed on all known family members of Nagib Jaber, in case contacted them. He added that as there was no indication Nagib was a member of any Palestinian terror organization, so that finding him would be difficult unless he was stopped before crossing into Israel.

David recalled that Eugene told him about the polygraph examination Nagib was subjected to in Los Alamos and said Nagib denied during the interrogation that he belonged to any organization or movement. This could have changed, of course, but it was possible, so far he had worked independently of any Palestinian organization.

The "Fish" said the smugglers in Sinai did not concern themselves about the motivation of the people they smuggled across the border as long as they paid cash, but commented that Nagib would have to seek help once he reached Israel or else he would be stuck in the middle of the Negev desert after crossing the border from Egypt. He added ISA will have to increase its level of operations in order to locate Nagib and stop him before reaching the heart of Israel.

July 30, Los Angeles

The Department of Homeland Security issued a special notice to all border crossings between Mexico and the United States with a description of Alia Jaber, aka Fatima Abu Jihad, bearer of a Pakistani passport.

Eugene, who had personally briefed the chief of field operations of the DHS, expressed his opinion that Alia would not use an official border crossing to get into the U.S. but would probably contact one of the drug cartels, like Tijuana, La Familia Michoacana or Sinaloa, and pay the fees like any other illegal worker.

There were literally hundreds of tunnels that ran across the border as well as areas that were not sealed properly by electronic fences. Once in the United States, Alia would have no problem to be absorbed in the crowd as just another young American woman—after all, she was born and lived almost all her life in the United States.

Therefore, Eugene concluded, the only place that they could surely expect her to go was the Pakistani Consulate in Los Angeles. It was located at 10700 Santa Monica Blvd and the DHS promised to post human surveillance as well as cameras to check anyone who entered the Suite 211 during office hours.

Eugene asked if the DHS could monitor the phone calls that reached the Consulate but was answered by an indignant shrug and a statement that the Consulate had diplomatic immunity, and this was strictly forbidden. Eugene thought the very reason for founding the DHS was to prevent repetition of terrorist acts like 9/11 and here was a much larger threat to the homeland and its security and the DHS was helpless. He said nothing and decided to go to the FBI and seek their help in tapping the Pakistani Consulate phone lines.

PART 5. GETTING SET FOR THE BIG EVENT

CHAPTER 16

July 30, Cairo, Egypt

The Embassy of Pakistan in Cairo is located at in Ad Doqi district, close to the Nile River, and is the only official representative of Pakistan in Egypt. Employees of the embassy suffered a high incidence rate of headaches and disproportional amounts of mosquito bites due to the proximity to sewage treatment plants, so they sought every excuse to get away from the embassy building.

The Cultural attaché, Sadiq Ul-Haq, who was in fact the senior representative of the Pakistani intelligence services, was surprised to receive a twenty-nine-inch suitcase with instructions to store it in a locked metal cabinet and not to open it under any circumstances.

The fact that the suitcase arrived as part of the "diplomatic pouch," was nothing out of the ordinary—many foreign office staff members used the diplomatic pouch to transport personal and restricted items into, and out of, Egypt, but the instructions, signed by General Masood himself, were quite irregular.

However, Ul-Haq knew better than to disobey such an explicit directive and did as he was told. In another note that was sent separately, he was instructed that a man carrying a Pakistani passport with the name Munir Abu Jihad would come to claim the suitcase and he was to provide him with any assistance he requested. The note also outlined a verification procedure that Ul-Haq thought was more appropriate for a 1950s Hollywood B-movie from the cold war era or a cheap thriller than for twenty-first Century espionage games.

Munir Abu Jihad, as Nagib now called himself, arrived in Cairo and was in no rush to claim the suitcase. He checked in to a small hotel and presented his Pakistani passport.

The proprietor had not seen many tourists from Pakistan and was glad to see that Nagib spoke Arabic with an accent he did not recognize and assumed it to be Pakistani, while in fact it was a Palestinian accent with some American influences.

Nagib paid cash so no further questions were asked. Nagib was aware of the restlessness that permeated the Egyptian capital due to the ongoing tension between the Muslim Brotherhood and the regime that was largely controlled by the army. This did not bother him too much as he tried to stay away from demonstrations and street riots.

He had to first make arrangements to get himself and his precious luggage into Israel. He had several options, but each had risks involved. The most obvious and straightforward would be to contact smugglers in Sinai that specialized in crossing the Israeli border with drugs, munitions or people and joining one of the groups.

The main problem was they may simply murder him, steal his luggage, and bury him in the middle of nowhere never to be heard from again. Another option was to travel by public transportation to one of the ports in Sinai, take a ferryboat to Aqaba in Jordan and cross into Israel either in an assumed identity through one of the controlled border crossings or clandestinely with smugglers or terrorists.

This option offered a safe trip for the first part of the journey, but the second part was almost as risky as the first option. A third option was to try and penetrate Israel's long shoreline by a fishing boat or by a small rubber inflatable fast boat. He knew that Israel's maritime borders were closely watched by electronic measures as well as by naval patrols and in view of the size and weight of the suitcase he would have to reach the shore without swimming.

The easiest and quickest entrance route depended on his ability to obtain a foreign false identity, board a flight into Ben-Gurion airport, and hope to get on the plane and through Israeli passport control without being apprehended. He also considered an option that would minimize his personal risk but had a high probability of failure. The idea was to send the suitcase separately, either in a shipping container with other legal merchandize or as unaccompanied luggage that was erroneously not sent to Tel Aviv, and then try to enter Israel, legally or illegally, without being encumbered with the suitcase.

He knew he would, at best, receive limited assistance from the Pakistani official delegation in Cairo and was quite sure Pakistan was not very popular in Egypt, despite its possession of the only atom bomb that Sunni Islam had. So, he had to make up his mind which of the options he considered would best serve his objective and then make the necessary arrangements.

For example, if he wanted to get into Israel through the Sinai Peninsula he would have to contact the Bedouins that controlled the smuggling operations, and then find a guide who would lead him to the area controlled by the Palestinian Authority where he could hide for a while until the time set for the act.

Getting in touch with Palestinian activists in Jordan seemed to be simpler and he seriously considered taking a sightseeing trip as a tourist to establish the necessary contacts, and then return to Cairo to fetch the suitcase. After some further deliberation he ruled out the naval option as unrealistic without considerable support of an experience commando unit. He also assessed his chances of getting into Israel with his suitcase as an innocent passenger on board a flight from Europe and thought that with airport security in the city of departure and especially in Tel Aviv his chances of getting away with this were extremely slim.

Finally, he decided that sending the suitcase as unaccompanied luggage or in a shipping container was not an attractive option because he wasn't sure that the slight amount of radiation emitted from the suitcase would not be detected.

The bottom line was that he believed the Jordanian option,

with the help of Palestinians to cross from Jordan into the Palestinian Authority and from there into Israel presented the best alternative. So, he decided to stay away from the Pakistani embassy until he returned from his exploration trip to Jordan. Unbeknown to him, this turned out also to be the safest route to avoid capture.

He checked the bus schedule and saw there were three daily trips by bus from Cairo to Nuweiba port via Taba. The bus trip was long, about thirteen hours, but it was much cheaper and safer than the flights to Sharm El-Sheik. Taba was a crossing point into Israel but Nagib knew he stood no chance of passing Israeli security, with or even without his suitcase, and anyway as holder of a Pakistani passport he wouldn't allowed into Israel.

For a fleeting moment he considered getting some innocent tourist to act as a courier and transport his suitcase from Taba into the Israeli resort town of Eilat, but was afraid it would be lost, or even worse, confiscated. So, he booked himself on the morning bus to Nuweiba and decided to look for a ferry to Aqaba once he arrived there.

July 31, Nuweiba port, Sinai Peninsula, Egypt

Nagib was exhausted after the long bus ride from Cairo. He had expected a rough ride but was favorably surprised by the comfortable, air-conditioned bus that was packed with European tourists who wanted to spend a vacation on the wonderful beaches of the Red Sea.

However, there were many roadblocks set up by the Egyptian

304 | CHARLIE WOLFE

army and for a large part of the trip the bus was accompanied by a military escort to assure that it was not attacked by Bedouin supporters of the Islamic State that terrorized the Egyptians in Sinai. Fortunately, there were no unpleasant incidents and when the bus arrived at Nuweiba all he wanted was to find a place to lie down and rest. During the long ride, a couple German girls took an interest in him and tried to involve him in their conversation and vacation plans. They told him they had just arrived in Egypt and were headed straight to the beaches of the Red Sea that were famous as free-for-all tourist resorts.

Nagib, who had always been faithful to Alia, was invited to accompany them to their hostel and was slightly tempted but thought better of it and declined. Instead, he headed straight to the small Nuweiba port to check the schedule of the ferry to Aqaba on the north-east shore of the Red Sea that was the only seaport Jordan had.

He found an appealing catamaran ride that offered reasonable prices including all marine fees, departure tax from Egypt, and even a soft drink and croissant on board. He saw that tickets needed to be booked at least twenty-four hours in advance, so made a reservation for departure in the morning of August 2nd and went to look for a hostel for two nights.

He entered the first hostel he saw and checked in. He left his room to find a restaurant, have dinner, and ran in to the two German girls from the bus. They greeted him with smiles and asked him if he knew where they could eat and when he said that he, too, was looking for a restaurant they invited him to join them.

They walked along the beachfront until they came across

a quiet place that had a large veranda facing the Red Sea. The evening breeze was very pleasant and after the heat of the day abated it was a welcome relief. They ordered an assortment of salads and freshly caught fish as the main course. The girls wanted to order some beer, but the proprietor said there was no alcohol, but he offered them strong, bitter coffee and a nargilah.

They were not familiar with the word, so Nagib explained to them it was a water pipe used for smoking flavored tobacco, and said it was also a kind of social recreation when the tobacco contained other substances. They said they wanted to try it and asked him to teach them how to use it.

Nagib called the proprietor over, and with a wink, asked him to add some of his special flavored tobacco. The German girls, who were no strangers to Marijuana, understood what was involved and invited Nagib to take a seat between them and they both put their arms around him. They passed the water pipe from one girl to the other and each time Nagib took a deep breath and inhaled the flavored smoke, so after a while they were all a bit intoxicated.

They paid the proprietor and went for a walk along the shore hand in hand. They found a secluded spot and the girls invited Nagib to sit on the sand beside them. Nagib could no longer resist the allure of the two girls when they suggested that they all go for a swim. Bathing suits were not needed, of course, so he simply joined them.

They entered the water gingerly and were surprised by the warmth of the water. The full moon highlighted the white bodies of the girls against the dark background of the water and when they laughingly encircled Nagib their blonde hair and white arms were like snakes beside his darker skin. The two girls took turns kissing Nagib and each other and he felt as if he had reached heaven.

At present, he had his hands full with the two girls who were obviously not virgins and he could only imagine what it would be like with the seventy-two virgins promised to Shahids who sacrificed themselves for the grandeur of Allah and Islam.

They returned to the beach and for a short moment they couldn't find the spot where they had left their clothes. The girls giggled when they saw the look of consternation on Nagib's face and then one of them spotted the clothes and they chuckled at the transformation of his facial expression from dismay to relief. As Nagib started to get dressed, the two girls said they had a surprise for him and asked him if he would like to be the meat patty in the hamburger they were just getting ready to prepare. Once again, they laughed when they saw the look of confusion on his face and one of them said he need not worry they would be the buns and both just hugged him.

Nagib thought this may be his last chance to make love in this life and succumbed to their gentle endearments and ministrations. They returned to the hostel as good friends and arranged to spend the next day together.

Nagib felt some remorse for being unfaithful to his beloved Alia, but then thought they would never see each other again and mumbled that a man has to do what a man has to do.

The three of them spent the next day relaxing in the sun,

but as the evening came the two girls apologized to him and said they were invited to a small party by a couple of English youths that had promised to bring an ample supply of booze.

Nagib felt some relief, considering his age was almost the same as their combined age, and in any case was preoccupied with worries about the near future and the trip to Jordan.

August 3, Cairo, Egypt

The frustration of the CIA agents that had been posted close to the Pakistani embassy grew from day to day. There was no sign of Nagib or of Munir or whatever he called himself and sitting for hours in a café, a public bench or a parked car took its toll.

The mosquitoes were particularly vicious, and unlike most members of the species that were active only after sunset, the brand that rightfully earned the name "Nile Tigers," due to their miniature dark stripes, were bloodthirsty 24/7. They were very small and agile and presented an unbearable nuisance. An outside observer may have been amused to see two grown men waving their hands and occasionally even striking their own face in a futile attempt to wipe out the little torturers.

The Mossad agents were aware of the American CIA agents fared no better. They complained bitterly about the assignment but obeyed their orders and kept an eye on the Pakistani embassy. Mossad knew that the "cultural attaché" was in fact the mission head of the Pakistani intelligence services in Egypt and watched him but didn't discern anything irregular in his behavior. There was no point in following him around the clock, something that would require a lot of effort with little potential gain.

August 3, Ciudad Juarez, Mexico

Alia's eighteen-hour flight from Islamabad to Mexico City was long but uneventful, except her excitement when she discovered the shortest route was over the northern pole.

She used her Pakistani passport to enter Mexico, spent a couple of nights in Mexico City and then made her way by public transportation to the border city of Ciudad Juarez. She preferred the anonymity of the twenty-six-hour bus ride over the one and half hour flight, assuming correctly that whoever tried to trace her movements would find it practically impossible to follow her trail.

While living in New Mexico, she had travelled to Ciudad Juarez a few times to get a taste of lively Mexico. Some people jokingly regarded the Mexican city of Juarez and the Texas city of El-Paso as twin cities separated by the Rio Grande, but no one in his right mind would ever think of them as identical twins.

Juarez at one time was considered as the murder capital of the world as the rivalry between the drug cartels and the police and between themselves led to the indiscriminate murder of gang members, policemen, and mainly innocent bystanders. She stayed at a small hotel near the center of the city and within less than a day, with some help from the man at the front desk, arranged a meeting with a shady representative of one of the organizations that smuggled people into the United States.

He was surprised she couldn't speak Spanish and her English was with an American accent and didn't seem to believe her story about an estranged husband who was haunting her, but as long as cash was involved he didn't ask too many questions.

He told her the next group would be crossing the border the following night and she could join it for a reasonable fee. She said she needed to get to Tucson, Arizona, and he said that would double the price as there were several roadblocks on all the highways leading from the El Paso border area into the United States and she agreed to pay the additional fees.

August 5, Amman, Jordan

Nagib's boat trip from Nuweiba's small port in Egypt to the large port of Aqaba in Jordan was delightful. The mountains on both sides of this narrow strip of the Red Sea and the clear blue waters combined with the breeze created by the motion of the catamaran allowed Nagib to relax for a few hours.

From the boat, he could clearly see the two cities on the northern shores of the Red Sea, Jordanian, Aqaba, in the east and on the west shore Eilat, in Israel. They were so close together and almost touching. Each had many big hotels and it was practically impossible to believe they belonged to different countries. He thought of the night he spent with the two German girls and wondered if he would ever be able to share this foretaste of paradise with Alia. For a moment, he reflected if his betrayal of her and of his adopted country were turning him in to a multi-dimensional renegade.

He disembarked in Aqaba, and after showing his Pakistani passport was admitted into Jordan without any problem. As a former Palestinian he knew that it would be easier to find support for his plans in the slums and refugee camps near Amman than in the prosperous city of Aqaba. He checked the bus schedule and saw that the buses from Aqaba to Amman ran with a very high frequency, more than twice an hour during most of the day, so just walked over to the central bus station and boarded the first bus to Amman.

The bus ride took about five hours, mostly through sparsely inhabited desert areas although part of the ride was through spectacular mountains. Nagib dozed off and was awoken from his dreams when the bus came to a stop in the noisy and bustling central bus station of Amman. It was late evening and Nagib found a cheap hotel near the station. He was hungry, so he left the room and in a narrow alleyway found a falafel stand that was still open. He bought himself a super-size falafel sandwich wrapped in fresh pita bread and smeared with spicy sauce. After one bite and a sniff of the heady aroma he was transported, in his mind, to the time he was a youth in the mountain village near Hebron and the emotions were so powerful he almost burst out crying.

He realized he hadn't had a good falafel sandwich since he left Palestine more than a decade earlier. In the morning he headed to the Amman New Camp, that was one of the largest Palestinian refugee camps in Jordan.

The fact that Palestinian refugee camps still existed seven

decades after the 1948 Arab-Israeli War and five decades after the 1967 Six Day War was due to the self-perpetuating organization called United Nations Relief and Works Agency for Palestine Refugees (UNRWA).

In all other parts of the world where refugee camps were established the residents assimilated in the local populations after a few years, but the dependence of the Palestinian refugees on the handouts from UNRWA made it difficult for them to leave.

UNRWA was the only organization that allowed generation after generation of refugees to obtain benefits. In addition, the local Arab populations in Egypt, Jordan, Syria and Lebanon were not too keen to see their "Palestinian brethren" become full-fledged citizens in their countries. These refugee camps were a breeding ground for terrorists because young men who had nothing better to do than wait for their monthly food ration and pocket money from UNRWA had a lot of time on their hands and were fertile ground for radical ideas. The Amman New Camp proudly counted Ibrahim Nasrallah and Nihad Awad as two of its former residents.

August 6, Amman New Camp, Jordan

Nagib took a crowded bus from the central bus station to the Amman New Camp and went to a café that was located near the largest mosque in the camp. He noted that most of the streets and alleyways were named after towns and villages in Palestine like Nablus and Al Khaleel or in Israel like Yafa and Al Ramla. He sat down under the slowly revolving ceiling fan and ordered coffee and kanafe, a cheese pastry in sweet syrup.

The proprietor regarded the man who was obviously a stranger but spoke Arabic with a Palestinian accent from the Hebron region. There had been several agents of the Dairat al-Mukhabarat al-Ammah, the Jordanian General Intelligence Directorate (GID), who had come to the café to spy or carry out surveillance on Palestinian supporters of the Islamic State terrorist group. Some of them affected a Palestinian accent and some were really Palestinian working in the service of the Hashemite Kingdom of Jordan.

Nagib noticed the distrustful attitude of the proprietor that was not unexpected and just quietly sipped his coffee. He ordered another cup and when the proprietor brought it over to his table, he asked if there was someone of authority he could talk to about some important business deal that involved the homeland.

The proprietor now noticed the slight American accent and regarded him suspiciously but said he would see what he could do. Half an hour and two coffees later, three stocky men entered the café and approached Nagib. Their leader asked him to accompany them and led him to a short, dead-end alley in which the three men frisked him.

They found his Pakistani passport and asked him about it, as he was obviously not a Pakistani, and Nagib told them that he was a Palestinian who had lived in the United States for many years and the passport was an assumed identity. This appeared to grip their attention and they blindfolded him and led him to a house that was surrounded by a two-meter-high wall. A couple of men stood at the gate and although no weapons were in plain sight, it was obvious they were armed.

Nagib felt a change in temperature as the blindfold was removed and he was led down a short stairway into a basement.

An old man was seated in an armchair in the center of the room and introduced himself. "I am Sheik Tawfiq. What business proposition do you have in mind?"

Nagib answered, "I have a very precious and unique package I need to deliver in Tel Aviv."

Sheik Tawfiq looked at him as if he had lost his mind. "So, why don't you send it by mail or by courier?"

Nagib laughed. "No sane courier would take this package. My package is the kind that no one wants to handle, that is why I must do this personally. I have an account to settle and this will more than compensate for it."

The Sheik thought about this for a moment and asked, "Obviously, you are not a Pakistani as you had admitted to my people. Who are you?"

Nagib gave him a short version of his childhood in the village near Hebron, of his studies in Las Cruces, work at Los Alamos, and briefly described his trip to Pakistan and the agreement he had made with them. He went into some detail about his brother's martyrdom in the service of the Palestinian people and the price his family paid. He stated, "I now have the perfect means to avenge my brother's murder by the Zionists and to wreak havoc on them in the name of the Palestinian people. All I need is a way to get into Tel Aviv with my package."

"Nagib, I am impressed by your dedication and brilliance.

How big is the package you wish to deliver and when do you want to do it?"

Nagib described the suitcase and added, "I think the best way for our people to celebrate Eid al-Fitr is to see the Israelis and the Americans count their dead. The blood of the tens of thousands of infidels will cleanse the streets of Tel Aviv and Los Angeles."

The Sheik nodded and smiled. "You shall have our full cooperation."

Nagib bowed slightly and said that he would be back with the package at the end of August. He asked the Sheik if there was somewhere safe for him to spend a month in prayers and prepare himself for the ultimate sacrifice, and Sheik Tawfiq assured him he could remain in the Amman New Camp with full immunity.

August 6, Tucson, Arizona

Alia found a small motel in a quiet area of Tucson in which she could rest and relax after the border crossing from Juarez. The crossing was by far the scariest thing she had ever experienced, not so much because of the risk of getting caught by the U.S. border patrols or arrested at one of the roadblocks but due to the fact that the two guides that led the small group of frightened people kept arguing with each other in Spanish about something she didn't understand but felt that it concerned her.

The younger guide consistently tried to get her separated from the group and when they were alone tried to force himself on her, while the older guide told her to stick with him and never leave the group. There was a loud exchange of words and expletives between the guides, and the older guy even drew a knife and threatened the younger guide to stay away from Alia.

The rest of the group didn't utter a word when all this was going on and she was greatly relieved when the younger guide took the rest of the group toward El Paso on foot while the older guide accompanied her in a battered pick-up truck driven by a drunk Mexican. The driver seemed to know his way and used dirt roads to circumnavigate the roadblocks and get to Tucson.

Alia thought she would be safer in Tucson than in the Los Angeles area and decided to abide her time and make the last leg of her trip just three or four days before Labor Day of September 2nd. She figured she would have time to go to the Pakistani Consulate, collect the luggage, and find a hotel.

That would also enable her to case the target area—a large shopping mall in the greater Los Angeles area, buy clothes that will help her blend in with the shoppers, plan where to leave the suitcase, and decide on her escape route.

August 28, Amman, Jordan

Nagib spent almost a whole month in a safe-house in the middle of the Amman New Camp among Palestinian refugees. There were very few original refugees from 1948—most of the old generation had passed away during the last seven decades—there were many more from 1967, but most of the

the camp's population consisted of their second, third, and even fourth generation descendants.

There were much larger newly created refugee camps in the north of Jordan that were populated by refugees from Syria that managed to escape the ongoing conflict there that indiscriminately persecuted Syrians of all classes and religious beliefs. These camps were in much worse shape than the more established Palestinian camps, and there was no UNRWA to come to their relief only a few volunteers and some contributions from European countries.

Nagib spent most of his days studying the Koran and praying—something he had never devoted time to do in the U.S. or in Palestine—and studied the potential targets in Israel. He decided that a nuclear strike in the heart of Tel Aviv would bring the Zionist state to the verge of annihilation as it was the commercial dynamo and cultural center of the country.

Furthermore, a similar strike in Jerusalem or Haifa was bound to include many Arabs in the death toll, while in Tel Aviv there were only a few Muslims and he believed that Jaffa, in which many Arabs resided, would not be heavily affected by the blast or fallout. He focused on the beachfront as it was always crowded and close to the American embassy.

The embassy had been officially moved to Jerusalem in 2018, but the building in Tel Aviv remained the real hub of American presence in Israel, and where most of the diplomatic and consular business was conducted. This would be like killing two birds with one stone.

He noted there were many hotels along Yarkon Street and some of them about one hundred and fifty feet from the embassy and decided he would check in to one of those, arm the bomb then try to get away from Tel Aviv. However, when he checked the availability of rooms in his selected hotels, he found there were no vacancies in most of them, so he decided to take a calculated risk and reserve a room at the Lusky Suites Hotel that was just across the narrow road from the embassy. He used his American credit card to make the reservation believing it was no longer under surveillance.

He had made a quick trip to Cairo to retrieve his suitcase from the Pakistani embassy. The Cultural attaché, Sadiq Ul-Haq, told him they had almost given up on him and he had consulted General Masood and asked him what to do with the weird suitcase. The general told him to wait until after Eid al-Fitr and send it back to Islamabad if it was not claimed by then.

Nagib smiled apologetically and said the timing was crucial and he wanted to stay below the radar of the U.S. and Israeli intelligence agencies for as long as possible. Sadiq led him to the basement, handed him the suitcase, and wished him luck, adding that he had already forgotten about the suitcase and Nagib...

The journey back to Jordan was uneventful—no friendly German girls on the bus this time and no fun and games in Nuweiba port. No one took a special interest in his suitcase and he made his way back to the Amman New Camp with no hassle from Egyptian or Jordanian authorities.

Sheik Tawfiq's people waited for him and told him that everything was set for crossing the border into Israel the following night. They also informed him that the Sheik had arranged for the suitcase to be carried through the King Hussein Bridge—that was formerly known as the Allenby Bridge—terminal in broad daylight by the driver of a tour group of Christian pilgrims on their way to the holy sites in Jerusalem. The driver, who was generously paid, didn't know what the suitcase contained and was led to believe it was just another load of illicit drugs.

Nagib didn't ask any questions and said he would be ready for the journey. The following evening, four Arab youths arrived in a four-wheel drive Land Cruiser and unceremoniously told Nagib to put on the dark clothes they had brought with them and sit quietly in the back of the car.

They drove for a couple hours along paved highways until they reached an area on the west side of the Balqa district, close to the border with Israel. The lights of the car were switched off and it slowly approached a deserted area near the low cliffs overhanging the Jordan River. They got out of the car and walked quietly to the edge of the cliff.

The leader looked at his watch and told Nagib to get ready for a short sprint in fifteen minutes. Exactly fifteen minutes later a series of detonations were heard from positions north of their location. Several flares were launched from the Israeli side of the border in the vicinity of the detonations.

The leader grabbed Nagib's arm and told him to hurry and the small group waded across the shallow waters of the Jordan River, cut a small hole in the security fence on the Israeli side and quickly dashed to Highway 90 on the Israeli side of the border where a truck loaded with chicken cages was waiting. A clearing was prepared in the middle of the chicken cages and although the stench was overbearing, Nagib was glad to be sitting down between walls of cages filled with chickens that were furious about being disturbed in their sleep.

The truck headed south and within twenty minutes they were on the highway leading from Jericho to Jerusalem. The sleepy Israeli soldier at the roadblock checked the driver's papers, took a cursory glance at the cages, wrinkled his nose at the stench, and waved the truck through. Thirty minutes later the truck came to a halt in an enclosed yard and the human cargo was unloaded from the truck, while the chickens were taken directly to a slaughterhouse.

Nagib said he needed a shower and fresh clothes and his wish was fulfilled by the attendant Palestinian host. He was told he had time for a short nap and in the morning he would be driven to the hotel in Jerusalem where his suitcase was waiting to be picked up.

CHAPTER 17

August 30, Los Angeles

Alia managed to find a small local car rental agency run by women in Tucson that accepted her New Mexico driver's license without triggering an alarm. She knew that presenting that document at any national car rental agency would be flagged immediately so she avoided those. Using her credit card would have surely also caused problems, so she was pleased to pay a substantial cash deposit to the local agency in lieu of a credit card.

She once again used the excuse that her estranged husband was stalking her and that he had private detectives tracking her movements, so she couldn't use a credit card. A sympathetic woman at the rental agency accepted the story and even upgraded her car.

She enjoyed the drive along the I-10 through Phoenix, Palm Springs, and San Bernardino and took her time, stopping for gas, food, and coffee. She arrived in downtown Los Angeles and didn't like the area, so she continued west to Santa Monica and found a reasonable motel only a few blocks from the Pakistani Consulate. After a good night's sleep, she searched the web for shopping malls in southern California.

There were several places that looked as attractive targets, but she liked the Costa Mesa mall that looked suitable for her purpose.

The next morning, she drove down there to take a look at the place. The traffic moved slowly at first but once she was out of the center the pace picked up and it took her about one hour to get to the mall. It was in the heart of Orange County, a well-known stronghold of conservatives who had a reputation for not being great lovers of Arabs and Muslims, gave her another reason to select this shopping mall. However, she was surprised by the number of women wearing Hijabs and Abayas and some even covered their face with Khimars.

Alia found it quite amusing to see that these fully covered women were accompanied by men in jeans or teenagers in shorts, T-shirts, and sandals. She was impressed by the size of the mall and the number of shoppers who were taking advantage of the pre-Labor Day sales.

There were several hotels nearby, so she presumed that a woman with a large suitcase would not raise suspicion. She noticed there were no special security arrangements at the entrance to the mall and it looked as if the shop owners were more concerned with shoplifting than with security. In short, she thought, this would be an ideal target for her deadly cargo.

She suddenly realized that the Pakistani Consulate would probably be closed until Monday due to the Labor Day vacation and that meant she would have to rush to the consulate on Friday to collect the suitcase. She did see there was an option for emergency services on weekends and wrote down the telephone numbers but preferred not to stand out and bring too much attention to herself. So, she headed back to Santa Monica and got to the consulate just before it closed. It turned out that due to Ramadan, office hours were shorter than usual, and the visa section closed at three thirty in the afternoon.

She presented her Pakistani passport and was admitted into Suite 211. As in Brussels, there were not many people waiting in line for visas. She was asked what business she had at the consulate and when she stated she needed to see the scientific attaché she was directed to a small office. A young man, in his early twenties evidently attempting to grow a virginal mustache, was seated at a desk and noticed he was furiously clicking the mouse and watching the computer screen with such great interest he didn't notice her.

She coughed gently and he looked up with surprise and apprehension. She then realized he had been playing some computer game and didn't want anyone to see what he was doing. He smiled shyly and asked her in Urdu what she wanted. She answered in English she had come to pick up her suitcase and said, "Do you remember my cousin Junaid?"

The young man looked flabbergasted and then a large smile crossed his face and answered, "She just married Rahman."

She knew he probably worked for the Pakistani intelligence services but to her he looked just like a highly confused young man and she asked him if he was really the scientific attaché. He laughed and said the attaché was on vacation and he was a novice administrative assistant instructed to sit in the office just in case someone like her turned up with the correct code phrase.

He added the attaché had expected her more than a month earlier and they were all getting concerned they would be stuck with this strange suitcase, and she explained there was no reason for concern. He told her to follow him and they took the elevator to the basement of the building where there were several locked storerooms.

He entered a code on the panel beside the door and then took a large key out of his pocket and unlocked the door. She saw the suitcase stacked on a low shelf and when she had trouble lifting it, the young man helped her.

***

He was dying to ask her what was in the suitcase but knew that he shouldn't. They took the elevator to the ground floor and he offered to load it into her car. She thanked him and when she saw that he was in no rush to leave her, she asked if he could help her further with the luggage.

He looked at her and saw a woman a few years older than him. She was by no means good looking but after losing some weight in the last month she was now slim with a nice figure, and she had an intelligent face and pleasant manners.

He got the impression she was yearning for human contact and as he had nothing better to do he gladly agreed to help her.

***

Alia had not really spoken to anyone, man or woman, since

she left Islamabad more than a month earlier and had not gone out or even shared dinner or a drink with another soul.

Indeed, she wanted some company and the young Pakistani man was very pleasant in his shy way that she found attractive. She was pleased he agreed to help her and asked him if he had a car. He said that it was undergoing repairs after a fender-bender accident, so she invited him to get in her car and join her for the ride to her motel.

When they arrived at the motel, he helped her carry the suitcase up to her room and place it in the corner of the room. He stood up and looked at her and she looked at him and said, "You didn't tell me your name."

He replied, "My name is Salim, what's yours?"

Alia said, "Please just call me, Fatima."

Salim gathered his courage and with a slightly blushed face asked her if she would like to join him for dinner, after sunset, of course, when the Ramadan daytime fast ended.

She saw how embarrassed he was and smiled. "I would like this very much. Could I drive you to pick up your car from the shop?"

He thanked her and asked, "Aren't you worried that someone may break into your room and steal the suitcase?"

She shrugged and said, "If it is Allah's will it will disappear, but I trust it will be safe here."

During dinner Salim and Alia shared a bottle of California red wine and talked about themselves. Alia said she was separated from her husband, a true geographical fact but a complete fallacy from any other aspect.

Salim confided he was too shy to approach the California

girls with their free spirit and was waiting for some good, traditional, Muslim girl to come on to him as he lost his last shred of self-confidence in the company of women. It was obvious that each yearned for the other's company, although for different reasons.

Alia felt this could well be the last opportunity in her life to spend time with a man while for Salim this would be the first opportunity in his life to be with a woman. So, they left the restaurant and without any further words, by mutual consent they drove to Alia's motel and quietly entered her room and switched the light on.

The first thing they saw was the suitcase and both pointed at it with a sigh of relief and then she took the initiative, switched off the light and put her hands on Salim's shoulders looking up to him and parting her lips.

Salim didn't really seem to know what to do when he crushed her lips with his with so much force she recoiled in surprise. Seeing the look on his face, she told him to relax and kissed him very gently with their lips barely touching.

He was a quick study and when she guided his hand to her breast, he caressed it gently while she unbuttoned his shirt and stroked his bare chest. Her hands moved a little lower and he almost stopped breathing. Alia could feel his heart beating a storm and for a moment worried he would pass out when she touched his erection with the back of her hand.

She liked that he was so inexperienced and continued to guide him to undress her slowly. By now Salim was trembling with desire and she ordered him to stand still while she finished removing his clothes and let her hands ramble over his

326 | C<small>HARLIE</small> W<small>OLFE</small>

body, rubbing her breasts over his chest and abdomen, and moving lower making him utter low moaning sounds.

It was over before she could get him to lie on the bed. He wanted to run away or bury himself under the shabby carpet, but she took a towel from the bathroom and cleaned him telling him that she was proud of him and the night was still young.

September 1, Jerusalem

Nagib celebrated the first days of Eid al-Fitr with his hosts in East Jerusalem. He was sure this would be his last chance to rejoice in the festivity and did his utmost to enjoy it. He had collected his suitcase from the bus driver three days earlier and had checked everything was intact, despite the rigors of the trips from Cairo to Amman and then to Jerusalem.

He was a bit amazed how easy it was for him and his escort to penetrate the supposedly impenetrable Israeli border and even more surprised by the fact that a nuclear device could be smuggled in broad daylight into the country. He hoped the final stage of his mission would also go smoothly.

He wondered how Alia was doing and if she would be able to stick to the schedule they had arranged. He had no means of contacting her. He regretted they had not purchased prepaid cell phones for communication as they had done in Europe or enlisted the help of the Pakistani intelligence service to serve as mediator between them.

He assumed he would hear on the news if she had succeeded and hoped she would hear of his own accomplishment. He told his hosts he would be leaving for Tel Aviv in the next day and thanked them for their help, saying that perhaps one day they would meet under the grace of Allah.

September 2, Costa Mesa shopping mall, California

Indeed, as the night progressed Alia coaxed Salim to take his time and attend to her needs, so by the time the long weekend was almost over he felt like an accomplished Don Juan and she felt that perhaps she had missed her calling as a teacher.

They only got out of bed to have some fast food and she was amused to see the goofy smile did not leave his face for even a minute.

On Monday morning she told Salim he had to leave because she had some business to attend to. He had a mournful look on his face but without saying anything he helped her carry the suitcase and put it in the trunk of her car and then drove off in his car.

She returned to the room, put on an elegant maternity dress and stuffed a pillow under it. She packed spare clothes in her handbag and made sure she had the small set of tools she had prepared.

The drive to Costa Mesa mall was slow because the highways were full of holiday shoppers, but she parked in the handicap spot closest to the main entrance and opened the car's trunk to unload the suitcase. A guard came up to her to ask her if she had a permit but when he saw her large extended belly, he simply helped her take the suitcase out of the trunk.

She thanked him and headed to the mall. The time was just before noon in California and Alia hoped Nagib was all set for his part of the mission in Tel Aviv, where the time was close to ten in the evening.

***

The large, innocent-looking suitcase was pushed slowly on its four wheels by an elegantly dressed young woman whose bulging belly announced to the whole world that she was carrying a baby, or perhaps even twins.

Gentlemen who offered to help her were repelled by a fierce look and those bold enough to try and take hold of the suitcase handle were shooed away by a loud hissing sound emitted through thin lips enclosing her small mouth.

She struggled with the wheels that appeared to have a will of their own and looked as if they were arguing with one another about the direction in which to move. Finally, she reached the escalator leading to the second level of the large shopping center and realized the suitcase was too wide for the escalator stairs. She turned around, abruptly knocking over a toddler holding his mother's hand and, without an apology, headed toward the wide elevator. The toddler's mother sent a drop-dead look to the receding back of the woman who was entering the elevator.

If radiation detectors had been mounted in the elevator, they would be chirping like crazy with flashing lights, indicating a deadly level of radiation, but none were installed, so no one was the wiser about the imminent danger.

The woman entered the ladies restroom with her suitcase and barely squeezed into the stall reserved for the handicapped. She quickly removed the pillow that made her midsection bulge, changed her clothes to nondescript jeans and a tightly fitting top that accentuated her slim figure, removed the blond wig she had been wearing and passed a comb through her jet-black short hair.

She placed the pillow and old clothes in a plastic bag that she left in the corner of the stall next to her suitcase. She then set the combination locks on both sides of the suitcase to the code that would give her thirty minutes to get far enough from the shopping center.

She waited until she was certain the restroom was empty, opened the booth's door and exited. With a small screwdriver that she pulled out of her purse, she set the sign on the door to "occupied." She entered the next stall to relieve herself from the sudden urge to urinate.

She exited the washroom and made her way to the parking lot, went straight to her car that was still parked in the spot reserved for handicapped drivers, and without any visible signs of being in a hurry merged with the traffic on highway 55 and headed north on the I-5, trying to get as far away as possible from the Costa Mesa Mall.

***

Alia turned on the car radio and tuned in to a news station. She was near East Los Angeles when she heard the "breaking news" jingle interrupting the regular program.

The announcer sounded very distressed and after saying, "This just in…" Then there was silence for a moment before continuing, "We have just heard that a large explosion took place at Costa Mesa mall. There are several casualties and emergency crews are on their way to the scene. We don't have any details as to the cause of the explosion, whether it was an accident or an act of terror."

Alia continued driving noticing the shocked look on the faces of the drivers and passengers in the cars near her. A few minutes later, when she was near Glendale, the radio station continued with its "breaking news," saying, "First responders estimate that a small bomb went off in the women's restroom on the first floor of the Costa Mesa mall. Initial estimates are that the size of the bomb was quite small, only a few pounds of high explosives. The death toll so far is just over two dozen but there are at least five times as many people that were injured and several more are in shock. Wait a minute, I am being handed a note saying that the first responders have detected an elevated level of radiation and suspect that the bomb included radioactive materials. All people are strongly advised to leave the area and keep their distance. The police are pushing the crowd of spectators back using loudspeakers to announce the area may be contaminated with radioactive materials. Our correspondent at the scene, Diane Sacks, says the crowd has now dispersed—apparently the warning worked."

Alia turned pale—this was not supposed to happen—she expected to hear about a nuclear detonation, a mushroom cloud, tens of thousands of casualties, vast destruction, a national state of emergency, statements from the White House, threats of retaliation against the perpetrators… This sounded more like a small "dirty bomb" that spread a little radioactivity.

September 2, Lusky Suites Hotel, Tel Aviv, Israel

Nagib wheeled his suitcase in to Lusky Suites Hotel in the early evening. He had reserved a room in that hotel with his American credit card. He assumed that by the time someone could track the transaction, he would be far away and knew that his Pakistani passport would get him in to trouble instantly.

He had selected this hotel because of its central location on Yarkon Street, just across the road from the American embassy building. It was also very close to the lovely beach-front promenade with its restaurants, pubs, and thousands of fun-seeking Israelis and tourists.

He set the timer to go off at exactly ten in the evening and left his room. On his way out he chatted with the concierge, actually a fancy title for the girl who sat at the front desk and asked her if she could recommend a good restaurant. The girl, Nava Pullman, was in fact a Mossad agent who took over the place of the regular concierge, and asked him what kind of food he fancied and what would he like to spend on the meal because the selection was huge.

Before Nagib could answer, he was knocked down by two large security operatives of the Israel Security Agency and trussed like a turkey.

David Avivi and the "Fish" went up to his room, followed by the top bomb expert of the Israeli police, and saw the suitcase.

The bomb expert examined the suitcase without touching it and then produced a portable X-ray machine and imaged the contents of the suitcase. He was a bit surprised by the fuzzy image and when he mentioned this, David quickly figured out this must be due to spontaneous radiation emitted from the contents of the suitcase. A portable radiation detector confirmed this.

The bomb expert said there were no booby traps, sophisticated triggering, or tamper-proof devices, and as far as he could tell from the image the explosives charge was to be set off by a crude timer. He asked David if he wanted to remove the suitcase and dismantle it elsewhere or to do it on the spot, and David said there was no telling when the timer was set, so it would be best to it then and there.

The bomb expert didn't even perspire when he neutralized the timer and carefully removed the conventional explosives that were placed on both edges of the metal tube. When David told him the metal tube contained a few pounds of plutonium, the bomb expert started trembling and sweat burst out of every pore.

The "Fish" showed how he earned his reputation and started laughing saying that dying of a nuclear explosion made you just as dead as dying from a simple detonation.

David added that the law of conservation of mass didn't deal with the number of particles into which you disintegrated.

The bomb expert said he didn't appreciate this kind of

humor and swore silently under his breath.

David called the director of the Israel Atomic Energy Commission (IAEC) and asked for assistance in appraising the device packed inside the suitcase. The director said this would be given top priority and instructed a couple scientists to attend to the matter urgently.

Despite the late hour, it was getting close to midnight, two of the top physicists arrived at the hotel. They studied the suitcase and the device and suggested it should be taken to the laboratories of the IAEC at the Soreq Nuclear Research Center.

David said he knew the place quite well because his mother had worked there until her retirement a couple of years earlier, and that as a youth he had spent some of his summer vacations in a science camp there.

The neutralized bomb and suitcase were loaded into a police car and delivered to Soreq, accompanied by the two physicists who couldn't wait to get a closer look at the device.

Meanwhile, the failed nuclear bomb in California was the hottest item on all news services.

David immediately saw the connection between the two incidents. He called his boss, Haim Shimony, the Mossad chief, and asked him to convene a meeting early the next morning to discuss the two incidents.

PART 6. GETTING EVEN

CHAPTER 18

September 3, Mossad Headquarters, Tel Aviv

All Mossad department heads, as well as a representative of the Prime Minister's office, the head of the anti-terror section of the Israeli police, and the "Fish" from the ISA, were gathered in Shimony's office waiting excitedly to hear David's report.

David started by giving them all the background on Dr. Nagib Jaber and his disappearance with stolen sensitive data from Los Alamos National Laboratory. He told them that Nagib had been suspected of being a rogue agent but was cleared after a polygraph interrogation.

He briefly summarized the route Nagib and his wife, Alia, had taken from New Mexico to Canada, then to Germany and Belgium, before getting to Pakistan. He added that the Americans never officially released the details of the information

Nagib had downloaded but he had surmised it included schematics and blueprints of America's most advanced nuclear weapons.

He stopped for a moment to allow everyone to absorb the ramifications of this type of information in the wrong hands, and then continued to state that the information itself was worthless without the possession of enough fissile material. David said the Americans were now trying to analyze the reason for the failure of the nuclear device detonated in Costa Mesa and the Soreq scientists were studying the device that had been seized in Tel Aviv, believed to be identical to the other one.

He started to say that he believed the device was an improved American version of the suitcase bombs that were allegedly developed by the Soviet Union.

As he was speaking, there was a knock on the door and Shimony's adjutant handed him a note and after glancing at it he passed it on to David.

David stopped his briefing, read the note, and said that preliminary analysis of the device confirmed his hypothesis. The note contained the results of the isotope analysis carried out by the U.S. forensic scientists of plutonium bearing debris and indicated that the fissile plutonium was of inferior weapon grade, just like the type the Pakistanis had used in their 1998 underground tests.

He explained it was possible to use "the football" design to obtain a large yield from a small, lightweight device if high-grade plutonium was used, but using low-grade plutonium could result in a fizzle as indeed happened in Costa Mesa.

Another knock on the door interrupted his narration and this time the director of the Israeli Atomic Energy Commission entered accompanied by his chief scientist, Professor Eli Halevy. The IAEC director apologized for the interruption while the professor inserted a memory stick into the computer and turned on the overhead projector.

He showed a series of photographs depicting the suitcase, the tubular pipe, and the blocks of conventional explosives on both ends. He then showed a series of photos in which the device was disassembled and two cone-shaped masses of a shiny metal that, together, looked like a football. He said that judging from the mass of these two pieces, a nuclear detonation could have wiped out every structure and human being in a radius of one mile and the radioactive fallout would have been carried for tens of miles inland and contaminated an area in which more than one quarter of the population of Israel lived.

David asked the professor if he thought the device would fizzle or deliver its full yield and the professor said he believed there was a fifty-fifty chance. He added that the plutonium core would be further analyzed in order to determine its origin but based on the preliminary measurements he was quite certain it was a product of Pakistan.

The Mossad chief said he would have to adjourn the meeting and present the information to the Prime Minister and his cabinet. He said that a great disaster was averted thanks to the efforts of the ISA and Mossad operatives, but the fact that a lone terrorist could almost single-handedly endanger the security, and perhaps the very existence of Israel was a warning sign to them all.

He added that Israel had already received an official request from the United States to extradite Nagib and the Israeli government had agreed in principle but first wanted to interrogate Nagib and find out more about the route he used to infiltrate into Israel with his suitcase bomb.

The "Fish" intervened and commented that the ISA was leading the investigation and Nagib's spirit was completely broken down because of his failure and Alia's partial failure and he is cooperating fully. He believed that there would be no more useful information coming from Nagib and, therefore, no reason to hold him in an Israeli prison any longer. Furthermore, he said, in the United States he would probably receive capital punishment as an accomplice for mass murder of shoppers in Costa Mesa mall while in Israel he would merely get an extended prison sentence and would probably become a hero of the Palestinian people in prison.

September 8, Los Alamos National Laboratory

The new Head of the Security Office, Commander (Ret.) George W. Haggard, who replaced Colonel (Ret.) Dick Groovey after the fiasco last June, had just completed a major revision of the security procedures at the lab. He was quite satisfied with the improvements implemented to secure electronic data and files and made sure that they were enforced despite the protests by the scientists and engineers that constantly complained it made their work almost impossible.

In addition to installing hardware that physically prevented the insertion of any removable data storage media he had purchased from a company founded by veterans of the NSA, a sophisticated software package that kept a record of every file was in use and of every change that was made.

The Commander, as everybody referred to him, was especially pleased that the Security Office budget was quadrupled, and the personnel doubled.

Dr. Eugene Powers who flew down from Washington, DC, to carry out an inspection of the lab's security, was not convinced these new measures would prevent the next Dr. Nagib Jaber from getting away with top secret documents. However, he knew that no system was completely foolproof, especially if it was supervised by fools.

The assessment of the death toll and damage to property resulting from the explosion in the Costa Mesa mall had been completed. The estimates of the number of conventional explosives contained in the device were between five and ten pounds—not a very large amount compared to the amount carried by human suicide bombers, not to mention booby-trapped trucks driven by suicide bombers.

Fortunately, the ceiling of the restrooms in the mall was built from very light construction material, so most of the force from the explosion was released skyward.

Furthermore, thanks to the fact the toilet area in the mall, where the suitcase was left, was built of concrete and not flimsy material, most of the force of the explosion was contained within that area or found its way out through the ceiling.

Structural damage was limited to the restroom and the surrounding stores on all sides of the toilets and to the restroom area on the lower floor below the explosion center. Only a small part of the plutonium contained in the metal pipe was dispersed by the explosion, mainly in quite large chunks, so the amount of aerosolized highly toxic plutonium was very small, and decontamination was expected to be costly but relatively easy to do.

The number of people killed by the explosion was surprisingly low—only two dozen or so died instantly, mainly women in the restroom and men in the adjoining toilet. About three times as many were wounded by flying debris or by the shock wave from the explosion. Several people were contaminated by the dispersal of the radioactive material, but probably none were exposed to lethal doses of radiation. Eugene and other NNSA staff members received the report of the damage.

In the post-detonation analysis, there was consensus among the scientists that a true "dirty bomb," with the same amount of explosives but made with powdered radioactive material, rather than solid metallic plutonium, would have caused more contamination and many more casualties. The bottom line was that the fizzle of the device was very fortunate, and some would go as far as to say it was the result of divine intervention.

Eugene had another reason for his visit to the lab and that was to get the report of the nuclear forensics analysis. The report summarized all the findings of the chemical and physical analysis of the debris collected from the site of the bombing. The conclusions were clearly stated, something that he found refreshing in view of the scientists' tendency to include several caveats in their reports.

Based on the forensic evidence there was no doubt that the plutonium was produced in Pakistan—they even pinpointed the reactor—and that the construction of the device was carried out at PINSTECH. Chemical analysis of the remaining traces of the conventional explosives also pointed to the Pakistani military industry and the remains of the metal pipe contained a clear signature of a composition made only in China.

The Pakistani attempt to blame the theft of plutonium as the source of the core of the bomb was laughable. Eugene met with the scientists from the lab and from Lawrence Livermore National Laboratory and was convinced that there was no room for uncertainty.

Furthermore, the Israelis sent samples from the intact suitcase bomb they had seized in Tel Aviv, courtesy of David Avivi, and these conclusions were unequivocally verified.

September 9, Islamabad, Pakistan

The U.S. insisted that all copies of the advanced designs of nuclear weapons would be returned to the U.S. or destroyed and threatened that any violation of this would be severely reprimanded.

The Pakistani government was aware of the fact that a real nuclear detonation with tens of thousands of casualties would have led to a punitive counter-strike. After all, the dominant global power, not to say the only global power, could not tolerate a nuclear attack on its homeland without a suitable response.

The President of the United States, who was more of a politician than a history scholar, knew that the Roman Empire survived for five centuries by prosecuting and bringing to justice, Roman-style of course, anyone who harmed a Roman citizen.

Under persistent pressure by the United States and intimidation of retaliation for the unconventional terror act that was supported by Pakistan, a major change in the Pakistani intelligence services was underway. The senior members of the anti-American faction were sent to prison or placed under house arrest and intermediate level officials were transferred to remote posts where they couldn't do any harm.

General Masood was the most prominent figure among those arrested and was now awaiting trial for treason and probable execution.

Rahman Chenna was demoted and with his newly wedded wife, Junaid, was banished to Mingora in the Khyber Pakhtunkhwa Province where he was put in charge of a field office that included no underlings.

The scientists at PINSTECH that were involved in the construction of the devices were banned from attending conferences in the West and were not allowed to participate in joint projects. This more or less curtailed the scientific career of Dr. Anwar Usman but his consolation prize was his vibrant wife, Alma.

September 11, Washington, DC

Dr. Eugene Powers was summoned to the oval office in the White House and in a modest ceremony was given the President's Award for Distinguished Federal Civilian Service.

The reason for the award was never mentioned in the public records but was commended by those few Federal employees in the NNSA and intelligence services who knew what he had done. George (Blakey) Blakemore, the Islamabad CIA station chief, received the National Intelligence Medallion, and Linda Katz was awarded the National Intelligence Special Act or Service Award. They all saw the significance of the ceremony's date—9/11.

Alia Jaber turned herself in after hearing that Nagib failed completely in his mission and was, at present, incarcerated in California and waiting for her trial. She had mixed feelings about the fizzle of the suitcase bomb she had planted in the Costa Mesa mall.

Dr. Nagib Jaber was released from the Israeli prison into the custody of two Secret Service agents and brought to the U.S. in chains and shackles. He was sent to stand trial in New Mexico, although capital punishment was abolished in that state in 2009.

The Islamic Society of North America hired defense attorneys for both Jabers and aimed at using the trial procedures to focus on the alleged discrimination of Muslims by the United States globally and particularly in the U.S.

ACKNOWLEDGMENTS AND NOTES

First, and foremost, I would like to thank you for reading this book. I hope you enjoyed it despite the scientific jargon that I really tried to minimize.

I dearly appreciate your comments, so please send them to: Charlie.Wolfe.author@gmail.com

You may want to read some of my other books: "*Mission Alchemist,*" and "*Mission Patriot,*" also published on Amazon.

This book would not have been possible without the help of Dr. Wikipedia, and Professor Google, and Magister Google Earth. I also found a wealth of information in scientific articles and books. However, any misinterpretation of the technical and geographical information from those sources is my own responsibility.

It is unnecessary to declare that this book is a work of fiction and any resemblance to real events or people is not to be understood as anything but a coincidence. I apologize in advance in case any person feels offended by the plot.

Finally, I am grateful to Glenda Sacks Jaffe for editing this book and to my family and friends who read the manuscript and enabled me to improve the text thanks to their astute comments.

You may also want to read the Prologue of my next book, *Mission Patriot.*

.

Printed in Great Britain
by Amazon